THE
RISE
OF A
VISIONARY

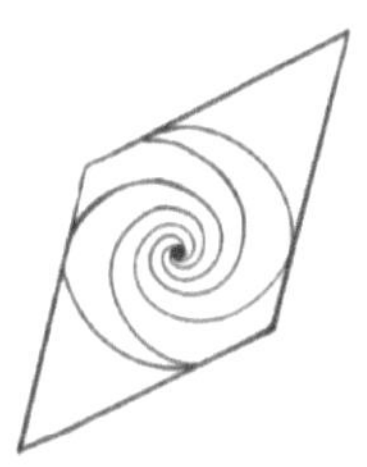

Putting the Fact in Fantasy edit by Dan Koboldt and Foreward by Scott Lynch

Mythology: Timeless Tales of the Gods and Heroes by Edith Hamilton

Description: First Edition | Special Edition | Denver: Audrianna Brownell, 2024 | Series: [Lost Isles Collection; 1] | Blurb; In an effort to punish his ex-lover, a maleficent God has separated mankind from the other half of their souls. Unaware, mankind is forced to pine after their mates. Their magic ripped into pieces, along with their hearts.

Identifiers:

ISBN (Special Edition Hardcover): 979-8-9915002-3-4

ISBN (Paperback): 979-8-9915002-2-7 ISBN (ebook): 979-8-9915002-1-0

Subjects: AC: Gods, Urban Fantasy, Greek Mythology, etc.—Fiction. | Love, Fates, etc. —(Philosophy)—Fiction. | Fated Mates—Fiction. | Greek Gods—Fiction. | Brothers—Fiction. | Adult Fantasy ISBNs: 979-8-9915002-3-4:(hardcover), 979-8-9915002-2-7:(paperback), 979-8-9915002-1-0:(ebook). Printed in the United States of America.

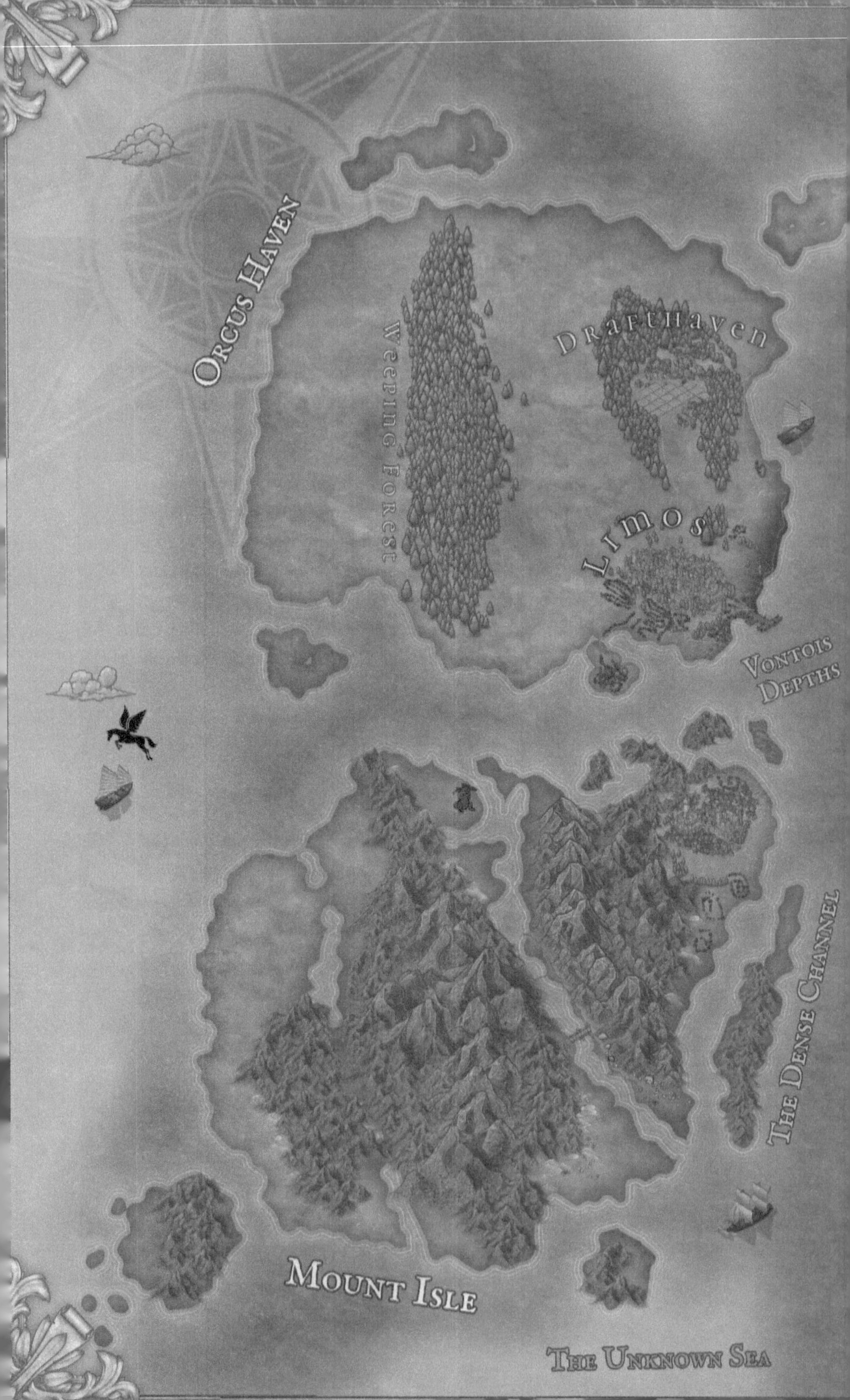

Orcus Haven
Weeping Forest
DraftHaven
Limos
Vontois Depths
Mount Isle
The Dense Channel
The Unknown Sea

LAFORNAS
ISLE OF MURR
THE DARK DEPTHS
RUTMEUSE ISLES

The Rise of a Visionary is a dark adventure fantasy full off liars, gray morals, and ruthless godlike behavior. As such, the story includes elements that might not be suitable for all readers. Violence, death (including the death of bystanders, children, and parents), inappropriate language, burnings, massacres, bombings, substance abuse, alcohol, sexual activity, gender-based violence, sex work, and suicidal intentions. Some elements boarder on graphic and others more imagined. Readers who may be sensitive to these elements, please take note, and prepare to lose everything for the cost of finding fated mates.

To Ashley and Alysha,
This book was inspired by all of our magical adventures and was brought to life in your images. I wouldn't be inspired to write such strong friendships without the two of you in my life. Thank you for reminding me that a male's point of view is only relevant if he has something intelligent to say, or if it's in the bedroom.

Prologue

Hades, the God of the Underworld, granted each of his three sons a singular gift once they reached the prime age of eighteen years old. He held little love for his many sired children, but these three sons, who had crawled from the womb of Persephone, had made him beyond proud as they grew into the ruthless beings they were.

His oldest, Nekiros, requested an army that could match the size and strength of any army Ares, the god of war, overruled. Hades granted him the use of all the bodies buried beneath the dirt. If he should one day need them, they would rise as zombies to do his bidding. Nekiros was delighted by this gesture and often boasted to his two young siblings that his gift would never be outmatched.

The second son of Hades, Skotadi, knowing he would need to be smarter than his older brother, was more meticulous in his choice. His dark nature made him lust for everything his brother had, and would ever have. When he reached the age of eighteen, he asked his father to grant him a marriage of his choosing. When Hades demanded he be clearer in his request, Skotadi clarified that he wanted his father to grant his marriage to Nekiro's first sired daughter. Hades agreed, finding his two eldest sons to be tiresome in their efforts to upstage one another.

Finally, his third son, Dolofonia, was of age and he patiently waited to hear what his favorite son would ask to be granted. Hades admired his youngest son solely for his birth order, as it resembled his own. Hades wouldn't make the same mistakes his father did, favoring a son simply because they were born first.

Dolofonia spent a majority of his eighteenth year pondering his gift, only adding to Hades's initial intrigue. Hades often tried to ask Dolofonia what it was he wanted most in the universe. He often attempted to prepare Dolofonia to ascend the throne in his stead.

His favorite son's only reply was, " I would like to ask for you to have been granted ruler of Mount Olympus, but alas, that is not possible."

Hades often let his youngest son speak to him in this manner. Seeing much of himself in young Dolofonia.

Then Dolofonia decided on his gift, explaining to his father that he wanted a planet to be fully under his control. He requested that his father split the planet's patron's in half to increase their suffering, and cause them to search for their other halves. Hades pondered this, he had known of a planet forgotten by the gods long ago, he would be able to grant his son this wish.

"No one must know of this treachery, Dolofonia." Hades stated firmly.

"Then we shall blame Zeus, or have all the patrons forget their gods names, have them forget all their histories." His son replied in his desperate grasp for power.

Hades was more than amused by this wish of manipulating a world full of useless humans. He assured his son that their identities must remain hidden within the world, even from the other gods. Dolofonia's only reply was a wicked grin pressed between his chiseled cheekbones.

Hades granted his son his birthday wish, the planet of Lafornas.

To manipulate at his will.

Chapter 1

18 years prior

Stanis never wanted a mate.

He knew what he'd been told as a child. As all children of Lafornas were, Batar, the ultimate ruler over all humanity, was so angry with his betrothed, Itia (the goddess who granted him immortality), who he deemed responsible for the curse thrust upon humanity by cracking them down the center. Forcing them to spend forever trying to find the other half of their power, specifically, their mates.

Sounds a bit mythological, wouldn't one think?

Even if he were to believe that all humans had fated mates, he also refused to believe any of that shit was actually true. Humans were greedy and needed that farce to validate the fight for more power. His father, though low in society's eyes, had told him many times that power was the key to unlocking any secret. He knew little about the world, being only fourteen, but he knew his father was always right. Power would be his only admiration in life.

Although, as he stepped from the curb, a car slammed by, and it collided with him.

No, not the vehicle. Wouldn't that have been simply perfect, though?

To be murdered in the sandstone streets of Limos, in the city's inauguration, on the day of their arrival in their new lives. His freshly crafted young body mingled with the rust colored dust and piles of construction material, mere steps down from where they were now.

At that exact moment, his entire world was upheaved. A car running him down would have truly been a better outcome.

No, instead a female figure had stopped him in his thoughts, just long enough for him to barely avoid being killed.

The woman seemed to be in her late thirties. Her age and features resembled his mothers, but she had something dark behind her eyes. His mothers deep green eyes had been kinder, one's that made you trust her instantly. This woman's eyes were cupped with purple crescents that typically resulted from wakeful nights.

"What was her name? What did she smell like-"

"NO"

He stopped his running thoughts, startling his brother. Cole's stern emerald eyes beat into him, and with every fiber of his being, Stanis withheld his eye contact. Cole remained firm, gripping Stanis's elbow, while sporting an amused smile. His familiar scent of pine and their childhood cabin home lit with a warm hearth wrapped around Stanis, hugging him tight and refusing to let go.

He should have remembered that his brother was also there. But in his defense, he had forgotten all his thoughts in those previous minutes.

Well, actually, that wasn't true.

He had struggled to focus since his parents' brutal deaths only three weeks ago. Struggled to remember to eat. Struggled to get up in the morning. Overall, he struggled to see past the current moment of simply existing. The scent of ash and burning flesh filled his nostrils, replacing the previous calming memory, setting his blood a flame. Forcing his eyes shut, he hoped the image would fade.

His anger was also hard to control.

His head was in a constant gray fog, which didn't seem to lift.

Time.

He shook his head at the word. "Time will make it better."

Like they knew anything about loss. Maybe they did. Constant resentment often overshadowed the numbness he felt though, and he wasn't sure when that would lift.

"My thoughts exactly," said Cole, as he pulled Stanis back onto the curb. "What is wrong with you?" He pined Stanis in place with his emerald eyes.

But Cole already knew.

He grumbled a noise and ran his hands through his short golden tipped hair. The days traveling over blistering bright seas, on their passage from Mount Isle to Orcus Haven, made his hair a lighter shade than its usual dirty brown. Stanis knew the gesture was an attempt to get his attention.

"My foot slipped before I could wait for the car to pass." An obvious lie that he knew Cole wouldn't believe, even as he kept his voice flat.

He often feared that his little brother always knew a lie from the truth. Everyone in Lafornas lied, it was as simple as breathing; but Cole always sifted out the truth under the surface. His little brother, of course, never confirmed that fact, but Stanis being the spitting image of his father, was never wrong about these things. Cole wasn't mature enough to understand the severity of their situation.

"Maybe you should've been looking both directions and not at that woman over there buying lace and silver or whatever." Cole's emerald eyes burned the side of his head with deeper intensity.

Stanis decided to scan her instead, up and down, resulting in a wave of frustration and as bitterness coated his tongue. "That's not what she's buy—never mind." Stanis's face was a picture of disgust. "I wasn't staring at anything."

Another lie.

A flash of strawberry blonde curls roped in his attention. Thumps of hammers hitting nails rang up around them. Cars cast billows of dirt in front of them, curtaining their hideout in a haze of dust.

Cole stared at him quizzically and reality sunk back into Stanis's veins.

"Can we go already?" Stanis grunted through clenched teeth before checking his wristwatch. The three hands began to spin furiously. They should be here by now.

Stanis watched the woman, who he most certainly wasn't watching, as she spoke softly to the salesclerk at the stand selling scarfs. Or was it tablecloths? He shook his head.

Why did he care?

That's when he saw her instead.

The woman shifted slightly to reveal a smaller version of herself. Twelve years of age, maybe. Stanis couldn't breathe. That's why. Panic locked in his throat. Darkness caressed the corners of his vision. He needed air.

The woman reached out her hand to the strawberry blonde headed girl and tugged her in tightly, whispering something in her ear.

The girl smiled at her mother. It was her mother, right? It had to be, their resemblance was uncanny. The sound that left her mouth could stop any clock from ticking. All the air rushed back into Stanis with force, as the girl laughed again. A sweetest sort of laugh that one reserved for the most intimate of jokes.

No matter how hard he urged his eyes to move off of her, they wouldn't budge. All the humidity of the evening had to be suffocating him. The city was blanketed in an eerie feeling of seclusion that matched his previous loneliness. Finding no other explanation for his stop in breath, he attempted to draw another.

She wasn't beautiful, no, she was somewhat ordinarily plain. Oh, who was he kidding? She was exquisite. A sigh of relief left his chest, now that his previous confusion was dissolved. It wasn't uncommon to have a large age gap between you and your fated mate, but the idea of generations separating them made Stanis slightly nauseous.

One had to really be still to notice the girl's beauty, before the moment passed. Like a pond without ripples in the dawn of day, reflecting the orange and yellow hues, similar to the strawberry blonde hair that barely reached her shoulders. Her limestone colored skin whispered the need to be worshiped like an altar. Every inch of Stanis's skin was set ablaze by her presence.

He knew she was the most breathtaking girl he'd seen in all his fourteen years of existence. He realized she was the only reason he existed.

She was his mate. She had to be.

The thought struck him so hard all he could do was back away, stumbling on wobbling limbs, his motions slowed. Then without a word to Cole, he ran.

"There he goes again", was all Cole could utter to himself.

He didn't want to blame his big brother for his faults. After everything he and Stanis had just gone through, he wasn't surprised. Well, not by the running, but in the direction for sure. Stanis had never been one to run from their problems, he'd never even left their father's side before everything had happened. Working tirelessly to master his skills and laughing at jokes only the two of them would understand, leaving Cole out more often than not. Cole wouldn't remember much about his father, but he would never forget his father's excitement for Stanis's potential, and the love he held for their mother.

She was right there. His mate.

Stanis's, not his.

Definitely not his. If it were his, he'd be running to greet her, that much he knew.

Cole sighed, jogging in the direction his brother took off in. So much for waiting at the corner of the street for The Relaggin couple. He was going to have to apologize on behalf of Stanis, again.

Every day it seemed, since the death of their parents only three weeks ago, Cole was apologizing for Stanis. Even though he was the younger of the two, Cole had a "better attitude". Stanis left the worst taste in everyone's mouth, and luckily for Cole, he often overheard everyone's thoughts on the matter.

Running helped Cole sift through the muddled thoughts around him and extract them from his own. Focusing on his steadying breaths helped slow his brain down. He wasn't exactly super athletic, but after the many times he was chasing after Stanis, he prided himself on his increase in cardiovascular health.

He rounded the corner at the next street and peered around for a moment. The city was buzzing with sounds of infrastructure, casting the entire street in red dust and the scent of asphalt. Large men bellowed commands and he was forced to duck under flying rods of reformed Norilekcin rock.

Hiding behind the tall pile of rust-colored bricks. Mere steps down into the alley, concealed from most of the bustle of the market streets around them, was Stanis bent at the waist. His hands on his knees, heaving down heavy breaths.

Cole approached slowly, not wanting to set his brother off on the chase again.

"Would you like to tell me *why* we have taken a quick jog this morning?" Cole panted.

The scent of the murky alley and dread made his stomach churn, urging him to make Stanis get his shit together, so they could leave. Cole side-stepped around a puddle of liquid as he made his way to Stanis. Praying to the gods above, that it wasn't a homeless person's urine. The scent of ammonia rising to his nostrils wasn't reassuring.

"As if you don't already know," Stanis bit out. Rising to his full height, he stroked his hands over his face.

One.

Two.

Three.

Cole's only guess was that Stanis was trying to calm himself. Many people had petty things like counting, to help slow their mind. Mostly the adults around them growing up, especially when they attempted not to exert their anger.

Cole was unsure how to answer. He could be honest, which he knew was risky to do in public, and he never had uttered it aloud. Was excluding information considered a lie? His brain was hurting thinking about it. Not because he didn't want to, but because it was illegal to possess a power that was a threat to the Federation. But also because his mother had often told him never to lie.

"Well, you already know." Stanis said, the same expression in his striking jade eyes that their mother had gifted him. She was a bright star in the darkness and her eyes had always brought Cole great comfort.

He looked down at his older brother, who's posture didn't resemble his mother, even slightly, at the moment. Stanis's mouth was in a sharp line, and his jaw was still tight from clenching his teeth. His sandy skin appeared whiter. It was an odd feeling brewing in Cole's gut.

Pity.

But his brother was his idol. It was impossible to pity the one you also idolized. Many people thought the two boys were twins. It was odd how similar they looked despite the three years of age separating them. Cole wondered if he would ever stop worrying about what others thought of him. If he could ever act more in the manner that Stanis carried himself in, at least most of the time. He admired his brother's strength, and he strived to be just like him in every way.

His mirror image.

"Yes," he said softly, "but that's not the type of thing I whip out gently, Stannie, especially in public." Cole attempted to lighten the mood with a small half smile and a wink.

"Well, I don't want to discuss what happened either," Stanis bit out, his voice strangled.

Cole ignored him.

It was illegal for him to possess the power of telepathy. The Federation feared anyone who could manipulate them. The competition between their secrets wasn't equal in Cole's eyes. Stanis finding his mate, *and* being given the opportunity to reach his full potential. Other than aggravating his brother more, Cole didn't see a reason not to push him.

Cole took a deep breath, then before he could change his mind, spat out, "You saw your mate, didn't you?"

"Stop!" His brother was shaking now, his fists in firm grips.

Cole rushed out in one breath. "She was the girl at the cart, right? With that woman?"

"I said…*stop* Cole!" He snapped.

His brows pushed together as he watched Stanis begin to pace. Stanis clenched his knuckles firmly, turning them into opals. He wouldn't hit him; Cole knew that for certain.

Cole sighed, "she's your mate. This is a good thing, isn't it! We need to go back and meet her. Meet the Relaggins. Stannie please!" He waved his hands around in the air, hardly catching a breath. "We need to go back, and you can be with her. This is what's supposed to happen. We finally know why all this is happening, to increase your potential."

Breathless now, he sensed regret rearing its ugly head. He hated his own rambling, realizing Stanis thought the opposite of this being his destiny. How could it have been? Was their parents' death leading Stanis to his mate? Cole grimaced at his own presumption, instead hoping the world wasn't that completely fucked.

"They're old friends of dads. Please let them care for you." Stanis stopped gripping Cole's shoulders and searched his eyes, fully knowing Cole would hear him, "*and don't look for me*".

Then, Stanis did the last thing Cole expected.

He hugged him. Stanis hadn't hugged him in years. Not since they had beaten two bullies for pushing Cole in the dirt and spitting on him. Even then, that had been a half hearted grip with one arm slung over his shoulder. He released him from the hold, Stanis's hand finding his biceps. His face sculpted in the perfect calm.

So unlike Stanis.

It worried him to his bones. He searched his face for anything, dug into his mind for anything.

Nothing.

Then he released Cole's shoulders, turned and in a single blink, he warped away. As if he jumped in the air from one place to the next. Or more specifically, from one time to another.

Chapter 2

She detected it before she even allowed her eyes to fully adjust from the darkness.

His presence.

He always found her in her dreams. Her stomach churned and her heart rate pounded in her chest. She knew what she'd see when she finally let her eyes drift in his direction. The anticipation of it all was what made her wait to do so. The dream was always the same. Always ended in heartbreak, but maybe this time it wouldn't.

What if it didn't? What if she could finally see his face?

Her eyes fixed on the pinkish orange glow of the umber sun setting over the hill, making her breath hitch.

He was there.

Standing atop the hill of lush grass. His hands clasped at his back as he watched the colors paint the sky. Her gaze followed the length of his tall stature. His dark pants and deep leather jacket did little to conceal his beautiful physique. His broad shoulders rolled as he admired the view in front of him. She willed herself forward in an effort to bathe in the glory of the sunset alongside him. This particular one was her favorite.

Honestly, it was the only sunset that she'd ever really seen. Thunderstorms always concealed their glow in reality.

When she would close her eyes for the night, she welcomed sleep as she was swept away to the base of this very hill. Imagining the scent of fresh cut grass and freedom.

Fortunate to be with him, but forced to watch him.

Her mate.

She knew it was him. It had to be, why else would the gods show her this? This unique form of torture she found herself basking in each night. Tonight it seemed different, she wasn't sure why but her skin tingled in a new way. A sensation she desperately wanted to believe was instinct.

She had studied his figure many times, but it was his eyes she craved to get lost in. The sky wrapped him in a golden hue, setting him ablaze, signaling her dream was almost concluded.

His presence, always calling to her.

She could sense him, just out of reach, so she tried to will her feet to move. Unfortunately, like always, they seemed to sprout roots, planting her firmly at the base of the hill. A subtle breeze kissed her face and she managed to reach up enough to press her fingers to her soft skin.

That was new…

Suddenly, a call came from somewhere deep across the lands, so faint she could barely hear it. Her head craned towards the deep forest of pine.

The voice echoed in the wind again, as she frantically tried to move herself closer to him. The urge to wrap her arms around him, pushing her, but forced to stay immobile. Her heart pounded her chest as she stood frozen watching him.

There.

The voice beckoned her again. He swiveled his head towards it, seeming to answer the siren's call. As if it was caressing their souls so deeply, laced with conviction, and yet distinctly soft and feminine.

"Come..home..baby."

His feet lifted from their perch and he began to descend the opposite side of the hill, towards the voice.

Away from her.

Her heart began to pound more aggressively. Her rib cage barring it from escaping. She tried to scream out for him to wait, nothing came out but an exasperated gasp. The sensation of moisture dripped down her face, hitting her upper lip. She hadn't cried in years, she never let it truly happen. Now she couldn't contain them, they rushed from her eyes. Her throat ached from the deep burn of trying to hold them down.

Her shoulders began to shake, then her eyes opened.

"Arabella!"

The fabrics of her canopy bed framed the corners of her vision. Her palms found her eyes sockets, reaffirming her into reality.

"No need to continue screaming mother, I am awake now," Arabella spat, irritation lacing her voice. Faint light crept into her room, dancing across the ceiling as she watched it, allowing her eyes to adjust. Intentionally ignoring her throat's soreness from the coarse scream. Along with the moisture on her pillow. Luckily, she had stopped crying, only leaving a coating of salt on her skin that cracked as it began drying up.

"I wasn't the one screaming," her mother said.

She matched her mothers scrutinizing look with her own. Her mother's pale skin appeared translucent, apart from the typical dark purple circles under her eyes. Behind the sagging skin, fading cherry hair, and bone thin limbs, it was easy to see her mother had once been beautiful.

Biting down on her tongue to prevent her from lashing back at her, Arabella forced herself to let the scrutiny wash over her. Her mother didn't deserve unkindness, but she also hadn't ever been nurturing either. Arabella observed her mother as she placed her fragile hands into her lap gently, forcing them to wait for something to happen.

Anything.

She sucked in a deep breath preparing herself. Tugging at her deep seated courage. She never had trouble finding it, but handling her mother was different. Like watching a car crash into a brick wall, it wasn't terrifying until it was happening.

"I —," She sat up.

"Well you better get up, he's waiting."

Her mouth remained gaping open as she watched her mother stride from the room frantically, without allowing her to respond. Her soft cream dress brushed her calves as she departed.

Arabella rolled her eyes, letting out all the air in her lungs, before slumping back down into her sheets. Covering her head with their satin shield and scent of her own sweat. She knew she didn't have long, so she listened to her mother's receding footsteps. Calculated the minutes until her father would react poorly to her untimeliness, then mentally prepared to face reality.

Rain began to pelt the window, overpowering all the other noises around her. She flung the covers off of her body in one fell swoop, then remained motionless. She willed herself to take her time getting up, it was a small rebellion but one nonetheless. She let the rhythmic thumping of the rain guide her pace. Counting its pelts and following the design encrusted on the ceiling with her eyes.

Slowly she rose, swinging her feet to meet the deep wood floors, and pulled on the maroon cotton robe that hung on the hook at the side of her bed. Striding into the opal tiled bathroom, making sure her feet were slow paced, she let her mind wander. It often helped her take her time, and she definitely was in no hurry. Unlike her mother who always raced away from her.

Her mother hardly ever raised her voice and never got angry, but without fail, would flee. Her father, The Lord of Drafthaven, however, did get stern, aggressive, and disturbingly silent when provoked. So, Arabella left all the provoking to her brother. She needed her parents to remain content with her, so she tried her hardest to do everything she could to keep the house stagnant.

Arabella Drafthaven, an unmarried, Enkrateia born, but seemingly vacant was almost thirty years of age, graduated from her magic schooling at the prestigious Udethe School for Exemplary Women, and back in her hometown of Drafthaven. Now expected to fill a role in Orcus Havens high society, also known as the Aristoi.

As well as, find her mate.

Her father, Cornielious, was the self-proclaimed king of his own throne, always making his every desire clear. She wasn't sure how he had convinced Batar, the over ruler of all of Lafornas, to grant him any favors, but her father was Enkrateia born and mated, so therefore an inevitable force that was feared by many.

He seemed to be unbreakable but like everyone he had weaknesses, and luckily his daughter was one. Well, at least she had been for many years, until she returned and he hadn't been all that welcoming.

While she was away Batar, himself, had helped raise her father through the Federations ranks. He had granted him the growing city outside of Limos, in the countryside, which her father had decided to name after their family line; and what better name than his own, Drafthaven.

Arrogant, right?

He had also inevitably declared that Arabella's life was to be organized for her, to match their newly granted elevated status within the Aristoi ranks. The man she knew growing up was gone when she entered the giant estate that she now was forced to call home. Gone was the smile that she was hoping would greet her at the door, followed by a warm embrace and a tickling of a beard on her cheeks as he lay kisses on them.

Instead she was greeted by servants, whom she didn't recognize, collecting her things with quick fingers, as she stood in the large foyer filled with atrocious paintings and sculptures she didn't care about.

Feeling nothing but emptiness.

Eventually, she'd been graced with the presence of her parents, while they all sat in a grand translucent dining room, asking her questions about her studies and announcing her future plans for her. The room iced over, freezing her so deep into her bones, she wasn't sure they would ever thaw. Nodding along as she shuffled the food around her porcelain plate. Staring across from her at the empty chair that she knew would remain. Hardly speaking at all, to answer their questions.

Soon, her chair would make a matching set. She just needed to decide on a day, now that nothing remained here that she truly cared about.

This wasn't her home. Her childhood home was the small flat in the center of Limos that was circled by the bustling markets and noise of the vendors hawking outside her window.

All her father ever guaranteed her through all of the changes was a façade. A temporary one.

Her next three years. That's all he was willing to grant her for freedom.

Three years.

So she knew that she would make it count, finding an apartment with her two childhood friends, Abby Celesta and Aritzia Visha, after she bided her time. She knew it was odd that they all had names beginning with the letter "A," but she also found it endearing. Few things in Lafornas allotted that feeling.

Everything was calculated.

The three of them were initially inseparable. They had all gone to their primary schooling together, but then scattered all around the continent for finishing schools. Luckily, every Isle had a school. Depending on if a person's magic had surfaced or not, there was an option for everyone. Anthizo University of Plants, Minerals, and Elemental Magic, which Aritzia had attended prior to her private training in the Orcus Armada. Then there was the Center for Althos, which cultivated healers into organizations formed by the Federation like the Relaggin's House of Healing. The Federation provided some equality when it came to education, but only if a family could afford it.

Not every transaction was monetary either, something Arabella had figured out very young while observing her father interact with other society members. So, she was afforded the opportunity alongside many women of her standing in the Aristoi, to learn how to run a house for her future husband.

Some of those women were vacant of magical abilities, like she was pretending to be. But others, The Enkrateia, meaning those born to a mated pair, thus having almost completely controlled magical abilities also trained there, in the same classes. Being a high ranking Aristoi member was one thing, but being an Enkrateia in the Orcus Aristoi was the epitome of power under Batar.

Why it required three additional years of schooling, she didn't understand. Running a household came easy for her, so did the party planning, the pouring of tea, even the arranging of flowers. All while concealing her knowledge of her speculative dreams to herself.

All of it was frivolous and boring beyond comprehension.

She was top of her class, of course, but she was more than content for it to be over. She welcomed the release from her prison, and ran back to be reunited with her friends and her old life.

Now she was home, and no, not the death house her parents called a home, but with her best friends. They truly were a sanctuary where she was complacent and empowered. Which in today's age, despite societies and her father's backwards thinking, she was allowed to do. As long as she followed her orders after the three years. Being a member of high society had its privileges; which she, not so secretly, enjoyed.

Water splashed around her feet as she let the shower cool her down, the heat of the day was already seeping into the room. After the morning's treacherous rain slowed, nothing could contain the hot humidity that formed over the Isle.

Well, except for more rain. The heat was inescapable most of the time, unless one had the luxury of a purified cold shower.

She basked in the stream as it cooled her skin and watched as it poured from the head above her.

She was avoiding the breakfast table. If she at least showed an effort by letting the cleansed water run through the house pipes, then her father would hear that she was at least making her way.

Her father had stated clearly that a betrothal was the most powerful move for their family. That she would do them all a great service and her sacrifice wouldn't go unnoticed. She was Enkrateia born after all and could still provide any non-vacant offsprings. She tried not to consider the topic, she knew he would certainly bring it up.

Her new prison. One that would be a larger challenge to hide her abilities in.

But she also knew he was waiting to leave for the day until she made an appearance. Until then she would stall him, slowly, often without him noticing, so she could continue to live life like she always did.

Free.

But what about her mate? She cut off the water trying not to let that thought surface, wrapping herself in a plush navy towel and slowly stepping towards the vanity. Pressing her fingers into her eyes she forced herself to calm her anxious mind and push the idea of her mate aside. She didn't have her mate anyway, so what mattered more? Was that a lie, though?

She had a mate. She saw him every time her eyes closed at night. The same dream, the same hill, the same man. Only now it wasn't the same. This time he had left.

Walking away from her.

Infuriating her.

Hurting her.

Familiarity always beat her over the head, but he never seemed to reveal his face to her. She had a nagging heart, telling her that she did know the face. Sensing, in reality, this man existed but he resisted their connection. Everyone said mates find each other before the younger one's thirtieth year of life. The power that came with finding a mate was insatiable, becoming Enkrateia, not just born into the title. Even though it was common to find a mate, it was highly desired and deemed a huge accomplishment to have a powerful second soul, especially to Batar. He granted statuses only to members with high born genes and magical abilities to match.

Mostly the men.

She watched her silver eyes roll in the mirror, at the thought. Pulling a faint, toothless, smile to her soft apricot lips. Sweeping into her closet, she plucked her favorite blue dress from the hanger. Admiring the color in the mirror again, in this black and white world, she'd decide to be blue.

As the years passed, she often feared that her mate wasn't out there, so she reflected on her dream more than she would've liked. Shoving it into a mental box she had created, with the weakest locks she could muster, but still boxed up.

It took her a lot of self-convincing for her to not actually care about her *so-called* mate. In reality, she thought about what he looked like often. Mostly his hair, the dark curls at the base of his neck, because she knew that much for sure.

Dumb.

That was the word for all this fated mate's nonsense. The dumbest thing she had ever heard. She dried her wet dark blond hair with a single spell taught to her at school, flushing it back to its bright peach and copper tones. Then dressed quickly, a nagging feeling driving her to hurry. She knew deep down in her gut that she would be dealing with much worse at the breakfast table then a conversation about her proposal if she didn't pick up the pace. She accepted her fate, her impending betrothal, and the man she would face downstairs who held her life inside the brazen bull.

"My Belladona!"

Her father's pet name bellowed from his place at the head of the table. The dining room echoed his voice to her before she even fully emerged through the threshold. The scent of fresh baked pastries and imported fruits danced in the air.

She cringed at the name, fully knowing it wasn't a sweet plant to be compared to.

"Good Morning." She made her way to the table and reached for the large oak armed chair towards the middle. Her father's eyes, as gray as the streaks in his chocolate brown beard, and half smirk greeted her. Unlike her mother, her father's skin glowed in a deep tan. Everything about his outward appearance seemed warm, comforting, but she knew it had become an illusion.

The long oval table took up a majority of the room. The surrounding floor to ceiling windows making the space seem larger than it was. Her father had insisted that the entire room be made of glass. The only time she minded was when it poured from the sky, pelting the panes with a crescendo of violence.

Luckily the rain had stopped, so the room was bathed in dark red sunlight as it was shielded from the humidity that blanketed the air outside. She gazed across the vast caramel colored fields behind the mansion, observing the dark thunder clouds forming on the horizon.

"I have news, Bella."

She grimaced at the idea but fixed a smile to her face as she turned towards her father. "Really? What could it possibly be?" He had a solemn look as he observed her, so she forced her smile to curl further.

"I have made my choice, of course!"

"Choice?"

Thunder boomed in the distance causing her to break their eye contact. A waitperson appeared at her side and she recoiled at the sensation their presence forced upon her. She was still getting used to being back and having people wait on her during meals. If she had been born to vacant parents, would she be the one serving the wine, to a woman in a blue dress with no real world worries.

A faint pitter patter of rain hit the windows above, and the room dimmed a few lumens. She gazed around the dining room for any other indication of her father's so-called news, but came up short. She did however notice the life sized statue of their old butler, frozen mid stride near one of the doors. Apprehension seeped into her veins, as it did whenever her father showed his true strengths. The butler most likely forgot to salt something on her father's plate. It wasn't hard to upset him, but for Cornelius to petrify a butler meant he was in a bad mood.

Her father chewed loudly as the seconds ticked by between them. Then stated pointedly, "Lukas Hik".

"Lukas….Hik?" She repeated, willing her voice to remain aloof.

Her father was a man of few words and he always seemed to think that was the better approach. She found herself disagreeing with that fact every time they spoke. It could be said that he most likely possessed the same impressions, but she didn't want to upset him for obvious reasons, so she waited for him to continue. Pushing around the food on her plate with her fork she resisted her urge to ask the staff for a stiffer drink than the juice that was in front of her. Her father continued to chomp away at his food without looking up at her. She wondered if that was all he had to say, and if she could leave.

A grunt jumped from her father's throat, causing her spine to stiffen. "Batar's messages have asked me to make the pairing, so I have." The mention of the Ruler of Lafornas made her tongue become thick.

"So Lukas is his…"

"Son. His son."

"Um.. and I'm to marry him?"

"Of course, Belladonna! How else do you expect to become a full Enkrateia like your family, he's willing to overlook your *issue* as well." Cornelius attempted not to recoil at the word issue, but failed.

Questions raced through her mind at rapid speed, but only one mattered to her in that moment. "In three years, right?"

Silence.

She froze as the pair of them stared at each other. She willed herself to remain firm in her posture. She was no longer a child and she had a right to ask questions. It wasn't like she had said no to him. It certainly was beginning to seem like it, the way he blankly stared at her with sterling gray eyes, unmoved by her question.

"Sir." The voice of a new butler broke their stalemate, allowing Arabella to force air into her lungs, while her father turned his enraged glare towards him.

The tick in his jaw was sharp but remained for a flash, over lapped by the wave of his hand.

The new and, rather obviously, young butler glanced at her quickly before continuing, "Mr. Atler is here to see you," his breath shook with every word.

A firm breath was released from her father's nose as the butler stuttered over his words.

"Well, what are you waiting for?" His voice was firm but held a hint of irritation.

Relief began to wash over her spine at the thought of their new guest. She bit down on her lip to force her smile to stay hidden. Her father still hadn't answered her question so she wasn't in the clear yet. Hoping to cross the finish line soon.

Then he appeared, causing her breath to catch.

He glided into the room propelled by his strong form and broad shoulders. His emerald eyes found hers instantly. Her heart tripped over each beat, like a crack in the pavement. She forced herself to look down at her plate.

"Cole!" Her father exclaimed, "I have many items for you today, but first, sit."

Cole didn't hesitate to take the seat across from Arabella, despite the extra steps it took to get there. She caught the scent of allspice and deep desires as he passed. He was intoxicating to her, and his presence was often unsettling.

She watched him as he sat and took his plate of food from the waitperson, his bright white smile causing them to blush back at him.

Her face was warming at the sight as well. She quickly shifted her head down.

Fuck, why was he so handsome.

Cole's deep laugh shook the room, and forced her to make eye contact once more. He never let his eyes leave her.

"Morning Arabella," Cole was the picture of calm as always. As his emerald eyes traced her features, forcing her to forget her manners.

She nodded, but her voice refused to leave her lips.

Cole smiled wickedly, causing her veins to warm. "I heard you are seeing Abby today."

She noticed how it wasn't a question, and she couldn't help but become thrown off balance by the comment. He always asked about her time at school first, how she was feeling, and then… maybe…about her friends.

"Why would you care?" She said, at a speed that surprised even her.

He smiled, placing a mug to his lips and watched her squirm, sipping his coffee slowly.

Black coffee.

Why did she know that?

Cole's laugh grasped her attention again. A nagging sensation made it appear like he was waiting for her to finish thinking.

"Are you done now?" He asked.

"Done, what?" She stated, her brows furrowing.

A wolfish smile gripped his chiseled face. "If you're done pondering ways to make me fall in *love* with you." He dragged the vowel sounds out of "love" with exaggeration. "Then I could remind you that Abby left her sweater at my Mother's house yesterday."

He knew what buttons to push for sure. His last statement had also caught her father's attention briefly. Causing her to freeze. The lord resumed feasting on his plate and she turned her gaze towards Cole again.

She cleared her throat, forcing herself to remain removed. "I hadn't realized she was still helping at the Relaggin's Healing House."

A lie.

"Where else would a healer, like her, work?" He asked, as he took another sip of his coffee.

Relaggin's Healing House was a not-for-profit hospital that his adoptive mothers had set up a decade ago in their own home, in the heart of Limos. After a deadly virus had swept through the Isles a few decades prior. The oldest citizens, unfortunately, had it the hardest, wiping them to complete extinction. Now the non-profit house was a place for children with minor injuries or diseases, ones that the main hospital in Limos didn't consider serious or couldn't afford to help.

Mortality wasn't a huge concern in Lafornas but some had required attention from common ailments. It was also the only "hospital" on their Isle, Orcus Haven, that actually cared for the children for long periods of time. Which was Abby's main goal in life. To heal all the children, to have a bunch of children, really anything to do with children. Arabella smiled as she thought about Abby, because one could not love Abby instantly upon meeting her.

"Sir, I will meet you in your study, there's something I need to do first." Cole stated, bowing towards Lord Drafthaven, who simply grumbled a noise towards him. At some moment in her delirium, he had stood, already having handed his plate off to the hands of an awaiting staff member. Heading for the door, deliberately rounding the table the long way, attempting to catch Arabella's gaze but it was firmly on her hands settled in her lap.

"I'll see you soon," he whispered in her ear as he passed.

Her skin blazed alive at the sensation of his breath across the back of her neck. Arabella decided now would be a good time for her to leave as well. She shifted in her seat and willed herself to casually stand.

She didn't even think to hand off her plate. Unlike Cole she didn't care to be courteous to the wait staff; who seemed to come and go through a revolving door at the rear of the house. She didn't want to be ungrateful, but she also never seemed to see a familiar face amongst them.

"You will be attending the ball with him, Belladonna." Her father's words stopped her retreat.

He couldn't possibly mean Cole, only she thought about him for more than a brief moment. He was her father's employee, his lackey if anything. No, her father meant, "Lukas?"

More grumbling answered her.

"Yes, sir," she nodded, even though he wasn't even looking at her as he ordered her around.

"I can't protect you forever, my Bella." She waited for him to state anything else. Her feet firmly planted in the ground.

"You may go."

She swiftly headed for the door, trying to regain her breath and hide her pace, as she retreated from their battle. A pit in her stomach formed as the idea crossed her, he never had answered her question. She had time to worry about that later, as of right now...

She had somewhere to be.

She headed down the hall towards the stairwell when firm hands grabbed her and yanked her into the hall closet. The action didn't surprise her. She grinned wildly as the darkness and the scent of allspice surrounded her.

Cole's mouth crashed into hers, and she struggled finding a barrier to hold her upright while they stumbled into the black.

His rough hands suddenly found their way to her lower back. He pulled back the urgency of his kiss slightly, and she moaned. His hands found their way down around her ass and lifted her onto a crate of table settings. The box rattled, and she tried to contain her laughter.

Cole's hands made their way to the hem of her dress, and she gasped at the feeling of his warm touch on her upper thigh. She pushed her hands up into his thick hair. The length of it disappointed her, but she pushed the thought aside. She wrapped them around his neck instead. Lifting her hips up as Cole hooked his fingers in her lace thong and pulled, allowing it to fall to her ankles.

He kissed a line down her neck as he thrusted his fingers inside her. Her breath hitched, and she bucked closer to the edge of the crate, begging for him to press deeper. He found the spot just inside of her that made her skin tingle, and she threw her head back in ecstasy.

She could always rely on him, even for a bit of fun.

"Fuck, Cole." She moaned as he increased his pace and covered her mouth with his hand. She could sense his urgency through his pants and he pressed up against her inner thigh. The friction of his jeans created a frenzy in her mind. Just as she squeezed around his fingers to find her release, he removed his hand. Forcing her head to go blank.

"Damnit."

She knew he was smirking, she could hear the purr of the zipper as he removed his pants. The darkness surrounding them made it impossible for her to visualize, but she imagined him freeing himself, and pumping himself with his hand.

Seconds later, he pushed inside her, and she gasped. The feeling of him filling her to the hilt immediately caused her heart to race. He increased his pace and the power of his thrusts. She reveled the recklessness of their entanglement.

Arabella willed herself to find her own rhythm again but was failing. She knew he was close to finishing, by the way he was panting in her ear, and didn't want to be left unsatisfied. So she closed her eyes as his lips found her neck again and she let her mind take her.

She wandered away from reality, away from the closet, and into the warmth of the arms of another man. Where he was worshiping her with his mouth, and he let her take more control.

Let her straddle and ride him.

She drifted into his embrace, which was frantic, imagining he was desperate to hold her and caress every inch of her skin. Her arms would circle around his neck as he kissed and licked her everywhere. Praising her with the words she could only imagine men thought about her. Her hands bathed in his long hair as she sank down in her seat and filled to the brim with his presence. Her heart singing as it propelled her over the edge, clutching down around him.

Cole jerked inside her, as she eased her shoulders and found herself back in reality. He unsheathed himself, leaving her feeling more bare despite being fully clothed. She listened as Cole readjusted his own garments, she knew from past experience, he would be avoiding her eye contact. Moisture seeped between her thighs and she quickly forced the gap closed, squeezing tightly. He was out the door not a minute later. The dim light from the hall illuminating her wantonness.

A joint between her lips was the only item missing from this picture. Hoping to avoid her father's wrath, she jumped to the floor, pulling her thong off of her ankles and whipping it between her legs. Readjusting her pale blue dress, she hid the soaked crumble of fabric in her pocket, casting a spell around her torso to ensure whatever remained of his seed inside her met its demise.

Her heart sank as she tried to catch her breath. She still ached for more, but he never stayed. It was always that way with Cole, quick and emotionless.

Chapter 3

Hours had gone by and unfortunately, on days when she waited until the next task, her mind would often wander. Following her around the halls and extending into their own tangents until forcing herself to reign them in. Her stomach was in knots as she tried to evaluate everything about her life. She would think of Cole, about how she was eager to be in his presence again. Then she would remind herself that he wasn't returning her feelings.

Wasn't he, though? He was near when he needed her. Did he need her? Or release? Was that enough for her? Her mind was often not nice to her. The consistent mean girl telling her she was worthless. Her tongue grew thick against the roof of her mouth. She tried to remind herself she wasn't. But what was she worth? Just enough for a good fuck in the closet every few days, obviously.

No.

She was worth more than that. She had her friends and her family.

Well, mostly her friends, who were her family.

She had Abby and Aritzia, and that was enough. Wasn't it? She pondered how their life would change if they ever found their mates and didn't need her anymore.

Arabella found herself in a delicate room, looking out the window. She hadn't remembered how she got there. Her feet just propelled her through life in a neutral state.

She thought back to why she was worth her given existence. What did she have in her life that was valuable? She recalled her familial duty, she would be valuable to her father again. She was doing her part for them by agreeing to marry Lukas Hik. The third son of the supreme ruler of Lafornas would be an effective match for her future and would ensure her family's success. She thought about what that entailed and she hoped he would at least be attractive enough to get her to reach her climax. If rumors were true, he was handsome. All the Hik's were deviously handsome

She could be successful in her role. Her schooling had ensured that part, even if he didn't lust for her in return. Would she lust for him? Her head was spinning again.

"Excuse me, Ms. Drafthaven, you have a message," announced the butler from the arched doorway. Crossing the room to meet him, she noticed how she appreciated the interruption from her inner dialogue. It was becoming too depressing, anyway.

"Thank you," she stated, as she picked up the envelope from the tray and turned away from him. Once she was sure he was gone, she unfolded it and read the word on the page.

She didn't need to worry about that. She was about to become an agent for the Itia Liberation Confederation (or the ILC for short). She had just become an unofficial member, and was entrusted in uncovering secrets for their fight against the Federation. She often questioned why they thought she would be effective in this role. She knew they wanted access to her father, and she didn't genuinely care if that was the case. Her father was boring and even if his work at the Federation mattered, he wasn't hiding any huge secrets.

She now had the code word for entry to the club and she knew her next step was to deliver information, which would be her driving force to get her through the rest of the day. Tomorrow she would inevitably contemplate her value in life again, but that was a problem for then. She tossed the card into the blaring fireplace and watched the paper burn into a small pile of blackened ash.

She thought about her mate.

She always came back to that, even if she didn't want to let it evade her mind. He was out there somewhere, but she could never talk about him with anyone who could actually help her find him. She would battle with the repercussions of finding him when the time came. She didn't know if she even cared. Most people in Lafornas did whatever they desired, so she would too.

Did she even deserve to find her mate?

She shook her head furiously as she continued to wander, finding her way back to her room. Deciding she should get ready to go out for the remainder of the day. The sky had cleared, casting an ominous rich wine color as the obsidian sun was pulling the fog away, revealing the ivory grass satiated with all its new found moisture. She cast a spell to help dislodge her scowl that had made its way onto her face. Her mask was always covering her true feelings. She ignored why that was the case, as she mangled her thoughts into a more productive place. Exhilaration seeped in as she let the magic flow through her veins. She wasn't able to use it often around her parents because she had convinced them she was a Vacant, not an Enkrateia. Eluding the unwanted attention that her foresight would inevitably bring was easier. Being vacant of magic would deem her less of a threat, plus, no one could prove lineage in Lafornas without the histories. All of which were lost generations ago; Batar having rid the need for any past tomes of knowledge.

She looked at her reflection in the mirror and decided she looked as perfect as one could in Lafornas. On the outside, she proved to be fierce and dignified. The hem of the dark blue dress kissing her lower thighs embodied the vanity that she kept on display for society, all while her fortified mask covered her true feelings, encompassing the pain that her existence held. She wished her façade was powerful enough to one day bury her weaknesses in a shallow grave and she would become truly worthy.

"Why would he bring that up all over again?" Aritzia asked, taking a sip of her drink. Her fierce chestnut eyes sat perfectly under her angular brows as she observed the small plate, filled of delicious sweets in front of her.

The coffee shop they now sat in encompassed them in warm woods. Bright light slammed in the windows at Arabella's back, followed by a resounding crash of thunder. She went into great detail about her escapades in the hall closet and loved watching Abby's sapphire eyes light up in excitement. She adored the laughter that resulted from making a mockery of the entire situation. They had replenished her after all pleasure seemed to have been stole from her that morning.

The scent of coffee and sweet conversations wrapped around them. Sweeping her away with the small talk and pleasantries of the patrons sprinkled across the small tables of the shop. They often alternated the shop choice between the three of them but always found themselves back at the Cere's Coffee and Tea House. The mystic decor drew Aritzia in the most. An oasis from the furious weather outside, the book nooks cut in the hallows of lifelike pines surrounding the space provided a haven. As screech owls and magpies nested in piles of brush along the branches, just out of reach.

Abby stood out in her bright white dress with violet flowers, flowy and backless. Opposing Aritzia's, which was dark red and tight around her thighs, with a single slight over her right leg. Arabella's blue fabric was simple as well, to accent her eyes, and the skirt sat higher on her hips and flowed longer around the legs than Abby's did. All three girls had variations of blonde hair, and most would think they were sisters until you saw them up close.

Arabella shifted in her seat and pondered the question Aritzia had asked. Her friends were forced to wait patiently. She was a bit taken back by the question, not because of what it contained, but because Aritzia had asked it first, not Abby.

Arabella had wanted to meet with them as soon as she heard the war report of the week. Fate urged her to see her friends as often as she could. With the threat of war between the ILC rebels and Federation looming over their heads consistently, she knew that her time with them was limited. Each day brought a new issue with the Batar and his Federation's rulings. Their constant blaring of vacant cleansing propaganda, funding his under lords to increase their standings, and increasing their efforts to expand the gap between the Aristoi members and the Social Rights class all fueling their rage.

Abby's parents, members of the Aristoi class, had already mentioned leaving to find refuge and taking Abby with them. Something a member of their standing could afford, the freedom of admiration. The thought of losing Abby made her want to hide in her closet and cry for days. But, it wasn't that simple. Batar never let anyone leave, and those who attempted it, he had exiled. Everyone was always exactly where he positioned them. She would never admit that to Abby though, the one person who put everyone above themselves. She had always admired Abby's relationship with her parents, even if that meant she had supported their agendas. Because it was strong, and rivaling in comparison to her own. It was her own fault though, having lied about her abilities, she had disappointed her Enkrateia parents by leading them to the belief that she had been born vacant of magic.

"I think he likes to remind me I'm not his mate." Arabella said.

"He seems to think that you are always thinking about your mate." Aritzia said from her right, causing her to crane her head to look at her. She perked up at the sight of Aritzia, tucking a stay hair back behind her ears.

Patrons shuffled in and out of the door next to them refraining from wicking moisture in their direction as they shook off umbrellas and coats.

Arabella followed her gaze and questioned Aritzia's line of thought. She had never talked about mates because she really didn't care who hers was. Aritzia frequently stated how she was perfectly content without a mate dragging her down. In her defense, she was Enkrateia, and pretty much the only woman on Orcus Haven that owned property before she turned twenty-three. Also one of only three women who worked in the government's infrastructure department right out of school.

"You should stop sleeping with Cole," Aritzia's deep brown eyes focused on her intently. And as Arabella met her fiery gaze, she decided it didn't sit well with her.

"Why do you suddenly care if I am having sex with him or not?" Arabella spat back, a furious burn coating her veins. "Or is it just sex in general?"

Aritzia's hands clenched, fighting the urge to make this a physical altercation. Aritzia was the feistiest of the three of them. That, topped with her background in combat training, made her incredibly intimidating. Her father, the General of the

Federal Armada, had been training her since she was a young girl.

"You know I couldn't care less about who you both have sex with, as long as it's consensual. I am just worried about you. I want you to give yourself to your mate fully when you find him."

"What does that mean?" Arabella released a breath. An altercation was avoidable, especially in public. Avoidance was a trait she wasn't familiar with though, and appearing weak was worse than the embarrassment of causing a scene.

"Maybe he can read your mind," Abby stated nonchalantly, but judgment laced across her face, as she stared at them. Her tone scolding them like small children.

Arabella didn't know how to respond but the tension seemed to be washed away by the wave of confusion settling amongst them.

Abby cleared her throat with a small laugh and stated, "Oh girls, I am only joking!"

"Possessing non-approved magic isn't a joke, Abby." Aritzia whispered, glancing around. Her eyes hardened further, until landing back on Arabella.

"It's fine, Ritz. No one knows, and it's better if we make light of it," Arabella said with a forced smile, avoiding the wandering glares from the other customers. She hated when she fought with Aritzia, and she detected a wedge between them that she wanted to force away. She made sure her tone was back to neutral as she cast her mask back onto her face. Aritzia deserved grace on her front, being the only daughter of a notoriously sexist general couldn't be without its challenges.

Arabrella had always been grateful to her friend for guarding their most treacherous secrets. Foresight, technically, wasn't considered "Non-approved Magic" in Lafornas. Especially if one could only access parts of it, and only through the dream state. Keeping that closed with a tight lid was the preferred approach. Being seen as a Vacant was advantageous, especially to her future husband.

Non-approved magic was controlling or manipulating; and worst of all, magic that killed people or the lands. Many famous tales reported magic that was deadly. Recent stories even depicted a man who could break someone's bones with a single thought. Her secret wasn't comparable. That was a long time ago, and that man had been exiled to the Prison of Norilekcin on the Isle of Murr. Magic didn't exist there, therefore people couldn't escape.

"Are we going to Filly's tonight?" Abby asks, completely ignoring the previous topic of discussion. Her deep sapphire eyes twinkled in the soft glowing orbs.

Filly's, the best club in Limos, played live music and offered an array of cocktails that were nothing less than magical. So it was an obvious escape from reality. The owner of Filly's, Marietta Glowrave, used her growth powers to create special herbs and spices that made her cocktails more than enticing. They were also bordering hallucinogenic, and one could never have a disappointing time while at Filly's, especially whilst seeing the sounds that drifted through the air.

Filly's also housed multiple secret rooms for the more risqué activities, which were only accessible to members and their close friends. The club was the epitome of pleasure and desire. It dripped with sex, drugs, and lust from all pores. Luckily for all of them, Arabella had the password.

"Of course," Arabella answered, straightening her spine.

People in Lafornas always strove for an escape. Arabella relished the idea that she wasn't the only one running from her life. It was widely accepted to have a devilish time when one could. Whether that meant doing drugs, drinking alcohol, or both. Men, and women, attended strip clubs and dabbled in sex with shitloads of people, especially within the confines of these luxury clubs. Limos was an escape from reality in itself, allowing anyone to dive into their deepest desires.

Federation operatives, the Aristoi, and Members of Batar's inner circle were restricted from giving in to the pleasures that the cities offered, but that didn't stop them either. Some people even whispered that they did the same things as the lower social standing members did, they just didn't often intermix with them while doing it, like most activities they partook in.

A nagging sensation weighed on her chest, this time would be different. She could sense it.

She tilted her chair backwards, pushing off on her toes, and closed her eyes; seeing her mate and his dark hair again. This time, she was running her fingers through the back of it. Uncertain, but she thought it might be soft, and she didn't want to open her eyes. She dove into the pleasure headfirst.

Returning home later that evening would be routine. She'd deliberately head straight into her bedroom, quickly changing into black pants, a dark cotton t-shirt, and the oversized soft navy leathered and white pin striped jacket that she had stolen from her brother. The silver threaded Band of Vipers crest stitched to the back. The scent of leather and inside jokes caressing her skin.

She'd cast magic to her face, painting it with a mask of beauty that inevitably hid her emotions, but brightened her face. Then be up and over the sill and out the window. Her feet colliding with the soil in the rose beds with a thump. Avoiding the thorns of the burgundy roses, while she ran across the yard and leapt over the fence with grace.

Running down the street with a genuine grin on her face as she ducked into the open door of the awaiting black windowed car. She'd embrace her friends tightly, as Aritzia handed her a glass of sparkling liquor. Her spine finally softening and sinking deep into the sultry leather.

Chapter 4

"He sends his best regards as well," Cole stated sarcastically to Mrs. Glowrave as he set a thick black envelope on the hard wood bar top. Sealed with a thick glob of maroon wax and stamped firmly with the Drafthaven Crest. Her piercings shifted as she raised an eyebrow at him skeptically.

Cole came to Filly's every once in a while to hand off papers for Lord Drafthaven. He was hired as the lord's delivery person ten years prior, when he decided he wanted to leave Limos and live out in the countryside town. As the lord's business grew, his need for more shady dealings increased, so Cole's list of duties did too. Oddly, his work now found him back in Limos. Moving back fully once he met his now roommate, Grant Eros. Originally, wanting to be out near Arabella more, but he knew he was playing with fire.

He had overheard a few bits of the conversation she was having with the Lord that morning, before he entered, but she wasn't thinking about much after that. He desperately wanted to ask her what was wrong, but the presence of her father inevitably stopped him. His own inner turmoil was also a factor in that. He knew that their friendship was complicated as hell, but he still cared for her. He wanted to do anything to help her, so he mentioned her friends and watched as her stern gray eyes lit up at the scent of jealousy.

He enjoyed the temptation, but something else in him wrapped with guilt when he let himself think about it for too long. Their friendship had started out innocent, but puberty had introduced a new set of desires between them. Ones they couldn't resist. He'd spent years blaming himself and his brother for her demeanor, until he discovered the side she hid from the world. The side that, instead, reminded him of his old companion.

"Thank you, Cole. Your usual booth is available in the back." She quickly grabbed the envelope, dragging it across the bar and sliding it into her bag. "If you want to sit, I'll send over Tia with your usual drink as well." The ruby red braid atop her head whipping around her curvy torso as she glided away towards the back offices.

Mrs. Glowrave, like many business owners in Limos, remained in line with the Federation, from an outward perspective. But Cole knew this "club" was the best in the city because it didn't give two fucks who came in as long as they paid and kept their mouths tight. The Federation ran most of the city with an iron fist, but also turned a blind eye to the lustful acts occurring at Filly's. Due to the ever growing number of higher class patrons. Cole never wanted to dive into those sorts of acts, but he loved a good strong drink and Filly's poured the finest liquors in all of Orcus Haven. His driving force in life was biological. To find his mate and didn't want any girls getting the wrong idea. If he thought of them for more than the few minutes it took for him to get them to climax, he became guiltier. He toed the line with Arabella because it was easy.

Easy for him to give into the urge of hurting the one person he knew it would most. He knew Arabella was aware of their lack of connection and often reminded her it was just sex, nothing more. Had he remembered to do that?

Filly's wasn't busy yet, it was too early, but Cole knew in minutes the crowd would flood in. Every Aristoi and Enkrateia member would be let in first, flooding the occupancy until the lower social class was forced to beg at the door for an entry. He didn't know if he'd get in if his circumstances differed or if he would care; because he didn't drink the tranquil drinks served anyways. His preference was the usual sort of brown bitter liquor that numbed the senses, not make someone manifest shapes.

As he sat and waited for his drink, scanning the bar. Past all the glassy eyed patrons. He wondered if a certain trio would be present tonight. He knew the answer already, because Arabella always gave into her temptations.

"Here you go, Cole," Tia exclaimed in an orotund voice.

Tia liked the way Cole looked. He knew that because he had read her mind every time she served him. Which now that he noted it, was more often than any other wait staff.

Not that he didn't like Tia, he was flattered, but she was clearly searching for her mate. Unlike him, who wasn't actively looking because he knew what happened when one found their mate. He'd witnessed Stanis see Arabella for the first time. It was an instantaneous and life altering event. So he knew that power was worth waiting for. He wasn't a romantic guy, per se, but he didn't like to hurt anyone's feelings either.

Which he knew when he did.

Emotions like anger, lust, and heartbreak were the strongest amongst one's inner dialogue. Imploring him to avoid encounters with people who dabbled in such sentiments.

"Thank you, Tia." The corners of her mouth quirked up. "Has anyone been in asking about me again?" He coaxed.

"Not for a while, no… I saw a guy come in earlier asking about special spices, but Margie turned him away." Cole drowned out what she was saying, because he didn't really care then.

Ignoring Tia's rambling, his senses sprouted around the bar. Groups of roisterers flooded into the crimson leather rimmed booths. Their affluence seeping from them in the rhapsodic neon lights cascaded from the ceiling and reflected off all the surfaces. Most of the patrons never held his interests for long.

It had only happened once. The bar had been so full, he'd hardly been able to actually talk to him, but the man had given him some entail on Stanis and his whereabouts. So Cole had paid him a generous sum to get more information. He'd spent years actively searching for his brother, and never being rewarded. He wasn't sure when he'd forgone the expedition entirely, but his relationship with Stanis had become trivial the longer he avoided Cole.

He was starting to think he had been cheated as the months drifted by, eventually turning to six of them, since he had last actively searched.

"Thank you, Tia" He stood, reaching his hand to her and dumping three coins into her palm. "I am going to head upstairs to the other bar instead tonight. Better view of the place and all." He made sure his smile tipped further up this time, forcing her cheeks to flush a deeper shade of pink. He liked the service people at Filly's and wanted to make sure they stayed working there, so some flirting was sanctioned.

Filly's comprised of three floors, a main dance floor on the bottom level, a rooftop dance floor, and six bars scattered throughout. The large staircase towards the back of the bar ascended to the second floor. The third floor, the roof, was accessible by another staircase just past the first. The extravagances of it all was meant to disorient and fully immerse its patrons. The rooftop access was always guarded, and one needed a password. Cole knew if he asked Mrs. Glowrave for it, she'd most likely give it to him. But he had never wanted to go up there before tonight.

So, he passed the guard with a short nod of his head in greeting and aimed for the bar that overlooked the lower dance floor. The crowd was getting larger, and the dance floor was filling up as the band played songs that made people lustful. Or maybe it was because the drink special that night was called "Slutty Delight", or something like that.

He couldn't remember.

The somber club became sweeter, and he knew they were pumping in euphoric scents to drive the masses to an orgy. He used a blocking spell that he'd learned from his roommate to help keep his senses clear.

He removed his pine colored jacket, hanging it on the wall behind him. Sitting on the far end allotted a view of the crowd while hiding him slightly from the eyes below. He got another drink from the person behind the bar, and they swiftly went off to assist the many other guests appearing in flocks.

That's when the air shifted.

Quickly scanning the crowd around him and then below on the dance floor, his eyes fixed on an individual. A gentleman entering the main door, wearing black pants and a dark brown jacket. Only pausing briefly before he headed straight through to the stairs. Alarm bells sounded off in Cole's head. He anticipated the man's arrival, with a huge pounding in his chest. The man looked exactly how he thought Stanis might have. To his disappointment, the man never emerged at the top of the stairs. Instead, three lovely blondes yanked Cole's attention, forcing a smirk to his lips.

Abby's golden hair strung high atop her head. The long strands still flowing to her lower back, with a turn sending the locks spinning around her, as she whispered to the girl behind her. She is always transcendent, Cole had always thought so, but he also knew she never thought of him.

Ever.

He rolled his eyes at the thought of the last time he flirted with her.

Crash and burn.

It was then he saw a flash of caramel blonde, Aritzia. Who was beautiful in her own way, she was rougher around the edges. Her indifference towards Cole need not be said, her feelings towards him clearly painted on her face. She never seemed to trust anyone, least of all him.

Then there she was, Arabella. She wore her brother's soft leathered navy and white striped motor jacket, which he recognized immediately, and her strawberry blonde hair flowing in curls around her face. Much like it was that morning at breakfast, but gone was the pretty dress he knew she only wore to please her parents. He knew she preferred pants and a comfortable top. Which he also enjoyed because she looked content in them.

He liked Arabella, but not for himself.

He preferred her for Stanis because he could see his brother in every conversation they shared. Cole could clearly see, through the personalities they obtained, how compatible they were. Every trait Stanis possessed matched with her. His brother needed someone confident, strong minded, and a little feisty. They were both intelligent and stubborn to a fault, somewhat selfless and determined.

Cole knew that she was confused, mixing her feelings for him with her foresight, not that he helped the situation. He hadn't meant to peer into her mind, but he couldn't help but wonder if she had knowledge of his brother's whereabouts. So, he always pried into her mind just in case because she'd never know he did so anyways. But he also pried his way between her legs because he could, and he was often unsettled by the resentment that brewed towards Stanis.

Keeping his smirk in place, he made his way to Abby. Quickly enclosing his hand around her wrist to grab her attention. He knew the action along with his next moves would anger Arabella, but he hoped he would rile her up. A man has needs after all.

"Looking delicious as always, Abby," he said, winking to really send the message.

"Ew!" She spat back at him, before she even turned fully. Her face scrunched, her scowl morphing her soft pastel lips from disgust to ambivalence in mere seconds. She was too nice for her own good, Cole reminded himself why he was harassing her so often.

"Can't blame a man for shooting his shot," he said, trying to keep his composure. He glanced over Abby's shoulder and faced Arabella's disappointment.

Success, he thought gleefully.

He knew she'd be searching for him later. Now he just had to figure out how to get upstairs with them.

"I'm surprised to see you here, Cole."

"You're always saying how much fun this place is," he tilted his head towards Abby. "So I thought I'd come see if you ladies needed any company tonight."

Abby and Aritzia scoffed, murmuring scathing and vile names telepathically.

"Hear that ladies?" Arabella quipped. "Cole seems to think he has more to offer a woman than a quick tumble in a closet."

"Glad to hear I'm memorable."

"You're not"

Cole sucked his teeth. She was battling her true feelings in an effort to protect herself, again.

"Well this is super fun…" Abby interpreted, "goodbye Cole, I'm sure you know when you're no longer wanted."

Cole wasn't sure what she was implying but nodded. Arabella would obviously have to reveal the coded word if they were to get to the roof, so he'd simply repeated it after them.

Batar.

Arabella thought the words before she whispered them to the guard at the door. It was almost too easy. He hoped no one else had a similar power to his in the vicinity because most people never put mental guards up and he worried about Arabella for her innocence to his magic sometimes.

The burley guard let all three girls enter the stairwell without a second blink. Cole stepped to follow them until he heard Arabella calling back over her shoulder to the guard. "Just the three of us, not that man whore who follows us around looking for scraps."

Damn

She was a good competitor, at least. Perfect match for Stanis, if he were to ever resurface on this plain of existence.

Well, he would not be getting in now, password be damned.

Making his way back to his place at the bar, he waited exactly six minutes before pouring the rest of his drink back. Astonished to find his jacket absent, he searched the ground but came up empty. He tried to see if anyone around had grabbed it instead, but that also resulted in nothing. He turned back towards the stairs, deciding to forgo his jacket search for now. Until he saw a flash of familiar golden brown hair. The tall man in a dark jacket passed the guard and vanished into the stairwell.

Stanis?

His head spun, and he wasn't sure if it was the events that had just occurred or if his drink was hitting him too hard. A huge wave of exhaustion crashing over. Absent-mindedly he searched for his keys, frowning at their vacancy. He needed to get home before Grant fell asleep and he wouldn't be able to get into the apartment.

Abandoning his previous quest he headed down the stairs.

Avoiding the glassy eyed partiers, as both men and women reached for him with desperate limbs. He smiled back at each of them briefly, before gently removing their relentless paws. Their admiration was tempting him but his one distraction was upstairs, most likely dancing with her friends.

She'd find her way back to him.

Arabella never missed an opportunity to rebel against her expectations, and after the marriage discussion he'd overheard this morning, she wouldn't resist him.

"No longer wanted?" He snorted.

He was the only person who helped her forget her obligations. Their friendship allowed him to gain her trust. If he was honest with himself, she often was solace for him as well. Allowing him to forget his circumstances temporarily.

He was in the street again before he realized, avoiding all the loud patrons fighting to get in line for the club. Walking aimlessly, he was forgetting which direction to go in. He needed to shake off this haziness, but he couldn't remember which direction to face.

What was in that drink?

He looked down and encased in his tight grip was the collar of a brown jacket.

He definitely needed to walk the whiskey off before he did something else that would confuse him.

Chapter 5

The rooftop on Filly's was something out of a sadistic dream, well, a normal person's dream. Not a dream of hills, and men with lush hair. Arabella rolled her eyes, willing herself to forget that idea for at least tonight. Maybe she'd find a man to help her with that.

The theme of the space changed frequently. Tonight, it was one that resembled a lighter side of desire, an oasis of sorts: The Garden of the Hesperides. The archways over the long bar, draped in thick flowers of various shades of metallic and inky vines. The floor spanning the roof carpeted with a thick layer of velvety violet moss. Small opal stones pathed their way through, leading to booths concealed with twisting black vines, velvet curtains, and small lights that cast the havens in an ominous glow.

Out of the moss, in the center of the space, sprouted a glass covered pool, colorful lights illuminated the shallow waters under the shell. Flowing rapidly at the beats peak and whipped heavily with the melodies under the feet of dancing patrons.

The DJ, atop a suspended silver cube, played the hottest music, keeping the exclusive customers animated. Rhythmic thumping cascaded over the edges of the rooftop and down to the scarlet streets below. An invisible dome encased the space, shielding it from the night's humidity. The air dripped with desire, the added element of innocence of the theme creating more intrigue. Which is how Arabella foretold what came next.

"I love this song!" Yelled Abby over the rising beat of the music. "I want to dance," frantically she grabbed for Aritzia's wrist, and swayed her hips, before her empty shot glass hit the table.

Arabella sucked her teeth, as the shot burned its way down her throat and into her stomach. She hated it when Abby picked the liquor for the shots. It was always something horrid tasting and extraordinarily strong. She hoped this one didn't contain any hallucinating properties. She wasn't sure if she could handle another night of that, in parallel to the drugs she had already taken.

Despite her urges dipping into the lust of the night. What would happen if she did give in to her desire to let go? To dance? Maybe it was the shot they just took. She tried to remember what it was called. Whore's desire?

They floated down the stone path to the dance floor, squeezing past all the sweaty bodies. Who threw their hands up and around, flowing to the music. Glossy eyes followed them as they bumped their way along the wave, swaying to the music. Huddling closer together, they joined the rise of the crescendo. They didn't intend to draw attention to themselves, but they inevitably always did.

Unfortunately, as they pushed their way to the middle, Arabella became a bit too enthusiastic about the beat. A hazy glow formed around Abby's sweet face as she mouthed the lines of the song blasting overhead. Well, she thought they were the words, because in actuality the world drifted away, and she regretted taking the shot all over again.

Abby's glowing seemed to be intoxicating to all the men around them, drawing them to her like moths to a flame. The swarms engulfed all of them in a huddle of infatuation. Arabella's sight jumped from one perfect chest to the next. Lost in the deviousness of hands on her skin, causing her skin to warm with their contact. Bathing in the rhythm, the reverberations from the bass shaking her bones and surrounding them in a sense of overdrive.

"Fuck," she gasped. She needed to focus. She could let herself be alive again, but she needed to do something first.

Not that she didn't want to have taken the shot, it was that she was there to accomplish a specific task. Which she had meant to do before she let Abby and Aritzia convince her to go along with their antics.

What if she couldn't spot the person for the drop? And even if she did, would she be able to hand off the entail without embarrassing herself? She needed to look for a person with pink hair and a white jacket.

Pink hair. White jacket.

She scanned the dance floor, then gave up, searching around the bar instead. She stopped and squinted. Was that jacket tan or white?

Definitely pink hair, right?

"Ugh," she grunted.

She couldn't tell from here, she had to get closer.

"Ritz, I'm getting a drink. Want one?" She screamed louder than expected as she leaned in towards Aritzia. Getting Abby's attention was out of the question.

"No, thanks!" Replied Aritzia, her lips forming a devious smile of perfect teeth, as she looked toward Abby, then back to Arabella. "I think she is doing fine, too!"

Abby had found a man who was lucky enough to be dancing with her, until she got bored.

Hesitating only briefly, "Okay, watch her please," Arabella pleaded.

Then, she was off towards the bar before she could catch a reply. A light show illuminated behind the DJ, throwing beams into the dark maroon sky. The house lights lowered as she emerged from the crowd, soaking the rooftop in a glow of the twinkling lights from the gigantic stars above. The scent of fresh cut flowers and envy consumed her. Back onto the lilac mossy ground, she found an open path to the bar.

The city line became a captivating sight, as it merged with the glow from The Pleiades stars running above them. The beams of light from the roof match other clubs across the expansive metropolis. She hoped that the beams and blasting of the music was the only major occurrence of the night. Hoping the reprieve would last, maybe even a ceasefire in Lafornas would occur.

Arabella let her eyes adjust before her boots dragged heavily along the soft moss carpeted the floor. She needed to find her contact as soon as possible. Pulling her eyes away from the constellations and slamming into a firm figure. Stumbling to a stop, realizing she had run right into someone's back. The smell of leather and something familiar…*cannabis*, engulfed her as she continued her gaze up his tall form, she noticed light sandy brown hair that curled slightly at the base of a strong neck.

She couldn't breathe.

Mostly because the man had knocked most of the wind from her lungs, but also because the sense of familiarity was too strong.

"S...sorry," she mumbled into his back. She dug her fingertips into her eyes, in hopes they would stop blurring and reset her reality. As she removed them, she stared in front of her at the emptiness. Unease hitting her instantly.

Her stomach now heavy, her feet even heavier, she stumbled. She shook her head and pushed forward again. This time she made it to the edge of the crowd and only a few people separated her from the tan wood countered bar. She decided against the drink endeavor, searching for the splash of pink hair in the darkness.

There.

To her right, a person in a white blazer with pink hair. Speaking to someone tall, with lilac hair that glowed in the soft light orbs. Her sharp rounded cheeks flexed with every word out of her mouth. Arabella couldn't help but stare at her, her gut tightening as the seconds ticked by. She pushed her way towards them, but a group of girls passed in front of her.

"Fuck!" The pain from a stiletto heel stabbed through her foot and seared up her leg. Her black boots took most of the attack. Frozen with shock, she managed to shift her head down quickly to review the damage. These boots were brand new. Her anger gnawed at the cages in her head, and she tried to breathe deeply to will it away.

She made her way the last few steps and tapped the person in the white blazer on the shoulder.

"Excuse me, do you have the time?" She said. Turning before her was not a woman, but an exquisite looking man. His flawless brown skin sparkled with a highlighting glow that bounced off his cheek bones, with his equally perfect pink hair unmoving.

He tilted his head slightly and squared his shoulder. "Actually, I do, but time differs from isle to isle, doesn't it?" His mouth was a firm line of pink gloss, as he observed her for a moment, assessing her with only his eyes.

"You're right, I should've been more specific," she retorted, as she reached out her hand to extend to him the small white envelope she had been keeping inside her jacket pocket.

He took it with silk glove covered hand and slid it into his small opal bag that hung off his arm. "Obviously," he said with an eyebrow raised and pouty pink lip. She thought the encounter was over until he smiled like a cat back at her before heading away.

Pride washed over her as she relished her accomplishment. She turned to walk away, but stopped, remembering the other person. Veering back, but instead being confronted with two short women leaning over the soft-colored wood bar to order a drink.

Arabella sucked in a breath. Spotting her friends still thoroughly enjoying themselves, she aimed towards the back of the club, intending to splash some water on her face. The world was in a permanent lavender haze, and the roof was a kin to a rocking ship in the stormy Vontois Depths.

She made it about three steps before a hand gripped on her elbow, steadying her. The nausea brewing in her gut indicated she was swaying; the sudden lurch made bile rise to her throat.

She sensed the heat of the hand burning through her sleeve and she stared at it like it was going to burst into flames. Sand colored skin, sketched with bulging veins, flexed as it clasped her forearm. The grip lightened softly, and the scent of cannabis and indiscretion hit her again. His presence engulfed her, every point on her body came alive under his attention.

The skin across her spine tightened as the large and muscular male body pressed against her side. She brushed every indent of his chest as he pulled her in tighter. She definitely knew this was a man, but it didn't bring out the same fear that usually came with unwanted attention from strangers. Instead she was filled with a sense of calm, steadiness, and oddly a lightness was budding in her chest. Something deep in her was being set free.

It must be the edible she ate, in the car, finally hitting her.

She leaned into his touch. Enjoying a good grinding every once in a while, wasn't a crime. A rough breath that tickled the back of her ear interrupted the feeling of ease. Her eyes rolled to the back of her head and her lids closed. She needed to breathe, but his closeness was making her vulnerable and the muscles between her legs tightened.

"Ara, you need to leave," demanded a deep voice.

Well, that wasn't exactly what she was expecting.

The confusion snapped her back to reality. She realized she hadn't looked up at his face yet. Before she could do so, he turned and led her through the glassy eyed crowd. His large figure wrapped in a tight black shirt, revealing his muscle lined arm, as it pulled her further from the crowd. At some point, he had let go of her arm and grabbed her hand instead. She stared at it again. His large palm engulfed her fingers.

She was in a trance.

Questions raced through her mind. Who was this man? How did she know him? He had called her by her name? Sort of, not really. But he assumed to know who she was. Why was she following him if she didn't know him?

Reality bitch slapped her, leaving indents across her cheek. Stopping her dead in her tracks, she tried to release her hand. He stopped, but didn't turn. She waited, but he didn't look at her as she struggled against his grip, then suddenly he moved towards her. He closed the distance quickly and pulled her in, pressing her back into his chest.

"What the fuck?"

He let his arms fall, but he kept his fingers lightly pressed to her skin and he grazed down her lower arm to her wrist. Tingles shot through her entire body, and she froze, bathing in his warmth and comfortability again. She leaned back into his embrace.

"Ara, you need to get your friends and leave this bar in the next eighteen minutes or less." His voice in her ear was more urgent this time, still deep and firm. The urge to do the exact opposite tickled her heart.

"Please, Beautiful." She could sense the desperation in his voice, and she heard its vulnerability. Men never said please when they wanted to hurt you, right? Men in Lafornas never said please at all.

No, she wasn't that naïve, but she could sense he wasn't being dishonest or acting selfishly. She had an odd sense to trust him with her life. That was important to her, she realized, so she shook her head.

"Okay," she uttered, the surrounding air suddenly chilled. She needed to know if it was him. "Cole?" She asked in a faint voice.

She turned to face him, but he was gone. She couldn't see him anywhere, it was as if he had run away intentionally before she could reveal his identity. Devastation washed over her like a violent wave.

"There you are!" Abby's eagerness knocked her off balance. "We need to leave. I don't feel too well."

"Yeah." Arabella choked out. She cleared my throat. "Yeah, we do."

She noticed Abby was holding Aritzia's hand, as she encouraged Arabella to turn towards the exit. She grabbed Abby's hand and led their chain of attached limbs towards the exit, down the flights of stairs and out the front door.

The humid air clung to their skin. Despite the hour being late, the city was buzzing alive. Street vendors selling their late night delights lined the curb. The smell making Arabella's gut tug. Fresh air filled her lungs and rejuvenated her soul. They weaved through the crowds that blocked the cars, who began blaring their horns. Their hired vehicle was nowhere in sight.

"Ugh, we have to walk." Abby whined, tugging at her heels.

Arabella bent to offer up her boots, only to be stopped by Aritzia thrusting a pair of freshly woven sandals across her, into Abby's grateful grasp.

"Thank you, bestie." Abby's sapphire eyes twinkled.

"Come on."

Arabella aimed for the transit stop a few blocks away, searching for a service booth, to contact their driver.

BOOM!

Arabella clutched her palms over her ears, ducking instinctively. When she finally dared to look up, hands cupped to her head, she found Abby and Aritzia doing the same. They had only made it a couple of blocks when a blood curdling crack broke across the sky.

She looked back towards the noise when a second sound crashed through the surrounding air. This time, she saw where it came from. Back at the club, the front side of the building of Filly's shot across the street, sending chunks of red cement, mounds of flesh, and metal flying in every direction.

Chapter 6

The Present

He'd known that she got out.

He watched her as she guided her friends down and out of the building. Following them for a short time before taking off in the opposite direction. He ran down an alley, shielding himself between two eerie buildings.

When he had arrived at the club, he knew his time was limited. He'd hurried through to meet the contacts, intending to run out quickly before he had to repeat the events of the night over. Before he was forced to return again to get the outcome right. He enjoyed doing things efficiently, and one attempt in this present timeline was enough for him.

He'd seen Cole, and thought about speaking to him outright; wanting the eighteen years laid bare between them to be washed away. Once he explained where he had been and why he was stuck away, his brother would understand.

They'd obtain normalcy again. One day.

So, he had drugged him, not enough for Cole to pass out, but enough to draw on exhaustion. He couldn't face him and explain everything then. It would just hurt him more.

Forcing the script was easier, because he could then shield his brother from all the pain. From the death of his parents. And definitely from the tormenting his own heart forced upon him. The resentment of that dragging him back to this time in the present, to Arabella.

Cole didn't need Stanis to stay to protect him, he had needed him to leave. So he had done just that, and so far Cole was safe. He made sure of it often, checking in when he could. But making sure that he lived under the radar in this time. Never staying longer than needed and always lying. That was how it had to be. He wasn't a devious person at heart, but he had become some one his mother wouldn't have been proud of.

"Remaining true to your own heart will keep it pure in the threads of the Moirai." His mother always reminded him, but he was unsure what he would do if The Fates had decided his heart was pure enough or not. Like the fictional concept of mates, he never wanted to believe in them.

But his mate was real.

He had touched her for the first time in all the years of watching her at a safe distance. He had to warn her; he didn't think she could get in that night. What was his money worth if it couldn't pay off the guard?

People never ceased to fail him.

Did he have time to go back?

Checking his wristwatch, the three hands spun furiously.

He needed to stop thinking about her. He had more urgent things to accomplish. He should look into the leads from his father's journal and start getting back. He couldn't get the image of her smile out of his head. The smell of her hair, coconut, and something floral, roses maybe. She was intoxicating, and he was a certified addict. He pushed his hands through his dark golden strands that swept over his face, flinching at the pain in his chest as it shoved its aggressive fists through him.

Of course, he'd seen her smile before, but when he had finally pressed his skin to hers, he imagined he was Adonis. Reborn and forever youthful, not a man on his deathbed.

He lost all control. Pulled her into him, two halves yearning to be forged. He'd also detected all his need for her pressing in his groin, which was a true indicator. Her warmth was like sunshine dancing on your face when it sat high in the sky on a summer day. She embodied the feeling of home, one he hadn't had in some time.

One he couldn't have.

His heart had shattered when she tried to look at him and had uttered his brother's name. She said it soft enough that she probably didn't intend for him to hear it. He gritted his teeth at the memory. Stupidly, he had thought that Ara had waited for him. She never seemed to have any interest in other men when he'd observed her. If he had, he would've made a list of all their names. He'd seen Cole with her, but they never touched. Or had they? His stomach rolled.

A heavy blast resounded in the distance. Stanis forced himself to slow his pace. The large city center opened up in front of him, reminding him to remain inconspicuous. Shifting his hands into the pockets of the pine colored jacket, to conceal them from the moisture wicking his skin, he clasped his fingers around a set of delicate metal keys. The shoulders of the jacket resisted against him, a smile tugged at his lips. It was fine that it didn't fit, the entire stunt was worth his personal amusement.

"Stannie?"

Only one person would have called him that. He should've cast an illusion around himself the second he left the club. The thought immediately scrambling to materialize into a mental barrier.

He looked up, and in front of him, clutching his rust colored jacket in a tight fist, was Cole. Gone was the sweet little brother that he once knew. He no longer had soft green eyes. Replacing them were the cold dark emeralds, sharp as knives.

"Cole."

The embodiment of strength wafted off his brother, squared shoulders paired with tight lips, Cole always had a better handle on his emotions. Stanis mentally congratulated him on the amount of willpower, but mirrored his brother. Who stood at his full height, which he was delighted to see was still three inches taller than Cole. "That's where my jacket went…"

"A jest?…Really?" Cole interrupted, throwing the lump of rust colored leather towards him with the force of a gust of wind. Stanis caught it in one hand, never breaking eye contact. He lacked confidence with that approach, but what else was one to say after not seeing their brother for over a decade?

"Learned a few new tricks, brother?" Cole said, impatiently awaiting an answer. It was a question, but danced like a challenge.

"One must adapt and all to…," Stanis retorted with a smirk. He had perfected it over the years, encountering smug strangers. "Well, you know, stay alive". In an attempt to avoid more pestering he fiddled with the joint in his pants pocket, before removing it, and placing it to his lips.

"Oh, stop it Stanis, if you won't let me read your thoughts then you're going to have to actually talk to me," Cole's voice was rising now. "You left without any reasoning and expected me to just move on without you! We were both orphaned, Stannie, but you completely abandoned me!"

"Surprisingly,…*Cole*, most people don't enjoy having their minds intruded upon." Stanis leaned back, pressing his back against the cold cement building. He scanned the surrounding street, flicking his lighter awake, fearing that someone would overhear them. "Can we please talk about this somewhere else, or change the subject?"

Cole eased his posture, following Stanis's gaze around the street. "My apartment is four blocks from here. Can you get there without disappearing again?" Cole pinned him with a glare.

Stanis nodded and noticed the moisture lined Cole's skin. "Here," Cole was still his brother after all, he couldn't let him run around without a barrier from the acidic rain. "It's about to rain again."

"Thanks" Cole snatched the garment back, throwing his arms into the holes as he led Stanis through the city. Silence pulled them into her shadows, even their footfalls on the harsh cement path were smothered.

As they ascended the stairs of Cole's apartment building, Stanis checked his surroundings and mental shields again. He didn't want to keep secrets, but in a way, he also became apprehensive around his, now grown, brother. He definitely didn't want him to confirm where he just came from. For multiple reasons.

Faint screams resounded in the distance. Cole's fist overpowering them, with the banging on a door atop the landing.

Stanis raised a brow and found an opportunity to tease his little brother. "Did you forget the password?"

Cole ignored him.

Bitterness stung his tongue at his brother's lack of retort. They had always been joking as kids, and he wasn't sure what would happen when he returned, but he didn't expect this. He knew Cole would be mad, but he was never mad for long, and he always washed away issues with a smile that only Cole could master. His mother had always said Cole was the charmer, but Stanis was humble. He laughed to himself, drawing Cole's attention but only slightly. Stanis could sense him bumping up against his barriers, trying to invade once again. An enviable ability, but then he remembered he was the more unique of the two. *So much for humble and noble thoughts, right, mom?*

"She never said you were humble," Cole stated as the door swung open.

Framed within it was an exceptionally toned man, adorned with raven hair. His brown skin painted with ink on every visible surface of his arms. Tales of angelic beings and winged creatures danced along his muscles, dipping under his short sleeves, and out of view. Even though he was built up around the chiseled thick frames of a god, he also had a softness to him.

"Thank you, Grant," Cole's tone became unrecognizable.

Stanis scowled, forced to use a few steps to maneuver around the brute in the door frame.

"My keys got stolen, along with my jacket at the club." Cole headed for the kitchen, tossing a glare towards Stanis.

"Oh, and this is my brother, Stanis."

Glasses clicked.

"Yes, that Stanis."

Cabinets slammed shut.

"Of course I'm safe, as always."

Stanis watched, his face frozen with disgust, wondering what Grant's voice sounded like, because he sure hadn't opened his mouth yet. He reached in his pocket and clutched the set of cold metal keys.

"He knows?" Stanis nodded in Grant's direction, while he wandered the small room around him. Floorboards creaked under his weight, his fingers flicking the scabs on the wall, causing flecks of wall paper fluttering to his feet. "What's your extended name, Grant?

"Grant Eros." He stated, pride flushing over his features.

"Interesting."

Deep onyx and emerald eyes trailed his path around the room. The apartment wasn't exceptionally large, but clean. He could see that there were two bedrooms on either side of the open space, which consisted of a couch and two chairs. He couldn't deduce where the bathroom was from where he was standing. The entire room shook as a transit train slammed by the window, dust cascading from the ceiling.

Seizing the distraction, he lightly set the keys from his pocket onto a dish next to the couch. The black ringed sun peeked through the few buildings to the north, flooding the sky in its crude wine glow.

"There was a bombing at Filly's, maybe half an hour ago," Grant briefed. "My radio's picked up the Federations static about it."

His voice was deep, but Stanis didn't think his composer matched. He looked as if he could not only beat a man with his fists but also encompassed some intelligence. Possessing knowledge that would be fatal to any man who crossed him. Grant carried himself in an honorable manner, making Stanis dislike him instantly.

Cole lifted a glass of liquor to his lips without dropping eye contact. "Stanis, why are you here?"

"You invited me," Stanis replied as he continued walking around the room, putting as much distance between himself and the window. "Do you have another drink? I have a feeling we are all going to need one."

"No," Cole jabbed, as another glass hit the counter sending whiskey splashing over the rim.

Chapter 7

Annoying, that was the only word that Cole could use to describe Stanis at the moment. Well, maybe also aggravating. Stanis was absolutely annoyingly aggravating. Great. Now he had Cole thinking in alliterations.

He stared at Stanis and willed all his disapproval to burn into his brother. All he wanted was to know where he had been. In the past years, he had worried if he were alive or not. He had worried if he'd ever return. Now that he was in front of him, he had to remind himself that being mad at Stanis was the priority. Which wasn't hard, since his dear brother had been wearing *his* green jacket when he found him.

He wasn't certain if he had actually seen him at the club, but now a million questions raced in Coles' mind. He knew his brother would evade every single one he threw at him. Stanis was annoying in that way. If manipulation was a talent in a contest, Stanis would win a medal.

Sliding the glass across the counter to Stanis, he finally managed to remove his disapproving gaze, nudging his head in Grant's in question.

Grant nodded in thanks, but silently asked Cole. *"What happened at Filly's?"*

Cole found jade eyes avoiding him once more. He wanted to respond to Grant. He desperately wished he could do so telepathically, but failed. Well, he never tried too hard, anyways.

"Stannie, I need to know what you are doing here. Your timing isn't exactly a coincidence, is it?" Cole didn't know if he wanted the real answer, but they were brothers, that had to mean something to Stanis.

"I missed you, brother. I needed a hug from a family member." Stanis said with a smirk.

A growl crawled from Cole's throat. Fists would definitely be thrown soon if Stanis didn't quit joking around.

"I had some business in Limos, and I thought I'd knock down two birds and all that."

Stanis never finished a metaphor fully. He was definitely aggravating Cole more now. There were two sides of business in the city, either his brother served the Federation or the Rebels. Either way, both options were gang related, and he didn't put it past Stanis to get into something illegal.

Limos, being the largest city on Orcus Haven, had become a watering hole for radicals that wanted to join the Itia Liberation Confederation (or ILC for short). Either way, people justified it, it was a cover for rival gang activity. Grant had been tracking their movements for months now and convinced himself that if he could find a member, they would have to let him in, solely on the argument that he had uncovered their secrets. Every duration of lack of success led Cole to believe the IFC may be an illusionary concept.

Grant Eros was someone he had met by chance, maybe fate. They had met in a bookstore years ago when Cole was working undercover for Lord Cornielious Drafthaven. Grant was a person who he knew was trustworthy and loyal without hesitation. His mannerisms and intelligence were nothing short of admirable. He was the type of person who people wanted to be friends with in light of all the dark, and Cole had ensured he became his closest ally.

He and Cole had tracked all the Federations' secret messages through the limited radioactive waves that flew over the city. Grant had been working to get a head of the Federations moves in parallel with the ILC, hoping to find one of the members. Cole was the ground agent and Grant, so far, had remained with his ear to the static. He enjoyed this work in between the gangs more than his work for the Lord. In his opinion, neither organization led with the Isle's people in mind. The bombings proved to be a result of that malice. There wasn't a week that would go by without some sort of act of distraction or a counterstrike.

Grant's dark eyes found his, "What kind of business do you work in?" He demanded of Stanis.

"Oh, mostly deliveries, packages and such," Stanis winked at Grant, "mostly hunting them down."

"For fuck's sake, Stanis, a clear answer please." He knew that would hook Stanis by the throat. He had prided himself on his clarity as a kid and Stanis had been notably a fair fighter.

"Fine," Stanis ground out as he sat on the couch and threw his drink back, taking a huge gulp.

"I'm not sure how much Cole has told you about me, but I possess magic that isn't exactly…accepted in most circles." Stanis observed the pair of them for a while before continuing.

"I have been searching for a few items that my father was working on finding. Let's call them treasures. He was a bit of a treasure hunter, you see, before he died."

"That's not an honest answer, Stannie." Cole ground out, his eyes flipping under their lids, then regarding Grant for confirmation.

"It certainly is truthful! You saw father's research. He never shut up about it." Stanis boasted. "Yes, it wasn't his job, but he was killed for the maps he created."

"I'm getting confused." Grant looked towards Cole.

"I'll explain the entire story later," Cole reassured him, which he would, but he'd be leaving out some minor details. "But you can't just assume he was looking for something real, Stannie. No one has ever clarified that treasure is in the tomb with Itia."

A small lie wouldn't hurt, right?

Stanis regarded the room. "How secure are we to speak freely here?"

"Gods above." Cole cursed. Stanis loved to redirect the conversation at any opportunity.

"Grant has secured the apartment, his technology surpasses most of the Federation's inventions." A smile gripped Cole's face. He had always been so glad to have met Grant. He was like a brother to him. Well, a genuine brother in arms to him. Grant had been there since Stanis had left him. Frustration laced his veins, Stanis was questioning him and Grant's intelligence.

"The Federation has been searching for the tomb for months." Grant offered. Knowing Grant, he had only offered partial information in order to bait Stanis.

Stanis took it. "The Federation?" Stanis stood, knocking his knee on the table in front of him. "What do you mean?" It didn't seem to faze him. "Why would they want to find the tomb?"

"The Federation has been after the ILC for the past few months. The radical's main goal has been avenging Itia by removing Batar from his throne." Cole offered, also waiting for Stanis to reveal a bit more information.

Fury gripped Cole in her white knuckled fingers, when he saw Stanis running, it was a mirror image of when he had last seen him. Stanis deserved to drown in that too.

"I know about the ILC," Stanis said, his eyes scanning the walls. Cole reached for his mind again, only to be slammed with a wall of brown fog. "Removing a god chosen mortal from his throne isn't an easy task."

"Communication works both ways, Cole." Stanis's eyes met his. "Reading minds doesn't." He ground out through clenched teeth.

"Stop evading the questions!" Cole said.

"I've answered every one!"

"Well, you have also asked more than you are warranted!"

Their arguing wasn't getting them anywhere.

"Ask him directly." Cole glanced at Grant. His rough voice tickling his insides. *"Or I will."*

This wasn't Grant's fight, but he knew he was also getting impatient. Cole could hold out for the entire duration of the war but he doubted Stanis would agree.

"I'm going to ask direct questions now. I want a simple yes or no, Stannie." Cole asked calmly, rolling his neck. He was starting to yearn for Stanis to trust him. It was becoming obvious Stanis had secrets, and he was working ridiculously hard to hide them.

Stanis looked between him and Grant, then nodded.

Cole counted in his head while easing the air into his lungs with each number.

"Do you work for the federation?"

"No."

"Do you work for the ILC?"

"No."

Grant nodded after the first question, but walked towards the kitchen.

"He's lying!" Cole could hear the disappointment in Grant's mind.

"I don't believe you, Stanis." Cole pressed.

"I don't have any reason to lie. I work for myself. I know of these gangs, yes, and I'd rather die than work for the Federation, but no, I don't work for either." Stanis's jade eyes softened granting him slight trust from Cole. He knew when Stanis was lying, but more importantly, so did Grant. His brother was a good liar, but something in his eyes resembled a bit of… pain.

"I'm confused why the Federation seems to think they have any right to the treasure," Stanis finally spat out.

"Fine. Where did you go? Or more accurately, when?"

"That's not a simple question." Stanis turned his head towards Grant, who had reentered the little circle, sitting on the couch next to him. His brother looked like the weight of their world was on his shoulders.

The silence between them was starting to become unnerving, even for Cole.

He pelted a smile in Stanis's direction, preparing for his brother's next reaction.

"Stanis is a traveler, more specifically a time bender," Cole stated. "There. Secret is out, now tell me."

"I can detect deception." Grant stated abruptly. Cole traced his features in confusion, wondering what had propelled Grant to reveal a secret to Stanis.

Stanis shifted back in his seat and a smirk rolled across his face. He took a drink.

"That's an interesting tactic," he huffed.

"It's not a tactic. I'm serious. I can differentiate between lies and truth with pinpoint accuracy." Grant retorted, his shoulders solidifying.

"He understands. He's just trying to frustrate you." Cole said, throwing a glance at Grant to help settle him. The need to redirect the conversation back to Stanis nagging at him.

"Stannie, answer the question."

Stanis sucked his teeth, "Fine."

Then minutes dragged by, well maybe not, but they felt like they had sat there staring at each other for a while.

His brother was testing his patience intentionally. Holding Cole in their stalemate hoping he'd break, but Cole had learned to grow tougher even without the guidance of his older brother.

"I went back to stop the fire."

Cole's eyes widened. "You know you can't manipulate the past."

"I didn't!" Said Stanis.

Another exceptionally long pause stretched the expanse of the room.

"I couldn't anyway. The Federation was behind the attacks, and they had almost discovered me when I tried to intervene."

Cole's heart sank as Stanis continued to retell the events of their parents' death in their small mountain village, with pinpoint accuracy. Cole's skin tingled along his arms, his eyes swelling. It was as if Stanis had witnessed it a thousand times. He had so many details to share, enveloped with so much pain.

Cole pushed down his feelings, a lump lodged in his throat, altering his voice slightly, "so you stole dad's journals instead?"

"It wasn't stealing. They are rightfully mine," Stanis said, "now that dad is gone."

"Where are they?"

"They're safe."

"So, you say."

"Again, why would I lie?"

Cole huffed a breath through his nostrils.

"I don't know Stannie, you haven't been here for over a decade and now this conversation is taking forever to get to the fucking point. We need to ensure that the people, the ones being targeted by the Rebels, from the club are okay," Cole paused.

"It's convenient that you think the Radicals are the problem here," Stanis huffed.

"What's that supposed to mean?" Cole's eyebrows pinched together, he didn't have time for Stanis's games. "We need to do something now!" Cole grew chaotic. He wasn't sure where the act of compassion came from suddenly. Then he remembered who the *people* at the club were, specifically, three individuals. "Arabella," he uttered, worry streaking across his face.

"What!" Stanis stood up again. Cole could tell it was not an intentional reaction, but an instinctual one. Cole's heart softened again for his brother.

"Arabella was there, with her friends." Cole said calmly, so as not to set Stanis off running again. To his surprise, he stayed put.

Stanis's eyes searched the floor. "They're fine, I made sure." he said. He ran his hands through his hair and pinned Cole with a nasty glare.

Befuddled by Stanis's audacity, Cole swelled with questions. Was Stanis really there? If he saw her, did he finally speak to her?

Before he could attack him with questions, Stanis said something unexpected.

"Did you fuck her?"

It was a direct hit to Cole's chest.

Chapter 8

Arabella had never run so fast in her life, or for such a long duration. She knew Cole had an apartment in the city, but she couldn't find the way to his building.

Abby and Aritzia slammed to a stop next to her as she took a moment to search the street crossings again. The air around them thickened in a heavy fog, then the streetlamps began dying out.

"Ritz, please help again," Arabella choked out.

Aritzia grabbed the lamppost next to them and it instantly blared brightly. Illuminating the stone signs on the surrounding buildings with her elemental magic, making them more legible.

"Not too bright, we don't know who will see," Abby stated, her voice hollowing.

"It's fine. I'm done. I know where we are. We have a few more blocks." Arabella said and Aritzia let go, letting the light flow away again.

"Why don't we just go to the garage?" Aritzia's question wasn't spiteful, but curious.

"No, we need to find Cole."

"Why?"

Arabella didn't have the answer exactly. There was a tether pulling her towards his apartment, after the explosion had knocked them into a run. Abby had run first, grabbing Arabella as she simply stared in awe down the street to Filly's. She let Abby guide her until her heartbeat thundered in her chest, then she stopped, stating she knew what to do. They had been fortunate up until this point, and the bombings had only occurred in the slummed areas of Limos. Avoiding them would be harder now if the Federation was targeting clubs like Filly's.

A soft sob left her mouth, all those innocent people had been murdered all because the ILC had messaged routes throughout it. The girls had agreed but questioning would inevitably follow. The best of friends always did question each other a little.

"He was there, I saw it," she stated again.

"You know it because you saw it in a vision or because you saw him?" Asked Abby, cautiously.

When Arabella didn't answer right away, Abby continued to ramble, but Arabella tuned her out. She took a deep breath and tried to interrupt Abby. That was an impossible task, so she waited until she finished a thought. Attempting to rub off the ash that painted her skin in streaks of rust.

"We need to go there because we saw him at the club, remember? Then I danced with him upstairs, well I didn't see him exactly. I felt him, and he spoke to me…. intimately." She let the last part out as a small breath. Her thoughts were becoming a tangled mess of ribbons. The drugs and alcohol did not lend any help.

Aritzia caught her whispers. "What does that mean?" Her eyes perking up.

"Ritz, I apologize for our argument earlier." Arabella said. "I don't know how to help you see that we can trust him. I know deep inside me, that I'm right about this," she pushed all her regrets to the surface.

"I'm sorry too." Aritzia finally retorted, embracing her. Abby's nibble arms encircled them as well, a result of her never missing out on an embrace.

Arabella quickly retold the events from the club. The street began to grow warmer around them, brushing away the fog, and the heat began drying their slicked hair. She spotted flecks of umber rays from the sun kissing the city skyline. Her friends took a few moments to consider everything, which was predictable, both of them were far smarter than she was.

As her friends processed the details, she closed her eyes and remembered the feeling of warm arms embracing her. The heat of him on her back, his scent, and how smooth his voice was in her ear. She willed away the feeling of desire, now that the drugs had worn off, she was becoming slightly embarrassed that she had let them take her to that ecstasy.

Her friends were both just staring at her now. Abby opened her mouth as if to speak, but then snapped her pink lips shut. She gripped Arabella's arm, narrowing her sapphire blue eyes in her direction, and she could sense her friend's magic trying to aid her.

"I…," Arabella started, but a wave of magic weaved through her fingers. It shot up her arms and into her neck, sending her head back as her sight blacked over.

She was seeing through a separate set of eyes. Staring at Cole, who was being slammed against the wall, pinned under a forearm at the throat. She realized she was his attacker. Fear latched onto her like a virus.

She tried to pull the arms back, but nothing happened. She heard shouting from behind her.

"Get off of him," she knew that voice. It was Grant's. Cole's roommate was also there, but she couldn't see him. She knew it was Cole's apartment. Frustration seeped in, but she willed herself to let the dream continue.

Not a dream. She was seeing this play out in front of her in real time.

It must be concurrent. She didn't know how she could tell, but it was as if her soul had just jumped from one place to the next.

Focus, she told herself.

She immersed herself in the details until she could see Cole's face clearly. His eyes were filled with fear, but then he smiled. A callous and calm smile. She was familiar with this mood of his, he was taunting his attacker. Why would he do that? Urgency kicked her in the gut. She knew Cole had a secret, and she hadn't been certain what it was but, after what Abby had said about mind bending, she needed to know if he could be a telepath.

Dipping her voice with a bit of panic, hoping it was enough to garner any man's attention. Men liked to be the savior's, and she knew Cole could never let a girl be in distress for long.

"Cole?"

It was simple, but she willed as much of her own voice through it. His face didn't change.

She tried again.

"Cole, it's Arabella. I'm hurt." It was a lie, but it was worth it, because this time Cole's eye shifted, aimed directly at her. He tried to speak but couldn't. She wasn't sure if it was the force of the arm still at his neck or her speaking to him that caught his attention.

She prompted the arm to release, and this time it seemed to ease a bit. Then she saw it, the fist at the end of this stranger's arm. Peeking out of a deep pine sleeve, was his hand. The hand of the man from the club, the hand she thought was Cole's. The one that enclosed hers with such grace and warmth. It wasn't Cole's, it was someone else's.

A tsunami of air filled back into her lungs with a force that rocked her back into the realization that she was actually in the rusty streets. Her friends stared at her. Abby had even been holding her arm, but she hadn't felt it until she looked down at her hand.

"What the hell was that?" Aritzia backed away, then scanned around them quickly to see if anyone else had seen them.

They were alone. But Arabella was now conscious of how exposed, in the empty expanse between the buildings along the main road, they actually were.

"How long..." She dug her fingers into her eyes. "No, what? No." She was fumbling her words, they were odd on her tongue. She realized she needed to speak, to pull herself fully back to her own body.

She engulfed a large breath before stating, "How long was I like that?"

"A few minutes," stated Abby, looking more concerned. "Has that happened before?"

"No, well, not like that, but it resembled my dreams." She said, her voice in a hushed whisper. "I had more control this time. I could drive myself to stay and the details were clearer."

"What did you see?" Aritzia asked. "Also, can we maybe get off the street before we get attacked?"

Arabella wasn't worried. Aritzia was trained to fight off anything. She was worried why Aritzia had asked it, though. Sometimes she could anticipate things others couldn't, not much unlike Arabella.

Their footsteps crunched along the side streets, but Arabella couldn't focus. So she stopped, pushing her palms to her temples. "It was Cole's apartment," she whispered.

Abby was in front of her, stopping her again, her arms on her wrists, "Is it your ears, again? Do you need me to heal them?" Abby had helped them eliminate the ringing in their ears, one of the many results of the explosions. She was incredibly grateful for everything her friends were doing for her at that moment.

"No, I am fine." Arabella shook her head. "My vision was of Cole, at his apartment. He was being strangled." She didn't want to go into more detail than that, knowing she would confuse them. She would confuse herself, too.

"You saw his apartment for sure?" Abby asked. She seemed to have gotten past the whole *new visions in the middle of the street thing*, rather quickly.

Abby sensed her confusion. "You mentioned it was his apartment. Do you think you saw enough to indicate that precisely?" Abby reframed her question. Abby always entangled her voice with the concern of a mother. Arabella knew Abby was a confidant, so at that moment she also knew honesty was the best course of action.

"Not exactly, but I heard his roommate's voice, Grant. He hardly ever leaves their apartment. I've only met him once, but his voice was recognizable," she stated calmly to Abby.

Abby observed her for a moment longer than backed away, still holding onto her arm. She looped hers through Arabella's, then reached for Aritzia to do the same on their other side.

"Okay, then let's go to Gra…Cole's" Abby said. Arabella noticed her slip up, but ignored it.

Arabella gazed at Aritzia across Abby for a moment. She hadn't seemed to notice.

Arabella had met Grant once. That was true. She didn't remember him really, though. Not until she heard his voice again. She made a note of all the details that stood out to her in her vision. It puzzled her why certain things seemed more imperative than others, but she made the mental tallies, anyway.

Her friends hadn't judged her at all in her new crazy antics. They believed her, and she realized that was important to her.

As they walked the rufescent streets, aimlessly, she pieced together the events of the night and her vision. This man she had interacted with was definitely someone important and he knew Cole. Along with the danger at the club. Information sunk into her fast, and she hardly realized where Abby was leading them.

Her eyes surveyed the short building facing them, and familiarity coated her skin. Had Abby been there before, too?

She had the strange urge to ask her, but when she beheld Abby again she realized she was rambling on about something to Aritzia; and had little way of knowing where she was leading them. It was almost impulsive, so Arabella must have been leading them.

Arabella rang the single red button. She knew it went to Cole's apartment. She remembered something about Grant having installed it as a prototype invention.

"Cole, it's me Arabella…… I'm here with Abby and Aritzia. Please tell me you're in there." She said, pressing closer to the machine. She wasn't sure how loud she was supposed to speak into the damn thing.

Static rang back to them.

"Maybe he isn't home," stated Aritzia with a questioning tone and she observed the mechanical device.

"He is."

Sweat coated her spine. She needed to ensure he was alive more than ever now. Her gut always guided her towards Cole and tonight was no different.

Chapter 9

Stanis had never physically attacked his brother before, but Cole's smile told him he had wanted him to react to her name. Now that Cole's throat was pinned beneath his forearm, something feral flickered awake in his emerald eyes. Stanis was unsure if it was shock or concern.

Stanis's emotions fluttered away from him.

He released Cole, backing away, to create much needed distance between them. Shrugging out of the tight jacket suffocating him, he tossed it over the hook near the door. Cole hadn't verbally answered him, but the smirk on his face would've made any man feral. At least that's what he told himself to ease his anger.

"Gods, it's hot in here, no?" His under arms had become uncomfortably clammy and the cool air felt nice through his short sleeve black shirt.

"Seem's cooler now," Grant said, finding his seat again. "Maybe we could refrain from acting like children?"

Stanis turned back to Cole. Still pinned to the wall, his eyes scanning the floor. He rubbed his throat, clear dysphoria eating away at him.

"Cole?" Stanis began.

"It's fine" Cole didn't let him finish. Emerald eyes slashed Stanis across the face. Cole pushed himself into Stanis's mind, and this time he dropped his mental barrier.

"What?"

Cole's head shook. He was deducing something.

The breath Stanis held flooded out rapidly. "Cole! What is wrong? If it's about Ara, I asked because I need to know, actually I don't think I want to know, but I-."

Cole forced out an acerbic laugh. "You saw her?"

Stanis's mouth fell open, but in an attempt to recover, he wedged his tongue between his teeth. "No, well, yes." Stanis thought about all the times he did in fact see her.

He was standing in her street hidden behind a tree, the Drafthaven estate looming over the rest of the world. A crack of light illuminated the sky followed instantly by a thunderous grumble overhead. Creating a shadow of himself tucked under his cap, his fists flexed impatiently as they rested in his pockets. He didn't think anyone would've recognized him in this damn city, but here on the outskirts of town he looked out of place amongst the more noble patrons.

The air thickened more furiously in the countryside, the ivory grass fields behind each estate swayed soundlessly. Scanning up through the canopy that enclosed him from the pelting rain and thought about how much he loved when it rained.

A reflective flash of a window opening across the street captured his attention. Then as if he had manifested her appearance, she slumped over the edge of the sill and tipped her head back. Allowing her strawberry blonde curls to sop up the rain, until they transformed into a dark shade of brown.

"Arabella, please, if you don't at least consider it, I'll never hear the end from your father." He recognized the woman, who now towered over Arabella, immediately as her mother.

"Would you stop that nonsense?" Her mother scowled, observing her daughter's behavior. In a flash Arabella splattered her damp hair across all nearby surfaces, whipping her locks behind her in one fell swoop. Orienting her gaze out across the open space beyond the tubular posted gates that lined the estate. He ducked quickly back behind the tree, his heart jumping into his throat.

He couldn't hear the rest of their conversation, but he knew it didn't matter. Arabella. That was her name. It was oddly well suited, but it was a mouthful.

Ara.

That's what he would refer to her as, His Ara. Unbeknownst to him, it was the last time he would gaze his eyes upon her for a while after that.

She was his, wasn't she? No, she couldn't be. He couldn't have anyone. He was alone and for a good reason. She didn't need to know about him and his crazy notions of finding treasures and bending time to get the answers. He couldn't stay here anyway, with her. He had to keep up his search to avenge his father. He had to find the treasure for several reasons, but mostly for his father's sake.

He wasn't sure how long he had been standing there like that, stamped to the tree trunk. It was much darker now. The street lamps had lit in a umber glow. Peering around the tree again, he expected her to be where he last saw her, or to have shut the window. But to his surprise, when he did build up the courage to look, his scowl reformed at the sight of Ara, a fully grown woman now, descending the wall of the manor and disappearing from sight in the bed of blackened roses.

"You were here less than a year ago?" Cole's voice laced with so much hurt as his emerald eyes flicked over Stanis in disapproval.

"I…" Stanis struggled to find his words, forcing himself to avoid Cole's gaze.

Her voice pierced through the air, surrounded by static. "Cole, it's me Arabella…… I'm here with Abby and Aritzia. Please tell me you're in there."

Stanis craned his head in the direction of the siren's call. The small box next to the front door reverberated in a low static. Cole stepped forward, but Stanis's arm flew across his chest in an effort to block him. A lump formed deep inside him, sinking slowly reverberating a tremble though his soul.

"Stannie?" Cole asked, reading Stanis' expression.

"She doesn't know who I am. She thought I was you," Stanis muttered, slight panic in his voice. He needed to leave; he couldn't see her yet. She wasn't ready. What would he even say to her?

"Why would she think I wa…", Cole's brow pinched into a tight line.

Stanis lowered his arm but blocked Cole with his body. "Why would she seek refuge with you, Cole?"

"She must be here because she has nowhere else to go after what happened at Filly's."

Flashes of anger seeped from Stanis's mind. Deep and tortuous thoughts wrapped in dark shadows, but Stanis welcomed them. Knowing they would bounce around inside Cole's mind as well. Stanis's anger seeped from under his skin. *"Maybe there had been no other men around Ara because there was only one man, maybe that man was Cole."* Figurative images of

Arabella underneath his little brother formed in the fog just before they were slashed with an invisible sword.

"Stanis." Cole warned, his voice strange. "It's not what you think."

His brother lunged. Cole dodged him, finding himself on the other side of the room.

"Stanis!" His voice was firm. "You have my word, I won't touch her again, even if you don't actually want her."

That stopped Stanis from lunging at him again. Cole's eyes revealed no truth behind them, but he didn't know that for sure. He hadn't been with Cole since they were children. Cole never lied to him back then, so would he now? He didn't know what to think.

Don't want her. Stanis shook his head, as it began spinning. Trying to latch onto a truth, but lacking to find one. He caught a look that Grant threw at Cole as he shifted uncomfortably on the couch, observing them. Of course, he had wanted her. He lay in bed at night and thought about all the ways he had wanted her. How soft her lips would taste brushed against his, against other parts of him.

"Stanis, I'm going to need you to put those mental walls up again."

Stanis cursed.

Arabella's panicked voice rang through the air again. "Cole, please be home! I need your help."

Stanis had two choices. Run or face his fate right in that tiny apartment, all five feet six inches of her. Instead, he made a break for Cole's room. Cole followed him without hesitation.

Chapter 10

"Maybe he's not home" Abby's honey silk voice of reason wasn't helping Arabella calm down. The second time she pressed the button and spoke, she drove it harder. Pushing with such fierce intent she thought it may break. Her heart certainly was breaking the longer the silence ran on.

"He's here. I saw it."

Her friends stared at her with slight concern but stayed firm in place next to her. Another blast rang out through the maroon soaked sky, from somewhere deeper in the city. It had been weeks since the last attacks occurred, now it seemed they were targeting the area where the rich also frequented, not just the social class. If someone didn't open this door soon, Arabella feared what would happen to them. Then, after what seemed like years, the static eased and in its place was a deep, familiar voice.

"Come on up." Grant's voice rang through the speaker as the door clicked unlocked.

Abby was the first to get to the door, pushing it open with ease, then leading them up the stairs.

"It's apartment B6", Arabella pointed to the door at the end of the hall as they hit the second landing. The hall was faintly illuminated by a flickering light dangling to the ceiling from one exposed wire. Most of the city had access to electricity but the district Cole could afford seemed to have a limited number of fixtures sourced. Adrenaline flooded into her veins as she stepped up behind her friends, staring at the flimsy wooden door.

Abby reached it first, again, and knocked thrice elegantly. She flashed a blazingly bright smile at her, "Don't worry Arabella, we are safe now."

The weight of that truth sat in her gut, burning deep inside her before turning rotten. She looked at Aritzia, who was giving her a look that didn't reassure her. It wasn't unlike Abby to be optimistic but she also had always slightly mistrusted anything to do with Cole, until this point.

The door swung wide, and in it stood a mountain of a man wearing a casual attire. Muscular brown arms covered with tattoos flexed as he held the door ajar. He stared furiously at Abby with dark eyes.

"Grant...um," Arabella's voice came out scratchy. She cleared her throat. "I'm not sure if you remember me. I'm Arabella, and these are my friends Aritzia and Abby." She nodded towards both her friends, but Grant didn't shift his gaze.

"Abby." He finally said as he repositioned slightly, gesturing to them to enter the apartment. Abby glided under the arm gripping the door, his eyes tracing her as he followed her heels. The door swung at them fast, until Aritzia palm slapped it in place, allowing them to follow the show. Of course, the only thing he caught was Abby's name.

"Is Cole here? We are looking for him. We have an emergency." Abby's voice seemed to startle Grant as she eased further and he remained gawking.

The hairs on Arabella's arms tingled alive, warning her he was close. She had been here before, but this apartment seemed different somehow. It seemed to have a warmer feeling to it. She gazed around, spotting a coach, the kitchen, but it was the bottles scattered around the room, the half full glasses of whiskey stumping her.

"Grant?" Arabella asked. As he finally let his eyes leave Abby, he'd been tracing her as she walked around the small main room, looking at the photos hung on the back wall.

"Is Cole here?" She pushed.

"He'll be out in a minute." His angelic tone of casualness wasn't expected, she tried to allow her shoulders to loosen but the air was thick as smoke. Letting her eyes guide her around the small apartment again, she counted the number of half full drinks around her.

One.

Two.

Three.

She realized someone else was in the apartment, aside from it's residents.

"Would you like something to drink?" Grant asked, following her gaze.

"No, I am fine." Arabella, her voice weak and trailing off. Aritzia also seemed to carry her shoulders stiff. Something was wrong. The weight of her libs became noticeable. Anxiety bubbled deep in her gut, she'd learned to listen to instinct early in life. Her brother always warned her that her gut had the best intuition.

"I'll take one." Abby's bubbly voice appeared to be far away. She had made her way around and into the small galley kitchen. Grant was next to her with a few strides, grabbing a bottle from the fridge and handing it to her. The two of them held deep eye contact long enough for the room to warm with discomfort. Arabella tried to pull her eyes from the sight of the two of them standing close enough to share air, but it was like a car wreck.

In an attempt to distract herself she twisted away from the sight of them, tilting her head at the one before her instead. A pair of jackets slung on the hooks next to the door.

Suddenly, blackness hit her with a familiar wave through her fingers. Shooting up her arms and into her neck, sending her head back and her eyes blacked over.

A fuzzy image of letters on a tan page appeared in front of her. They were shifting and flipping over themselves. She willed herself to focus. Her vision changed a bit more. Shapes collided in a frenzy. Slamming into each other. Flipping around and over one another. The image became clearer; it was one shape repeating.

"What are you trying to say?" She felt her limbs grab hold of something, but she couldn't see them through the haze. They were distant, detached from her body. Her temples burned, and her vision became crossed as she focused harder on the shapes.

"The true prophecy, little shadow." A deep familiar voice whispered.

Then it all stopped, and she was back in the small apartment. Resting in one of her palms was a delicate black pen, the other firmly pressed against the table in the middle of the room. She hadn't realized that she had moved, or that she shifted to her knees.

She also hadn't realized that she had drawn the shapes that she had seen on the page in her vision. Was that what she had seen?

Her breath was becoming shallow. This vision felt otherworldly, unlike the previous. But that voice, she recognized the sentiment behind it.

Her chest tightened, and her heart beat rapidly. Searching the room she met a pair of eyes studying her. Abby and Aritzia slowly kneeled down on the opposite side of the table. Grant held firm behind them, his mouth forming a small circle and his brows knitted tightly together. Abby reached for her hand again. The familiar contact steadied her thoughts and eased her headache, reality was getting immensely tangled with her visions. Twinkling sapphire and chestnut eyes reminded her this was reality, wrapping around her soul, and her breath finally flowed from her lungs.

She stared down, finding the piece of paper that mocked her. Her friends must have placed it in front of her and handed her the pen. She noticed some ink etching the table's surface as well.

She stood abruptly, her mind reaching for anything to grip onto, something powerful pulling her towards the closed door across the main room.

"Where's Cole?" She asked, her voice laced with panic. She tried not to sound so dire, but she felt a deep urge to speak to him.

The door swung open moments after the words fell from her mouth and she propelled forward. When she reached him, she pushed up onto her toes, wrapping her arms tightly around his neck. Inhaling the scent of allspice and deep desires. Despite the closeness, she also felt a wave of hatred hit her. Opening her eyes, but before pulling away, she found the jaded eyes of the man behind Cole.

"The object of her feelings of disdain. The worst and most–" Her thoughts were instantly obstructed by a dark caress in her mind.

"The most beautiful man you've ever seen, right?"

Somehow, this man that had locked her gaze was forcing himself into her thoughts. She looked at him suspiciously for a moment, his fury cascading from his scowl.

"He must be a psychopath."

"That's not very nice, beautiful. You shouldn't judge anyone, especially a psychopath, before asking for their name."

She backed away from Cole slightly, looking up into his eyes, searching for an explanation. She nuzzled back into his arms as he returned her sentiment and whispered, "Cole, thank the gods you are okay."

Chapter 11

Six minute prior

Stanis stood with his shoulders ridge, unlike the crumbling musty walls of the small room off the back of the apartment. Looking out the window, estimating the height if one were to jump. A hooded figure loomed on the roof across the street briefly before dissipating into shadows. They were on the second floor. He could make that jump, right?

"You can't keep running, Stannie" Cole whispered. Cole cast magic around them to silence their conversation. What a neat trick, Stanis eyed his brother suspiciously. They had heard the three women enter the room. Even if he hadn't heard them come in, he felt her presence.

His mouth suddenly went dry.

He looked at the window again. He could just jump through time, but that wouldn't do much for his current situation, so he hesitated. The three hands on his watch ticked by at the speed of molasses.

He didn't want to leave.

Specifically, he didn't really desire to leave Cole again. He wasn't even sure if leaving Arabella was the answer anymore, they were destined to meet eventually and The Fates were clearly getting impatient with him.

Stanis looked at Cole, deep in his emerald eyes, across the heated distance between them."Promise you will help me find it Cole, for him. It doesn't have to be for me." He had to make sure that he continued searching.

He needed the information he had almost gotten from his brother and Grant before his world tilted on its axis. She wasn't supposed to have come here. He wasn't supposed to have come here. Tonight definitely wasn't going as he had planned. He needed more time.

He had panicked when he had first seen her, eighteen years prior, mostly because he was too young to have found his mate. She hadn't seen him then, so he knew he could avoid the connection as long as he stayed far away. Stanis had also just lost his parents. He needed to go back and stop the day of his parent's death. Having tried tirelessly, but he never could figure out how to do it without creating more of a disaster. His father had shown him the maps the night before the devastation gripped their town. He had memorized some, but he didn't have all the clues.

"We're so close, son." His father's deep hazel eyes had been filled with so much hope. His father had a knack for being right about these sorts of things.

"Of course," Cole whispered. "Without the bad, how can we appreciate life's treasures?"

Stanis met Cole's gaze. They were almost the same age as their father before he had died. Cole embodied almost every detail their father had, except for the deep green eyes. They both had been gifted those from their mother. His brother's strong jaw ticked the same way their father's had, when he was patiently waiting for an answer but didn't want to rush someone. Those were his fathers words, the exact ones he continuously told them when the world crashed around them and they lost hope. Stanis had forgotten about them until now.

Why had he run from Cole?

Every thought had pushed him to keep distant from his brother, fearing darkness would taint him as well. But now, he wondered if he could've used his help. He hoped Cole would forgive him one day. He hardly felt fear, but in this moment of complete terror, he knew that he didn't need to dread anything. With Cole at his side, more courage seeped into his skin.

He could face his mate.

He'd failed at most things in his life but that was before he fully felt like he was hers, he could be the best damn mate, if he simply tried. Arabella deserved to be at her full potential and if he was able to give her that, he would force himself to succeed. Protecting them would come later, he wasn't sure how to accomplish it, or if he'd have enough time, but at that moment hope budded inside him for the first time in years.

Memories of her soft skin played in his mind. His calloused fingers twitched as if to be reaching for her. She was on the other side of the door. He wanted to run to her and wrap his arms around her. He wanted to lay his head in her lap and let her run her hands through his hair. He wanted to have no other worries in the world but what they were going to eat for dinner, or where they should live.

He knew that would never be their life. Would she be upset by that? He'd heard of the idea of people rejecting their mates. He wasn't sure what happened to them, and he had a feeling he couldn't accept it even if she did reject him.

"Stanis?" Cole's tone seemed to be more urgent. "It's now or never." He eyed the door and his shoulders stiffened.

Stanis cursed, he hated lines such as the one Cole had uttered, but he knew he had a valid point. "What's she like?" The question flew out before Stanis could process it. He was stalling, but he had to know more about her before everything changed.

Cole observed him for a long moment, his brows forming a firm line. Why did he have to think so damn hard? Impatience was overcoming him. "She's your other half, Stannie." Cole finally said. "The rest is for you to figure out."

Relief burned away the last strand of doubt. When had his brother gotten so damn intuitive?

Cole smiled at him again, but Stanis instinctively pinned him with a warning glare, he wasn't ready to get all mushy with his brother quite yet. He wanted Cole to be right. He wanted to be more than that to her though, he wanted to be worthy. Worthy of her time and most of all her affections. He wanted to give her every second of the rest of his life and wanted to make it worth it.

He gripped the door handle, thrust it open, and signaled Cole through it first with an open palm.

Regret stabbed him deep in the chest.

Arabella was already across the room, aiming for them. She thrust herself, with open arms, right into his brother's open embrace.

The room was engulfed in a fiery red.

But, somehow, through the blood tinted haze, he locked eyes with her over his brother's shoulder. The urge to rip her out of his arms engulfing his entire body. Then, on top of this irrational display of affection, she had the audacity to be spewing hate at Stanis telepathically. There were obviously too many mind benders in the room now. How had he been unaware that she possessed magic?

"The object of my disdain. The worst and most-."

Well, he couldn't let her get away with that, now could he? Before she could finish, he blasted back towards her. *"The most handsome man you've ever seen, right?"*

Somehow, everything he had previously estimated about her burned away. Replaced with this vison of power that stood before them. She wasn't the girl exchanging jokes with her mother, or the one being scolded for fleeing her manor. She was a force beyond his comprehension and as her sterling gaze gripped him by the throat, he was reaffirmed by the connection to her. As delighted that he was for this new development in his life, he hated the words she was using to describe him. He wasn't even sure she was aware of it, letting her words flow without being filtered.

"He must be a psychopath."

Well, now, that was just pure hate. A psychopath, really?

"That's not very nice, Beautiful. You shouldn't judge anyone, especially a psychopath, before asking for their name, at least," he thought.

Instead of responding to him, she had the audacity to lift herself on to her toes higher, nuzzle into his brother's neck, and release a soft sigh. A sigh that Stanis believed was created solely for him, like she was. But she was dangling herself in the arms of another man.

His brother.

"Cole! Thank the gods you are okay," she breathed.

The gods definitely were dealing out the harshest of punishments at this moment.

Chapter 12

Cole didn't know what to do in that moment, other than hug her back.

He was grateful she was safe. His brother's presence had distracted him from any thoughts of her, but even after Stanis had reassured him of her safety, slight guilt gripped him.

He hadn't thought much about her after that.

Stanis was all he wanted to focus on, he had finally returned, and Cole had a brief hope he had come back for him. The thought of his stupidity, as it rattled around in his brain, of course Stanis had returned for his mate.

He hadn't thought they had actually spoken to each other. Was their connection made final? Was that how he had heard her through Stanis's mind? He was so stunned when Stanis had him pinned against the wall, but then he was simply curious to see how far Stanis would actually push himself. Cole was fortunate that in his anger, Stanis dropped his mental shields, but he hadn't expected to hear her voice ringing through.

He also hadn't expected Stanis to have lured him into hiding in his room when they heard her voice over the intercom.

He always just let Stanis push him around.

He really needed to stop doing that.

He thought back to their brotherly soaked promise. Obviously he had been propelled to agree, his brother was back and his expressions were desperate. He wasn't sure if he'd actually follow up on all he'd promised, or if he could. Part of him didn't even want to, his brother had been missing for years, the myths Cole created in his head weren't lining up. He would've understood if Stanis was mangled, or imprisoned, anything other than wandering around.

Unsurprisingly, he was fine, waltzing back into Cole's life, an abandoner with no worries of who they left in their path of hurt. He needed to be more of an authority figure, though. Stanis had no right to come back and start making demands when he didn't know what Cole's life was actually like now.

Or did he know? Cole had seen into Stanis's mind when he had retraced the days of seeing her less than a year ago. He hadn't meant to, but his brother kept avoiding the subject of her. His brother cared for Arabella, Cole could see that, but Stanis didn't know her. She wasn't the sweet flower he painted in his head, she was more of the poisonous variety, and Cole was all too familiar with her allure.

"What's she like?" Such a simple question for Stanis to ask. That's because to Stanis, she was simple. If he had grown up with her like Cole had, he wouldn't have been so naïve to her. Maybe it was the mating bond blinding him. Speaking of, was their telepathic communication their fated power?

Cole had heard about mates who increased in strength once they met. It happened every so often, but mostly when both the powers deemed equal. Which would add up for Stanis and Arabella, maybe. He wasn't sure if either of them truly understood their power, but neither he the expert.

"She's your other half." That wasn't a lie. He just didn't know how to tell Stanis about Arabella's lust for Cole. He knew it had grown more platonic over the past few years, he had made sure of that. He just wasn't entirely sure how Stanis would understand that, especially after he had slept with her so many times.

So, Cole hugged her back, praying to any of the gods who would listen, that Stanis would reign in his anger long enough to actually meet Arabella. He had always wondered what that would be like, to witness their initial meeting. Surprisingly, something deep inside Cole wanted to make Stanis suffer for all he'd put him through.

Cole pulled back slightly until their faces were almost touching, he waited to be pulled away but held onto the last moments painfully tight.

"I'd like to introduce you to someone very important," he kept his voice light. Desperately hoping she wouldn't misinterpret his rapid heart beating for excitement.

She pulled away from him enough to face him. Her soft features drew him in, until a low grumble sounded in Stanis's throat. The sound seemed to be oblivious to her. Cole searched for her thoughts, hoping their skin touching would help amplify it.

Nothing.

He searched her face for any familiarity but her gray eyes were shining, as if she were holding back tears. Cole's heart cracked, he didn't want to be the villain in their story but it was beginning to seem like he fit the role.

She gazed towards Stanis for the tiniest of moments, but firmly grasped her arms around Cole's torso, engulfing herself deeper into his chest.

Closing his eyes to hold onto *them* for one more brief moment, more guilt flooded into his soul.

They had to stop touching.

For the first time in his life her caress was like a curse, she didn't deserve to be tangled between him and his brother. He needed to put as much distance between himself and Arabella as possible.

In that moment, all his actions were catching up to him and he wasn't ready for Stanis to find out. His heart ached as it cracked open further, as it began seeping disappointment.

Forcefully releasing himself from her embrace, the air chilled around them, and he took a step away, adding to the distance.

"Stanis," addressing his brother now with his chin high and shoulders squared. He didn't want to show any weakness. "This is Arabella and her friends," he said. "Arabella is the daughter of Lord Drafthaven. I have worked for her father for many years now." His nerves snaked around his gut.

Cole sucked in a breath, realizing he used all the air in his lungs to get the words out. He forced his feet to carry him further away and into the galley kitchen, he reached for his half full glass, nestled on the counter. Peering back towards the drama he'd inevitably created. His hands shook as he gulped down. It did nothing for his nerves, but everything for his dry mouth, boiling his blood alive again.

He noticed Grant sitting on the couch, transfixed and unmoving, staring at the back of Abby's head while she sat at his feet.

"Oh, and this is my roommate, Grant. I know you've met Arabella. But yes..." waving his hand through the air. He didn't want to repeat himself. That was all the introductions, right?

Stanis was right, it was hot in here. No one else had said anything yet, so he leaned forward, his elbows resting on the cold surface of the counter. "A, why are you here? It's not a safe night to be out. There are bombings happening all over the city," he said as calmly as possible. He needed her to do all the talking now. Anything to ease the searing tension. Most of which was seeping from Stanis, who looked as if he might burst into flames, if Arabella kept ignoring him.

All three girls turned towards him in unison, realizing his mistake, he looked Arabella directly and gestured for her to sit. She guided herself away from Stanis's attentions and positioned herself on the mangled rug tucked carelessly under the short table. He hadn't cleaned in a while, the place didn't look dirty but he was starting to become embarrassed now that women had entered his place. He should've at least picked up the papers on the table.

Arabella's strawberry blonde waves fell into her face as she started detailing out all the events of the girls' night, with excruciating specifics. Every once in a while, Abby and Aritzia would nod or add a small helpful inquiry that she would forget. Cole willed himself to listen, but he just stared at the shapes all over the paper on the table.

He hadn't seen it before Stanis dragged him into his room. Was it there before? Had Stanis put it there? Stanis did like to move objects around. Cole had seen Stanis drop the keys from the jacket he'd stolen into their side dish, casually, as if he were just coming home from a day on the job and this was his apartment.

A weird feeling, a kin to dread tangled with excitement inside his chest.

He gazed at Stanis, who still hadn't removed his jade eyes from Arabella. His brother was leaning his shoulder on the wall, placing himself far from all of them. Cole tried to force him to make eye contact. Stanis didn't budge. He tried guiding into Stanis's mind with no luck.

Cole coughed slightly, and everyone looked at him. "Sorry, dry throat." He tried to recover with only brief hesitation.

Arabella continued with her story.

Stanis was looking at him with a deep scowl, so he tilted his chin towards the page. His large figure leaned forward off the wall to look over Arabella's shoulder. A creak from the floor cut off all storytelling, the sound causing Arabella to jolt as if Stanis had stabbed her. Their eyes met, and this time she didn't look away instantly, causing the entire room to chill over.

Cole frantically reached out to catch anyone's inner thoughts, hoping mostly for his brother's. He hoped he had seen the paper before getting pulled in by her again.

"Abby?" Grant's voice came out more of a squeak. "What magic do you possess?"

Cole's attention bounced between the two pairs, a bit startled by Grant's change of subject and by the topic. It wasn't "appropriate" to ask someone if they had magic, because some people never developed gifts. What was the matter with Grant? He was always so intentional in his speech, and always appropriate.

"I am a healer." Abby looked at him with soft eyes as she pulled her lower lip between her teeth. "I work at the Relaggin's House, actually."

"That's amazing," Grant stated excitedly, and she blushed back at him.

Cole decided he would ignore that until later. He needed to get Stanis to look at the paper.

Luckily, both his brother and Arabella had broken eye contact long enough to turn back to the group and were watching the interaction between Abby and Grant like it was the main stage now.

Cole cursed internally. He should just ask. He drifted into the living area, and sat on the chair across from Arabella.

"What's this?" He asked casually, grabbing the paper swiftly off the table. Everyone was staring at Arabella now, except for Stanis, who looked at the paper in Cole's hand like he was going to tear it from his grip.

"Um...," Arabella started. "Well, I have been having dreams for some time regarding," she paused, "um…regarding certain images, but tonight after the explosion as we made our way here, I saw something out of a dream state."

Fear must have been making her so shaky, she normally was well composed, even around her father. Was it possible Stanis had done something to her?

"You're a Visionary, then?" Grant's eyes glistened.

Cole whipped his head to Grant, then back to Arabella. A Visionary? Those were exceedingly rare; Cole had never heard of meeting one. Well, now he guessed he hadn't known he'd actually met one.

"I don't know what to call it," Arabella stated, cautious to continue.

"You saw a vision here too, right?" Grant exclaimed. "Before, when you were…" Grant trailed off, catching the glance from Abby. "Sorry, you tell it." Grant leaned back. Abby's bright smile washed over him as he relaxed.

Arabella was silent for a while.

"Be honest." Cole overheard her say to herself. His gut jumped.

"Yes, I had two separate visions tonight." She met her friend's eyes, they both gave her a reassuring nod. "The first was in the street a few blocks away. We were on our way to see you. Then I had a *vision*, if that's what you'd like to call them." Her eyes scanned Cole's face. "That you were being pinned against the wall and I heard Grant's voice pleading for someone to stop." She stopped, her brows knitted, pondering further.

She turned to Stanis. "You." She said, her brows knitting together. "You were the one pinning him." It wasn't a question. She looked down at Stanis's hands as he heaved a deep breath, forcing him to retreat to the wall again.

The silence was pliable, blanketing the entire room as Cole searched every observing face.

Cole desperately wished people would begin sharing some inner dialogue at that moment, but he couldn't seem to catch anything important. Grant was mentally listing a large number of words that described Abby's hair color. Rolling his eyes he shifted focus away from his obsessive roommate. He reached for Arabella's mind instead, just to be shut down. Stanis whipped his head to him, sporting a more furious expression. That was certainly odd. Cole's lips curled back into a snarl.

"So, you had a real vision then," he stated loudly to draw attention back to him. He leaned forward again, and began waving the paper in her direction. "Does this have to do with the second vision Grant witnessed?"

"Yes." Arabella said, turning back to Cole with a confused look on her face. "I didn't know I was drawing it," she stopped, and her eyebrows knitted together, again.

"We got her a paper before she thoroughly ruined your table," offered Aritzia.

Cole nodded with gratitude, but didn't hesitate to address Arabella again. "What did you see exactly?" His tone became firmer.

Stanis inched closer again. His fists knotted so tight his knuckles turned white.

She sucked in a breath through her nose. "Just that shape really, repeated multiple times on a sheet of paper."

"Paper? Not in a journal?" Stanis asked, his voice causing Arabella to jump again.

She didn't look at Stanis. She looked at Cole, straightening her back, and asked, "Is there a difference?"

"Yes." Cole and Stanis said in unison. Stanis had slightly yelled this time, and it overpowered Cole's words.

Arabella's face had been fixed into a mask, until she snapped. "I wasn't talking to you," she hissed back at Stanis. Everyone in the room went silent. Cole noticed in his peripheral vision, the other members of their little meeting were now watching Stanis and Arabella like they had taken the main show.

Surprisingly to Cole, Stanis didn't respond. It was uncharacteristic of Stanis not to argue.

Which meant Cole had to respond again.

"Yes, there is a difference. Our dad kept journals with similar drawings. If you saw paper, it may be a current representation of it being drawn."

"Or future." Stanis said firmly.

"I'm pretty sure Cole was talking, asshole." Arabella's attention was fully on Cole again.

Rain plastered the windows, sheets falling from the sky, washing an ominous wine soaked glow over the group.

Cole couldn't help but smile at the two of them, bickering the way they were. He wanted to hear all the thoughts Arabella had towards Stanis, but her damn mind was locked up. He needed to be more strategic if he wanted to get back at his brother.

"What do you mean?" She asked, her voice rising over the battering rain drops. "How do you know that?"

He told her the truth. He had never lied, but he felt like she should know his full story now. She obviously was having visions that related to him, so fuck it.

"Before we," he caught himself. "I, before I was adopted, I didn't live in Limos."

She looked at him with a look that expressed a sort of "no shit" attitude, so he rephrased.

"I mean, obviously you know that I'm adopted, but what I haven't told you is that our parents died, forcing me to come to Orcus Haven, to Limos." He paused because he wanted to make sure he phrased the next part correctly.

"Our parents were postal workers in the town of Gallouth on Mount Isle. They had intercepted some classified Federation letters, and that's when my father began spending all his time chasing theories." Stanis looked as if he wanted to jump in, but Cole pinned him with a threatening stare.

"Don't tell her everything!"

He ignored Stanis. Not appreciating the control his brother's had over sharing his thoughts. Of course, he would not reveal every secret they had, but he wasn't hiding anymore. He had promised Stanis he would help, but he also saw something new in Arabella. She was a stronger version of herself, which made sense if she was a visionary. How long had she possessed that ability? His fingers fiddled with the paper in his grasp.

He couldn't let either of them know his secrets now.

No matter how angry he was at Stanis, he knew that their combined wrath would be unbearable.

Cole continued, "Our father found maps and clues leading to a lost treasure. He would spend hours hunched over his work late into the night. He used to tell Stanis and I stories of the life we could all live if we found the missing jewels and bricks of gold, and he convinced us he knew where to find it."

Stanis turned towards the wall.

He could sense all of his brother's anger, even without reading his mind. He had managed to unintentionally set a trap perfectly. He just needed one more opportunity to really drive the wedge between them. Maybe then he'd be over his anger towards his brother. Then they could all move on without Stanis ever needing to know about their past. His lie to Arabella wouldn't matter either because she wouldn't want to be with Stanis then. Was that what he wanted?

The fragile walls surrounding them shook. Metallic flashes of the transit train slamming past, resounding off the walls, then it blasted the window with a wave of spray.

"Whose treasure is it?" This question was from Abby.

Grant sat forward again. "Well, legend says that Itia took all her shared fortune from Batar when he punished her along with all of Lafornas. At her death, her tomb became filled with all his gold and jewels to hide it from him forever." Abby seemed enamored with his tale.

Cole watched his friend as Abby gripped Grant's knee briefly. He wanted to brush it off, as if it was normal, but for Abby it wasn't. Abby didn't trust men.

Arabella's mind opened up..

He did seem to carry himself in a manner that was other worldly and he was kind to them, so she needed to trust her friend's instincts. She wanted to protect Abby, but she knew Abby wouldn't have allowed herself so close if she wasn't sure in her actions.

"It's not a legend." Stanis said firmly. He was clenching his teeth as he turned away from facing the wall. It was a short sentence but something in his tone reverberated through the small room. His presence had always been difficult to ignore, a flinch threatened to leap from Cole's skin with every movement his brother made.

"What?" Abby asked him.

Stanis turned slowly, then looked around the room. Landing briefly on Cole with an expression that, if looks could kill a man, would have ended him. Cole was aware they had a laundry list of issues stretched between them. Over a decade apart, and still the two of them hadn't managed to discuss the topic once.

"It's not a legend, I said." Stanis reaffirmed. "Our father had found maps to the tomb, and he was deciphering them, before the Federation set fire to Gallouth."

Everyone just stared at him. Arabella's mind trickled open again.

She was using the groups attention as an excuse not to avert her eyes, she wanted to see him fully. Her entire life she had been drawn to the idea of her mate but he didn't look like the man from her dreams. He was handsome, under his brooding features, she could sense that he harbored his feelings in a dark place far beneath the surface. He was devastatingly beautiful, especially when he spoke of his father, his jade eyes gleamed before he even spoke.

Cole scoffed, drawing the groups attentions to him.

A warmth crept under his skin, until Stanis summoned their eyes to him again. "I have been continuing my father's work for years, and using the maps I'm hoping to find what my father did, and it will lead me to Itia's Treasure," Stanis said.

"Is that why you are here now?" Cole was unsure why Arabella had asked it. The room warmed as the rain subsided behind the pane, his veins bursting as they sat waiting for Stanis's reply. It was as if her heart knew how specific her question was. Cole watched her with intensity as she shoved her shaky hands into her lap to conceal her nerves.

"No." Stanis said, peeling his eyes from her. The breath she held deep finally released. What was wrong with her? No man had ever rattled her like Stanis was, he hoped it was because Stanis was either extremely irritating or infatuating to her as well. If he wasn't, that meant that Arabella was being drawn to his brother, the connection pulling on the strings of the fates. Cole couldn't decide which was more dangerous. Looking towards Arabella, he searched her mind, but he couldn't seem to find the connection he had her prior.

Stanis didn't elaborate further at first. Unsurprisingly to Cole because he already knew Stanis always had multiple motives, along with his abilities to be in multiple time lines at once. Cole's fury matched his brother's, he had stopped looking at her a while ago, fixating on every word out of Stanis mouth instead. Searching for some remanence of truth, but only finding the after effects of poison.

Stanis was waiting too long for Cole to hold in his patience. He felt the paper in his hand crumbling under his strength. Arabella couldn't have known the depth of her question. The dominos were starting to tip, and Cole could see their inevitable tumble as the lie escaped Stanis lips.

"I returned to see my brother," Stanis finally stated.

"To include him in your get rich quick scheme?" Arabella joked.

Stanis stared at her for a moment, his famous scowl breaking, "No."

A monster had formed inside of Cole, Stanis didn't deserve to come back and win the girl. His brother had left his only remaining family, for years. He was reckless and it wasn't fair for him to come back and manipulate his way into anyone's hearts, even his own mates. Arabella was falling for his act, Cole witnessed the moment her facade had fallen. That's when the monster had become uncontrollable, he managed to keep it all in until he felt the dynamic between them shifting. He couldn't keep them apart, but he would never let Stanis continue hurting the people who would love him despite his flaws.

"Stanis can travel through time." Hate fueled his words as they trickled out of his mouth. Regret trailing after it immediately. Cole watched as Stanis's eyes went wide, but his smile curved into something wicked.

"Cole can read your minds."

Everything immediately went to shit. Cole was furious that Stanis had somehow got the upper hand. He reviewed everything in his head over again. Arabella's gray eyes flicked with hurt, her expression drowning out all the yelling erupting around them. He felt like he was suddenly the shortest person in the room with her looking down on him. She said nothing. No words were needed, he was fully aware he had severed anything they had before today.

Cole wanted to erase every hardship between them in that moment. He regretted ever letting her get close to him. He thought about all their intimate moments and how their friendship now lay shattered on the floor surrounding them. That was the first day he ever felt like the villain, because he was no hero, that was clear.

Chapter 13

Arabella adjusted herself again. Sitting on the floor was becoming difficult amongst all the tension in the dusty apartment. It was thick as oil, and had consumed her heart then spat it back out onto the hardwood floor.

Rich maroon light filtered through the window panes, Abby and Aritzia sat next to her in its warm glow. They had both removed their shoes and sat intimately on the floor next to Grant. Their comfort should've seeped into her, but she sat rigid as ever. They all had finally decided they needed to share all their powers with the group as well, since some people were being forced to.

She was fully aware of who Stanis was now. He was the man from the club, his warning had saved her. But he also was the man who had pinned Cole to the wall. Since he had drifted into her life so many things had changed, mostly how Cole was acting towards her.

Cole had never been heartless. He was honest and reassuring. They had at least been friends, but now she felt like she barely knew him. They had never embraced in public but she had dreamed it would be world altering. A symbol of his acceptance, and it would reaffirm her that she had been right, and he had been lying. After everything they had just gone through she hoped he would've been welcoming in his embrace. But he'd been stiff and before he could pull away for good, she held onto that hope tightly. Her arms constricted around his torso, bathing her in a flood of allspice, but it had been blended with deep scents of hesitation. Instead he hugged her like he was disappointed that he had accepted her embrace. She hoped he was just focused on his brother being back.

But something about their embrace felt spoiled, like it was to be the final time they would be that close and he was giving her time to realize it.

She tried to remember anything about Cole's brother. He had mentioned him before but she had assumed that he had died, the way Cole spoke about him. Unlike her own brother, who had also left, Cole never mentioned hearing from Stanis. Maybe he had kept that part of his life from her. They weren't exclusive, that was for certain, but she he had always dangled himself in front of her. Now he seemed to be icing her out completely.

Maybe her friends were right, she needed to stop sleeping with Cole. Now that everything was changing between them, she could see that being an option for her future. She didn't need to chase after a man who wasn't returning her affections. They never had talked out their relationship, so perhaps this was how it was meant to come to an end.

Silently.

Each of them had been given a journal to review, Abby had suggested it after the verbal boxing match that resulted from the two brothers revealing their secrets to the room. None of them could have predicted the vastness of their dad's collection. Which consisted of hundreds of leather bound scribbles. The journal in her lap mocked her with its lack of helpfulness, she couldn't find it in herself to even care what it said. Without Cole she had no reason to be there. She had come to him in fear for his safety and for her own, her gut driving her to him. But that wasn't true, he hadn't been in danger.

She glanced around the group again, all of them seemed so deeply invested in the task; even Cole, who seemed to be avoiding her gaze more now.

She was furious at Cole, but something overpowered it, she worried it was heartbreak. He was sitting across the room from her and kept shifting in his seat, running his hand through his hair, causing it to look messier. It looked longer now that it wasn't styled, like it usually was. He folded his arms across his chest again, and she admired his chiseled features and muscles flexing. She glanced away quickly, shifting her gaze back to her lap.

Arabella couldn't trust anyone now, especially Cole, he most likely had heard every thought she's ever had; and still denied her. The idea mortified her, recalling all the times they *were together*, she tried to remember what she had thought about.

That wasn't true, she could trust people. She trusted Abby and Aritzia more than anyone, so when they asked her to stay, she did. She even slightly trusted Grant after he admitted his gift made him drown in a puddle of guilt when he was dishonest.

Abby, on the other hand, had just gloated immediately, stating that she had known all along about his telepathy. Suddenly, Cole seemed less intrigued by her, his relentless flirtations with her friends had ceased when they stepped into the apartment. Arabella looked between him and Abby again. She wished she could speak to Abby telepathically, she needed her reassurance in her actions. Everything was falling through her fingers, she had started the night so sure she had a purpose but now that was unclear. The patrons of Filly's had all been murdered, her contacts with it.

She adjusted her legs again underneath her and focused on summoning a vision. She hadn't ever willed them to come about, but it was worth a try. Grant had called her a Visionary, and she desperately needed a vision to guide her. She needed it to tell her the people in this room could be trusted and she hoped even more it would tell her if this treasure hunting expedition was worth her time.

She, however, did not trust the man behind her, and no vision would help her get to that point. *"He certainly was such a…,"* her thought was severed off by a caressing cough.

His cough.

"I can hear you still, Ara."

"Stop calling me that," she retorted back, refusing to look towards him. He was still sitting behind her, she could sense his eyes burning into her back. Cole's eyes glanced up over the top of his assigned journal.

Her heart warmed momentarily.

She turned away swiftly, hoping his telepathy only worked when he was making eye contact.

"Also, get out of my head."

"I'm not sure that's how it works."

"How what works?" She huffed. Abby glanced her way, and Arabella reassured her with a soft smile. Then she returned her gaze down to the pages in front of her.

Fuck, the urge to leave was overwhelming her. A wave of water splashed the glass again as the transit train flashed across the window. She hadn't noticed it was raining again. She should just try to summon another vision with more details about the symbol she had drawn, to help them narrow down which journals were important. She had been unsuccessful thus far, but she would loathe herself if she were to back out of this endeavor before anyone else.

"I don't think that I am in that beautiful head of yours. I think you are in mine."

He was trying to get her to snap her composure. She gritted her teeth and pressed herself to ignore him.

"You are the one who summoned my attention."

"I did no…," she stopped again. She wouldn't lose to this infuriating man. So, she decided going on the offensive was the better approach. She never had feared assholes like him and wouldn't start today.

"You lied to me and tricked me into thinking you were Cole. Why?"

"That's pretty presumptuous."

"Big word for you. I'm surprised you even know how to wield it, being uneducated and all."

"What makes you think I am not educated about certain topics?"

"I'm not sure what you are referring to, but I know you seem to think you know everything. When actually you don't!"

She couldn't recall why she was sure about that, but she had known him for only one night. She knew that he had left Cole when they were kids. Sympathy was an option, yes, if he had reached out every now and then. The way they acted towards one another, it seemed that wasn't the case.

"I know quite a bit actually," Stanis voice became more laced with anger. She was winning this round, it seemed. *"I don't expect you to understand much about my situation, Ara, but if you let me, I can try to explain."*

"Why should I believe you? You have lied repeatedly, and you don't seem to understand our unfortunate predicament, either?"

"Unfortunate predicament?" His voice seemed to be tinted with a bit of hurt.

"Yes, your nagging voice inside my head is unfortunate for me, especially, if it isn't helping me with the task at hand."

"When my parents died..." he paused his thought. She hung on every word. She didn't know why, exactly, but she wanted to hear him finish.

"Please, go on." She felt her shoulders release some of their tension.

"When my parents died, it was my responsibility to find a place for Cole and me. I did everything correctly, per my father's instructions. He had a will, but it didn't include money. We had none, of course. Including a plan for after his death if it were to come. It felt as if he had known it was coming." He stopped again.

Stanis shifted behind her, and she could sense his heat closer to her now. She froze, hoping to conceal the hitch in her breath.

"My father had worked every second on finding this treasure. He felt it would solve all our problems, not just our money ones. All of Lafornas's. He told me stories about the generations of men before him and of how Lafornas hadn't always been so divided."

"Divided?" She asked before she could stop herself.

"Yes, divided between its magic sources. My father was never wrong about anything. So, I wanted to follow in his steps. It is the only course of action after his death. He had many journals and drawings, just like that one. That's why Cole recognized it from your depiction. Can I see it again?"

She grabbed the sheet of paper from the table in front of her, stopping to flatten out it's crumpled corners. The pause causing her to readjust in her seat and become unaware of him shifting closer to her side. She closed her eyes, hoping the sensation of ecstasy would pass. But as her eyes flashed open again, her stomach fluttered alive. His jade eyes, tucked under a single brow scar on the right side, poured into her soul. Her mouth dried from the heat between them; they'd been as close as they were in the club. His rough fingertips grazed her skin gently as she held out the paper to him.

"This symbol was always drawn this direction in my father's work." He turned that page slightly, revealing the symbol to look like a diamond with an infinite swirl inside it. *"But you drew it this way. Why?"* He turned the page, breaking their eye contact.

He was still cradling her hand slightly, along with the paper. Burns penetrated her skin where his fingers made contact.

"I need to use the restroom!" She blurted aloud, as she stood and hit her knee on the table. That would definitely bruise later, she headed for the open door behind Stanis in search for the closest toilet. She cursed herself in frustration.

"It's to the left," Cole yelled after her.

Arabella had made it much longer than he would have. Stacking his mental walls back up, to give her privacy.

She hadn't stumbled when they had initially made mental contact with their introduction. She hadn't faltered when he continued to push his limit on speaking to her directly. She hadn't even freaked out when he had broken the physical barrier again. She impressed him; that was evident. They had spoken little but he could tell she hid her knowledge well. She wanted to seem simple, to blend in, but she didn't.

She was gorgeous. He had always thought her beautiful, but as their eyes met, he was entranced by their sterling gray hue. Her nose scattered with tiny freckles, painted by the gods themselves. His heart had been beating rapidly when they had touched again; but he tried to will his composure to remain so she wouldn't be startled. He desperately wanted to know who she was, truly under all her jokes and cool façade. She had made him laugh internally, on multiple occasions, even if her jokes were sarcastic ones and were at his mercy.

He hadn't minded. He was enthralled.

He could tell that she was using them as a tactic to show how much she paid attention to the tiniest details of a person. He knew she wasn't malice, but playful and feisty, enlightening a side of Stanis that he had lost. The desire to kiss her when she wrinkled her nose in annoyance at him, was forcing him to madness.

His heart was leashed to her with a bronze tether.

She made him question everything. Now he was tempted to stay in one place and fight for something. Something with soft limestone skin, long legs, and a smile that lit up his soul. Stanis smiled widely, but sharp emerald eyes forced him back to reality.

"Shit."

His smile vanished immediately.

"What?" He croaked, brows furrowed and an extra layer of anger laced his tone.

"Not sure why you're smiling. She will hate you for a while." Cole glanced at Abby and Aritzia. Luckily, they were both enamored by something Grant was showing them.

Stanis leaned in towards Cole and said quietly, "you still haven't revealed how you would know so much about her, brother." His voice was stern, and he was aware of the ice in his veins forming.

Cole smiled, but it was withholding. Stanis knew it was a tactic.

"She doesn't even know me yet. She'll forgive me once she does." Stanis said confidently.

"You seem so certain of that, Stannie. Too bad she won't after you reveal your bigger secrets." Cole's eyes narrowed in challenge.

"What secrets?" Arabella said.

Once again regret, and prickles of slight panic, flooded Stanis's veins. He didn't even need to look in her eyes to know they were going to burn his flesh. The next few events happened without his notice. He needed to fix this, she was so close a moment ago and now she would drift away again.

He deserved this.

All his running had led him to a girl who would undoubtedly also run from him, he wasn't a good person, he'd done terrible things. He could conceal her from that, as long as his brother stopped bringing up secrets. Stanis' heart pounded relentlessly, rising with the chorus of rain battering the window. He hardly heard Grant speaking until he mentioned the ball. His eyes flashed to where Grant now stood, a boisterous grin gripping his face.

"...so, we should attend the Ball. It's the only way to get into the archives and find more information about the treasure."

"What ball?" Asked Stanis. Everyone looked at him with questionable expressions. He let their stares roll off, secretly hating the fact that he was allowing Arabella to believe she had bested him on his lack of knowledge.

"The Drafthaven Annual Ball. The one that celebrates the passing of the previous town's name onto the Drafthaven family name." Arabella said, without looking at him.

"It's held in my family's honor at the Orcus Museum, here in Limos, every year."

"Which also holds the archives on the history of Orcus Haven and some on Lafornas." Chimed in Aritzia, as she twisted a vine in between her fingers; creating a rod then concealing it.

"Yes, and it's in three days." Arabella examined all of them. "But only Abby and I have been officially invited." A wrinkle formed between her brows as she considered this. Stanis wanted to reach out and rub his finger over it with his thumb.

"So, get us on the list." Stanis remarked, bouncing to his feet, suddenly excited to have another reason to be close to her. His eagerness dimmed as he noticed the horrified gazes jumping off everyone.

"That's not how it works. It's for Federation Council Members and their family's only; and invitations went out months ago. I couldn't get you one, even if I wanted to." She hid her eyes from him. He could find the answer to this, he had to.

"Can you bring a date?" Stanis hated the desperation that seeped into his voice.

"We already both have one," said Abby. Her voice was sympathetic as she regarded Stanis.

"Fuck that! Bring me instead!" Stanis demanded through the connection he knew led to Arabella. Pinning her with his gaze, willing her to cooperate. He hadn't meant to snap but the thought of her going to a ball with a date was shattering him.

She coolly stated, "Abby and I will go, and we will report back to everyone after."

"Ara!" Stanis shouted. He looked down at her with frustration and opened his mouth to say something. He shut it, realizing they were in mixed company.

"Can I speak to you privately?" He said through gritted teeth, trying to calm his distress.

"No, we have to go now." She declared, her eyes devastating. He watched as she flung a deep blue leather jacket around her shoulders, noticing for the first time it fell just enough to indicate it was a couple sizes too large for her.

He stepped forward, gripping her wrist. "Ara, wait."

She wrangled out of his grasp in a swift motion, before aiming for the door. Her friends standing to exit with her, glared at him. Stanis didn't miss the final look she threw back in Cole's direction.

The lock clicked into place, a signal for Stanis to let out a huff of frustration as his fists met the counter. He sagged his head into his hands. What had just happened? He knew she had felt their connection. After the events of tonight, he couldn't think of anything else, even as they inched towards discovering more about the tomb and finding the treasure.

Wasn't that what he wanted?

Then why was it that all he cared about in that moment was that Arabella had a date to this fucking *ball* and that date wasn't him.

Chapter 14

"Are we going to talk about it, or not?" Abby asked Arabella as they grabbed their drinks from the open bar at the back of the ballroom. Her corseted dress with its flowing skirt touched the floor gracefully. The lovely shades of pink tulle made her hair even more golden as it flowed to her hips.

Arabella envied Abby's hair. Everyone they knew did.

Abby brushed off any talk of it, though, stating it wasn't all glamorous. Abby was often humble with those sorts of things. She admired Abby for being unapologetically different from every other woman she knew in Lafornas. She also adored corrupting her with all of their immodest escapades, she often noticed Abby actually liked all the parties and glamor.

The Limos Board of Commissioners in charge of planning the Annual Ball really had outdone themselves this year. Arabella thought to herself, as she observed the grand room. The Museum was always beautiful, its glimmering dome ceiling was painted with stories of the gods. Huntresses chasing deer whilst a bow was firmly secured in her hand. In a flash the story shifted to The Fates, snipping their taut string before being chased by the famed hero.

Chandeliers of differing sizes danced to the concert below, casting somber reflections upon the mural. Upon the grand stage, in the back of the ballroom, was a twenty four piece orchestra filled with men and women dressed in dark iridescent suits. Black one moment then a deep shade of purple as they yanked their bows across the strings.

Billowing shirts bloomed on the dance floor as patrons spun around with their partners. Arabella watched as sets of women were dipped back, their hair sweeping the floor just before they were whipped back up right. Dancing wasn't going to be on the agenda for her tonight, she doubted she could rangle that much passion from her date.

She did however devour the plated dinner, all six magnificent courses. Each plate was developed with a secret message that clued into the next course. When the time for dessert came she was stuffed full of Orcus game owls coated in black garlic and rosemary, the mountain of brown butter mashed potatoes, and the cheese plate that was more dairy than she consumed in a single day. Honestly this is the most food she'd consumed all week.

"Six layers of molten chocolate wrapped in a creamy fudge blanket."

She wasn't exactly sure how the cake would look but the idea of chocolate was making her hungry all over again. Each course was also paired with a beverage that was indescribably good, each one outdoing the last.

Arabella had watched Abby from across the room the entire time, wishing she had been allowed to sit with the rest of society, instead of up on the stage with her family. Unfortunately, she was stuck between one of her father's business associates and her date, her betrothed, the third son of the Lord of Limos, Lukas Hik.

He had been pleasant to look at, but he was a complete narcissist. Flirting with every woman at the party, married or single. His picturesque figure and deep black hair were a large part of the appeal. Accompanied by his asymmetrical smirk and quick wit, he was anyone's devious temptation. Arabella immediately didn't trust him, something deep in his cobalt blue eyes expressed too much was hidden beneath the surface.

They had, however, been a dazzling sight as they entered the elaborate party. The match of the century, paired in attire and striking features. She never felt as beautiful as she had under the admiring smiles of the Aristoi as they descended the stairs and into the pit of gossip mongers. Lukas had made her seem special for all of the twenty four steps they descended, but that had been the extent of their civility. The moment their feet hit the main floor, flocks of women engulfed him and his arm slipped from her elbow like the end of a dream; revealing it instead as a simple nightmare.

Luckily, the music and bustle of the crowd had been enough to distract from her abandonment, and Abby was there before too much embarrassment swallowed her up. None of this was going as she hoped, a small part of her thought he would be like most men, ecstatic to be in her company, needless to say she had little experience with rejections other than from Cole.

Her heart ached at the thought of him.

When they had left his apartment a small bubble of hope had formed in her chest. Hope that he would follow her and explain he acted the way he had because Stanis had been there. That he was still willing to try for them but he had to work things out with his, now found, but priorly long lost brother.

Before the ball she had ensured her outfit would be murderous, so Lukas would possibly fall for her instantly and she could forget the idea of her and Cole being together. She had molded her face in the perfect mirage to ensnare him but it hadn't worked, like her attempted relationship with Cole.

Lukas hadn't even commented on Arabella's dress, which she definitely found disappointing because it was one of her favorites. A black floor-length gown that hugged her hips and was slit up the right side, revealing a good amount of her thigh. She knew it was a bit shameless, but she also loved the kiss of rebellion a little too much for her father's liking.

Once dinner was set and they found their names etched in stone along the banquet table, elevated above all the rest of the round one encircled with Aristoi members, Arabella only hoped people would stop staring. but Lukas incessant waving and hollering to greet his friends was drawing twice as much attention as before.

Her heart would lurch when someone would address her, she never remembered their name and only hoped they would leave soon. It was odd how many people filtered by, just to wish them happy tidings and a passionate marriage. She didn't mind at first, but his stories about his cousin's best friend's sister went on endlessly. He always found a way to mention other women, no matter the topic. He was either trying to make her jealous or it was clear that he wouldn't be faithful in their marriage.

The longer the night dragged on she realized she had been more enticed by the food than him and that it didn't matter if he wanted her. She would rather eat sand and shit diamonds than have sex with him, no matter how hot he seemed.

What a joke the entire engagement and this ball was turning out to be. At least Abby was struggling to have an enjoyable time as well. She seemed to be open to the idea of her date before tonight, but when Arabella made eye contact with her from across the room, they exchanged a look that proved her theory very wrong.

Abby was nice, so she still played her part well. She smiled and laughed often.

Arabella had met her date, Lord Raron Salvo, he wasn't even that witty, so she knew Abby was really sticking to the act. She had noticed, however, Abby constantly glancing into her purse under the table.

"I don't know what you're referring to," Arabella said.

They had made their way around the room twice already. Then stated they were going for a walk around the grand theater attached to the museum. Some would say the lie was white but to Arabella it didn't matter because it was the perfect cover if they were to be discovered while on their actual mission of exploring the archives in the basement below.

"Oh I meant to ask you," Abby paused, clamping her teeth around her bottom lip, "Stanis, is the man from your dreams, no?" Abby avoided her direct eye contact. Instead they stared straight ahead, linking her arm with Arabella's, and began their stroll out of the boisterous party and into the grim hallway. The thick brown carpet softened their retreat but the silence that welcomed them was foreboding.

Arabella didn't respond, but that never stopped Abby from continuing, "he fits the description perfectly, and he has a connection to Cole, which would prove..."

"It proves nothing" Arabella snapped, a bit of anger building in her chest. She never raised her voice towards Abby.

Abby watched her now, searching her face with intense sapphire eyes. Her sparkling pink eye shadow made her appearance more striking. Abby pulled them to rest for a moment. She stared up at a painting of a maiden overlooking a cliff while large waves, akin to the ones in the Vontois Depths, slammed into the rock wall below. Its entire frame encompassing the whole wall next to them, and overshadowing the deep green wallpaper. Abby never pressed too much, but they wouldn't continue snooping until Arabella told her something. She wasn't sure when it had started but Abby had always managed to pull information out of her.

"We can communicate telepathically," Arabella whispered.

Abby was silent for a moment, then she asked, "I'm assuming we're talking about Coles's sexy new brother, right?" Her eyes lighting up with glee.

"He's not his "new" brother," Arabella said, giving her a side smirk. Abby always knew how to make her day better, even when the situation had no clear outlook yet.

"Well, no…but he is new to you, and it makes sense now, knowing that you were speaking to each other privately and all…" Abby was rambling. Arabella turned them to keep walking down the hall, and she tuned Abby's voice out as she searched for the entrance to the staircase.

When they arrived at the top of the stairs, Arabella registered what Abby was saying. "So that would obviously make you and him mates, which, like I said, made sense." Abby beamed, seeming immensely proud of herself.

"What?" Arabella stuttered.

Abby's feet began descending the stairs, but stopped once she realized Arabella hadn't moved. "I said, if you can communicate telepathically and you have increased your magic potential, you are clearly Stanis's mate." Abby's captivating white smile washed over her, uniting with the feeling emanating from the contact of their skin, and eased her rampant heart rate.

Mates.

Arabella hadn't registered the connection between her powers and meeting Stanis. She had assumed that his telepathic powers were his alone.

Something similar to Cole's.

She had reacted to Stanis in a confusing way, but she chopped that up to him being frustratingly attractive. For the first time in a while, she wasn't focusing on the concept of mates, or the idea of her becoming a full Enkrateia.

After the night of the bombings, her visions, along with the major life altering revelations at Cole's apartment, Arabella wrestled with her morality a bit. She had been at Filly's for two reasons, the first to deliver undercover ILC secrets. The second was to prove herself as ILC's newest agent. She was recruited by the radical group six months prior through a private letter. She had waited months for her first mission and was ecstatic that morning when she received the code word.

The two of them had been getting into the Filly's for years and she had made some contacts there, helping her use her status in society for something actually practical. It was no longer frivolous balls, flower arranging, and searching for a rich husband. She finally had a purpose beyond her birthright, and greater than birthing more Enkrateia.

After the first real vision, she had decided she would inform her ILC contact of her magical developments. She hoped that her first mission was unrelated to the bombings and that they would still allow them to work with her. She had done the drop successfully despite her condition and it was rewarding. She had even urged Abby to join soon after they returned to Drafthaven, but she was reluctant to join a group of "non-Enkrateia". What ever that meant.

When she sent the coded letter to them, she had also included a few minor details about the treasure. She hoped it would add a bit of motivation for the ILC to keep collaborating with her, and maybe they would even reveal more information regarding the story of Itia. She hadn't heard from them, though, and she was worrying they were rejecting her. So, she had refrained from mentioning the small details to Abby, a pang in her heart had followed. It felt deeply like the deception.

"Arabella?" Abby interrupted her inner monologue with a light grab of the wrist. Right. They had a task to accomplish, and they needed to move quickly.

"Sorry, I was thinking about what you said." Abby eyed her quizzically. "We aren't mates. I know for sure that he's just playing games."

A lie.

Abby's soft features challenged her until she eventually gave in again.

"That's fine. Let's just find those Archives and get back to the party. Surely your parents will notice your absence sooner rather than later." Abby stated as they descended the stairs, a smirk pulling at her lips.

Arabella was relieved that Abby had dropped the subject. She feared if they were to fully accept the truth, she would lose whatever pieces remained of her relationship with Cole, denying it was fully over between them.

Two large black doors with gold embellishments found them at the base of the stairs. Above the door scribed in bright gold letters flashed **Orcus Haven Archives and Written History**. Oddly the doors were slightly ajar, the sight tugging deep in her gut. She grabbed Abby's arm and placed a finger to her lips in a request for silence. Abby examined the doors with curiosity. They crept up to them and peered inside, casting silencing magic around them. Abby was right behind her as they moved around the perimeter of the room, searching for any signs of cohabitation.

Silent steps guided them inside, engulfing them in complete darkness. Moments passed before her eyes adjusted to the dimness of the room, small sconces around the Archives were already burning with maroon flames. The vapid spaces swallowing up the light in places, creating pockets of complete blackness. Shadows replaced aisles, blanketing them in an eerie sensation.

Books overflowed from the shelves, scrolls tipped outwards, barely held at the ends by the pressed book covers. Multiple books were placed backwards in the shelf, revealing no titles but a fray of dust and scraps of paper jutting from them. How could they possibly know what to look for in this mess? They snuck in between two of the shelving units, concealing themselves in the shadows, and scanned the cumbersome texts.

Nothing was sparking any recognition.

Arabella looked back at Abby in question. Abby shook her head, showing she wasn't getting any clues either. The murmurings of two voices slipped through the rows of historical texts like a small breeze. Whispers until they inched closer to reveal their secrets. The room finally appeared through the stacks revealing a small enclave.

"We need to find anything regarding the location of the entrance. Hugh's will not accept another failure from me, M." a male uttered softly.

As they peered through the cracks in the publications, Abby's hand stayed laced in hers. Across from the man who had spoken was a woman, or M as he had called her. M's soft brown skin and deep brown hair illuminated in the orange flames dancing in the glass lantern adorned to the table.

Thump

Arabella's jolted her attention to the book that M had slammed to the table. Only able to glimpse the cover briefly, the black binding contrasting the flouncy gold script patterning was too thin to read from a distance. The book flushed open in a wave of sprawling pages until it stopped near the center, enlightening the space further.

"They are hunting more than ever now. They need powerful magic wielders to do their bidding. We are looking for more than just the entrance on Orcas Haven, we need any other details we can find as well." M stated, her dark dress revealing as a shade of deep green in the book's light.

Arabella stared at the pair with intent curiosity and tried to process the information they were overhearing. Blonde bangs fell across the man's face as he too leaned in to observe the open pages of the text splayed on the table. Placing his hand directly over M's where it rested. Their gazes collided but Arabella was sucked deep into a dark fog, preventing her from seeing what happened next.

She was running down multiple hallways she didn't recognize. Glorious sunlight splashed through the colored glass windows while her feet continued to push her past them. She felt its caressing warmth, but she didn't stop. Bringing her hands to her face to glimpse any recognition, she was met with pale skin and petite fingers. Long platinum blonde hair whipped around her face, and white dress splashed around her ankles. Beneath her, bare feet padded along the lush carpet. Rounding another pastel painted corner, she heard screaming at her back. Panting, she willed herself to move faster, panic rising in her chest.

Relief flooded her as she made it to a small doorway; it was brief.

She grabbed the handle, but the door wouldn't budge. Looking back over the shoulders, her limbs began to shake.

"Hael. It's me. Please hurry." The voice that escaped her lips was angelic but panicked.

Just before frantic magic spilled from her fingers, the lock clicked, the small white door swung wide. She flung herself into the opening and shut the door quickly behind her. Throwing her arms around a boy with blonde hair and squared chin who stood firm as a prince. His fine blue suit reeked of royalty, with its gold embossments and medals drapping off the lapels.

Maybe he was a prince, Arabella had never met one but he seemed to hold the physical qualities. Hael rested under a small orb of light, his hand gently grabbing for hers. His smile softened everything in her corrupt soul, until she realized he wasn't real to her. He tugged her along the small hidden tunnel. His burly shoulders barely fit through the passage.

Without stalling, he spoke over his shoulder. "We have to go. The doorway will only be open for three more hours. If we hurry, we can make it there before the final split is complete."

"Hael, we can't just leave my family. They need me to stay and help them fight."

She tugged Hael back to stop him from pulling her further. In a few steps he was in front of her, worry streaking across his face. She realized his appearance wasn't as polished as she thought, his pale blue irises were dimming with faint crescents settling underneath them. His burning palms found the groove of her waist as he pressed her back against the wall. Her hands found his jaw, pulling his forehead to rest on hers. Repeating the moment from memory, she seamlessly wove her arms around his neck embracing fully their intimacy.

Her visions were becoming more vivid and realistic, and despite the hesitation she felt from invading on this obviously private moment, she let the vision pull her deeper. Arabella questioned the love in her heart at that moment, realizing it wasn't something she often felt herself. Relishing the moment of pleasure it brought with it, she sat back and watched the story unfold in front of her, not wanting to interrupt.

"I can't just stand by and let you both die. That's what will happen if we don't go. Laylah, please let me save us." Hael's voice was thick with desperation as he parted from her embrace, reaching down to place his hand on her abdomen. "We can hide from all of this."

Arabella found herself reaching down as well, placing her hand over his and feeling an unfamiliar mixture of emotions, mostly fear but also a small amount of liberation as she looked back into Hael's glorious gaze.

"She'll be born illegally." She could tell by Hael's softening expression that the concept of that would be heartbreaking for them both.

"No, she is an Astraea. We will guard her secret. Say that she is an Enkrateia, make her blend in with them, no one will ever know Layalah. I promise." Hael's eyes gleamed with conviction.

"Okay, let's go then. We shall fight for her, to protect her until it's time for her to return to Idyll."

Thump

Reality reformed in front of her.

Dusty air filled her lungs forcing her to cough, panic budding until she remembered the silencing bubble surrounding them. Next to her, Abby continued to peer through the stacks, so Arabella too, re-fixed on the show. The couple were packing up the books on the table. Abby's hand still clutched hers tightly as her other hand had found her forearm, gripping it gently. She seemed to be frozen as well, but completely transfixed by their spying. In the shadows, she could see so much of Abby's father in her.

She shook off the feeling and leaned into Abby quietly. "We need to leave," Arabella whispered, squeezing Abby's hand tighter. Abby was still staring at the pair through the bookshelf, but nudged along after her without question.

As soon as she reached the door, she yanked Abby through and around the corner. She fixed her composure and cast magic on both of their faces. She dropped Abby's hand, regretting the lack of comfort immediately.

"A, I have to tell you something." Abby's soft pink lips formed a pout. "I can't go back into the ballroom."

"Why?" Arabella frantically searched the hallway contemplating how to approach the next few seconds. They managed to wander into a dead end, the only fixture in the area was a small side table adorned with a large metal vase full of blackened roses. They needed to leave or they would be discovered soon.

"He wants to…you know." Arabella stared at Abby's wriggling brows vacantly, until sirens began to sing in her head.

"Who?"

"Lord Salvo. He's very…persistent. And I don't know how to tell him no. Well I've tried but he continues to ask… and I can't because…"

"I'll handle it."

"What are you going to do?" Abby's shocked expression didn't falter until they heard the doors of the archives slam shut around the corner. She reached for her arms again, looping their limbs together, dragging them to return to the main hall.

"Don't worry about it," Arabella whispered.

Bodies slammed into them as they rounded the corner, forcing her to lose balance.

"Oh, my gods, we didn't see you both there!" Abby exclaimed.

"It's fine." The man said coldly as he brushed the front of his jacket off. He quickly shifted out of their way and as they passed, his olive green eyes branding her skin. They seemed oddly familiar, and she forced herself to look away, fearing what would happen if she held his stare.

Continuing down the hall and back to the ballroom, Arabella glanced back at the duo, noticing the women staring at their backs as they departed. The man was still readjusting his clothes, searching for any dirt they may have left on him.

The orchestra had died down and a soft melody filled the air as they approached the main conservatory. Abby stiffened, her date was stalking towards them with a determined expression, but passing right by them. Tipping his head suggestively towards her.

She leaned into Abby's space and whispered, "Meet at the back of the west gardens in thirty minutes. That's where Aritzia said to meet her. Near the black roses that hang along the fence."

"What are you going to do?"

"I'm handling it." She turned and unlinked their arms, feeling the withdrawal of her comfort, before Abby could reply and slipped back out the door and followed him down the hall.

Arabella had found herself bent over a metal table in the back of what she assumed was a food preparation room. She thought Lord Salvo would be hard to persuade but she knew his intentions well enough. He had been slightly surprised, when she had rounded the corner instead of his date, but showed little resistance once she laid on the charm. His smiles were a bit too eager and she forced herself to ignore it. She liked when men wanted her, but this didn't seem like any of the other times she had sex with random men. She could pretend he was someone else, she'd done it before plenty of times.

So now that she was bent over and willing to accept their lack of intimacy, and her sacrifice, she willed herself to forget all the events leading to her indiscretion. She needed a few minutes of release, and why not do so with a man, who simply, wanted her. He was undeniably attractive, and he also was slightly interested in blondes; which at the time was the only two items of criteria. Fully dressed, her skirts pulled up over her hips, and her thong around her ankles she lifted herself higher on her toes. Her heeled shoes had been thrown in their initial entanglement. Which she regretted now, feeling his struggle to get their heights to match up. He wasn't exceptionally tall, but he was sitting high, and that deterred him from finding the right spot deep in her. He was just thrusting around, causing her focus to waiver.

She lifted higher, willing to forget the cramps forming on her feet. Crossing her legs at the calves, her thighs squeezed tighter. Only making Lord Salvo more excited, as he continued to thrust aimlessly. She had a feeling if she kept making the decisions, he wouldn't be able to resist his urges much longer.

She rolled her eyes at that thought.

She shifted her hips off the table slightly; enough to shove her own hand down to her core. She began working on herself; more than she had ever wanted to outside the privacy of her own room. She couldn't understand how men were so stupid sometimes.

She focused on herself and ignored the man's groans of approval as he did little to help her find pleasure in their situation. Not that he was small or anything. She had just been too wet to feel him after a few thrusts, and he made it clear he wasn't willing to put in much more work for the evening.

She struggled to stop thinking about him until her need was pushing its way to the surface. Instead she thought of herself.

How sexy she must look bent over for him and taking control of her own pleasure. She imagined what her thin spine tattoo must have looked like from his angle. How round her ass must be in this position. As she dove deeper into the feeling, panting harder, because her breathlessness was addictive. She bit down on her forearm that crossed in front of her. Sending pain into her knuckles and her arm simultaneously, pleasure shot through her body, and she held her breath as she dove over the edge. Gripping to the table aggressively, to force her to hold on to the last inhale. She willed herself to moan louder than the man behind her was, blocking out his noises. He pulled out of her and released himself into a cloth. She adjusted herself, bent down, grabbed her shoes. Then patted the man on the shoulder, fleeing before she was late for her next date.

The clock above the door indicated it was a quick endeavor and she was just on time to slip out and meet Abby.

Chapter 15

The Present

The ball seemed to wind down. From the lack of patrons on the dance floor, Stanis couldn't see the blondes anywhere in sight. Some stragglers were still drinking near the bar, as most of the staff were clearing tables.

Stanis ducked, as someone carrying a large tray passed. Entering the service hall they had used to access the Orcus Museum, he heard two moans sound from a room around the corner, forcing him to smirk. He felt the urge to listen in on the moment of passion, until Cole tugged him along, away from the moans. He wondered how many of these socialites were fucking around with each other at events like this.

The fitly dressed orchestra was packing up their instruments in between accepting thanks from guests and left over plates of food. Overhead the chandeliers dimmed, beginning their descent, as subjects in the mosaics rested from their performances.

"Seems like we have missed it," said Grant, disheartened.

"We can still try to see if the girls are in the Archives," Cole said.

"We should get a drink first." Stanis headed straight for the group of men surrounding the bar.

He noticed the tallest of the men first, a cocky-looking asshole in a stunningly nice black suit. His dark black hair pushed back, dark stubble lined his jaw, as he held the attention of his friends like a fallen god. He was flirting with the bartender as Stanis leaned over the hard wood, interrupting the provocateur to order. The man glanced his way, eliciting a click of his tongue in Stanis direction. Obviously irritated by the interruption, smoke billowed for his lips as he released the cigar from their clasp, wafting judgment in their direction.

Stanis had never been an envious man. So finding envy to be licking at his heels made him shift angrily. He adjusted his shoulders, hoping the action wouldn't reveal his sudden urge to puff out his chest. Not a single ounce of him was fearing the stares that branded him now. He smirked back until the rumbustious group severed their showdown.

The bar was now the only occupied space left in the open-air ball room. The scent of smoke and indulgence consummated the ball's finale. Stanis side eyed Cole as he refused a drink in favor of searching the open doors for any stragglers.

A deep laugh echoed around them. "Arabella Drafthaven will be my future wife and if this night goes as planned, then we will be fucking her soon." The man let out another hoarse laugh, one that reverberated into Stanis's soul. "Hopefully her cute friend in pink can join us, too."

Stanis flew down the bar, fisting the man's fancy jacket, and shoving him backwards. He felt hands grabbing at him, most likely the prick's friends trying to stop him, but his size prevented an interruption. His porcelain white knuckles refused to loosen the grip until the night air welcomed them into its embrace. Rain kissed their skin in small caresses attempting to cool them down. He barely recognized the scent of roses and hasty decisions dancing across their new scenery, his adrenaline taking charge, tossing the man into the ashen gravel path leading them away from the steps that brought them into the gardens.

"What the fuck?" The man spat up at him, his blue irises set ablaze with red rings. "I think you have forgotten that I am Lukas Hik!"

Cole and Grant flanked his sides, peering down at their victim. The three of them creating an impenetrable wall.

"You have zero idea what assaulting me will result in!" Lukas scrambled to regain his footing, embers flicking the tips of his fingers. Stanis closed the distance between them and punched Lukas in the nose. Then leaned down to whisper into ear as Lukas remained on his knees. Lukas attempted to stand, Stanis shoved him back until he hit gravel once more.

"You broke my nose, asshole!" Lukas cried, grabbing at his face as blood gushed down onto the grass. He spit the blood coating his mouth onto the stone next time him. Where hands met the gravel beneath him black prints stamped on the ground.

Cole descended the few steps, intercepting Lukas comrades attempting to jump into the fray. Stanis waited for Lukas to stand, placing both his hands into his pockets.

"I could not care less what happens to me." Stanis growled, pressing his forehead against Lukas firmly.

Lukas took the bait, pressing his head back into him, his rage bursting alive in his coal tinted irises as they ringed with gold and burned a deeper crimson.

Stanis thrusted his neck back, slamming his forehead into Lukas's. A load crunch occurred, then a sound similar to a grunt or a cry ripped from Lukas mouth as he crumpled back to the ground. His hands coated in more blood as it flowed from his nostrils and the gash now adorning his forehead. Splattering the gravel underneath him as he rested on his hands and knees at Stanis's feet.

The man in Cole's locked grip thrashed but was no match for his strength. Grant mirrored his actions with another brave soul who thought they could stop this madness.

"You seem to think you are betrothed to my girl," Stanis stated calmly as he bent over Lukas again. "So obviously you needed to force that thought out with a concussion."

"Who?" Panic elevated in Lukas's voice.

Stanis unfolded himself to his full height, forcing his feet to step away from Lukas, as irritation washed through him.

"Arabella?" Lukas mocked. "That whore my dad bought for me?"

Stanis sucked a breath through his nose and circled around Lukas.

This fucker.

Obviously, having no intention to stand against him again, Lukas watched Stanis with a devious grin. Maybe he expected Stanis to be stunned by this, but he couldn't seem to find it in him to be threatened.

"Yeah, see, you don't get to go around saying her name," Stanis said calmly. "She isn't yours to speak about, or even think about…" Stanis paused for effect. "Actually now that we're mentioning things that aren't acceptable. Women aren't objects that you can purchase. So, if you plan to think about her in the future, or her friends," he glanced at Grant and saw his approval, "then I'm going to have to remind you again." Stanis could sense his anger building. "And I'm afraid people won't notice your hideous new nose job if your teeth are missing as well."

"You're a psychopath!" Lukas howled.

Stanis crouched in front of him, removing his hands from his pockets. The infamous smirk uncontainable at the sight of Lukas flinching away under his threats. "Only my Ara gets to call me that." All emotion left him while he slammed a knife down into Lukas's extended leg, just above his knee cap. Lukas wailed as Stanis ejected his knife at the same pace. Confident that the discussion had come to its end, he ascended the steps. Cole and Grant presences followed close behind, after they released their captures.

Gravel shifting as they stumbled to assist Lukas as he laid on the ground clutching his wounds.

Air whipped past Stanis, along with the scent of citrus and enticement. Grant began chasing a woman in a green floor length dress, and more confusion encompassing him with every passing second. his adrenaline was fading, the feeling in his fingers tingling unsettling him.

It hadn't been a fatal blow, but still, the entire fight had been impactful. Anger flashed at the thought of Ara being betrothed.

"Stannie, are you alright?"

"Of course, why wouldn't I be?" He said vacantly, raising his brow as he looked past Cole's shoulder. Following his jaded line of sight, they watched Lukas and his friends retreating into the wine soaked night, through the arched gate leading into the heart of Limos.

"For one, you just head butted someone, then stabbed him," Cole searched his expression, possibly for any hint of self conflict. "Also, you still haven't told me about your interaction with Arabella."

Stanis hadn't been excessively violent through most of his life, but something deep seated within him wanted to burn the world down at the thought of Ara with another man. They had never come to blows, even as children. A part of Stanis, most likely, had been triggered by his destined bond to Arabella. Resulting in his lack of judgment, a tact Cole wasn't going to be able to relate to until he himself found his mate.

"I told you, there's nothing to tell. She hasn't really spoken to me since the other night," Stanis said.

"You called her *yours* back there. Are you accepting The Fate's decision now?" Cole pressed. "Does she know?"

Stanis stiffened, but before he could respond he caught Grant approaching over Cole's shoulder. "The girls aren't here. They went to the Fen's," Grant seeped concern from every pore.

"What is Fen's," Stanis asked, hating that he didn't have the answers, again.

"It's the speedway across town," Cole mouth a tight line. "A Drag Racing Speedway."

Chapter 16

Fen's Racing Speedway was something out of a car enthusiast's wet dream. Engines roared to life around them, while they weaved their way through to endless kaleidoscopes of colorful vehicles. Across the parking garage, which was obviously blocked off for this gasoline perfumed party, a DJ bobbed their blue mohawk while spinning disks on the jockey situated on an invisible elevated platform. The magic of it all still stumped Stanis, so he marveled at the floating controller hoisted above the crowd of grinding patrons.

Stanis never had an affinity for cars or gyrating parties, not that he could have ever afforded a vehicle for himself. Most cars in the city were owned by the notoriously rich, and distastefully snobby. The howl of engines grew to a furious volume as two cars slammed by, racing at high speed, then drifting around the crowd in a wide arc. The vibration sent his heart into his throat before the cars pounded away from them.

He traced his eyeline back to where Grant and Cole lead him through the crowd, catching glances from the surrounding women who bent their desirable figures on hoods. Their legs extending for miles; he found it hard not to look at how high their skirts rode up on their thighs. He was enjoying the views of cropped tops and ripped lace tights, but the desperation seeping from them was suffocating. His urge to find Ara was making his mouth dry; and the thought of her in this place was burning anger through his veins.

He fiddled with the lighter tucked deep in his jacket pocket, sweeping up with his other hand to find the joint he had placed behind his ear. He sucked in a hard breath as he ignited the roll. Smoke coated his lungs and his head lightened as he sucked it deep and held tight.

Stopping at Coles apartment prior had been the best decision they could've made, if they hadn't changed from their suits they would've drawn some unwanted attention. If their wardrobe hadn't, his bloody knuckles would have most definitely caused some glances, but alas he'd whipped all evidence of his brawl away.

His deep brown leather jacket brought him a better sense of comfort and he needed all his shields as they weaved through this battlefield of lust and headlights. Frustration licked the back of his mind; he was hoping to have found out what was in the Archives by now. Arabella didn't seem like the type of girl who would be sneaking into Archives or associating with people who smelled heavily of grease.

Cole nodded towards the elevators, and they stepped in. The doors collided just as another pair of cars slammed around the corner in front of them. Stanis caught glimpses of their glowing undersides while smoke coiled from the tires. Cole jabbed the bottom for the rooftop, shooting a concerned look at Stanis.

"What?" He thought.

"Try to rein it in." Cole's face lacked any bull shit. "She's sort of a big deal to these people, so don't go stabbing people."

Stanis furrowed his brow.

It was often unclear what his brother was thinking, unlike Cole, Stanis couldn't simply invade on people's mind. If his brother wasn't asking him incessant questions, he was accusing Stanis of something. He reluctantly had to agree with Cole in the slightest. He had changed from the last time they had been in each other's company. Stanis had been sharpened to a point, and Cole had been, well he wasn't sure really, but he had an edge to him as well. Even the way he glided through this function had Stanis questioning his honing.

"What's that supposed to mean?" His question fell flat as the doors flooded open revealing an extravagant number of bleachers piled full with an audience. Everyone in Limos had to have been in attendance, if not more from the outskirts of Orcus Haven.

His eyes transfixed on the glowing hills that now expanded around them, beyond the monstrous rows of patrons. The Limos's skyline created a canyon, the buildings barricading in the euphoric event. Stanis had very little experience with magic creation, most of his education coming from first hand experience, not a school. This oasis was one of the most spectacular he'd ever come across in all his times.

His feet pulled onto the moving translucent walkway, gliding above a bustling array of smoke coated card tables piled high with riches in all variations. Quickly averting his sight from the drop below his feet, he sucked down another puff of smoke, ogling the view that lingered in front of them.

Black tents hung onto the large canyon that cradled the long strip of asphalt, stretching out beyond his line of vision. The stars above them burned so brightly, that the landscape bathed in an infernal glow. Assisted by the neon lights that the magic orbs hanging at the entrances of each tent and headlights that filtered onto the track.

The crowd roared loudly at two cars placed on the starting line. Both drivers were viciously yelling at each other, taunting in preparation for the impending battle in front of them. A man stood in front of the cars thrusting his hands out as money flew through the air to his hands from all corners of the magical colosseum.

"All final bets needed, ass hats." The man yelled over the chaos, towards the drivers.

Each one tossed a roll of cash at him. Floating to him with grace; his magic calculating and displaying the totals above his head. Stanis tried to look away, but at the last minute, he wanted to throw the few dollars he had into that pot. Cole grabbed his arm before he could and pulled him along.

"Try not to be tempted by the persuasion benders around here. Most of them are using their gifts to collect bets."

"Bets?" Concern and smoke billowed around him. Cole stole the joint from his lips, placing it between his own, then sucked a long breath.

The pair stumbled from the conveyor belt along the sky bridge, being presented nicely in front of the largest tent, which was situated nicely above the finish line.

"Yeah, gambling's sort of the whole point of these drag races." Cole started walking away again, following Grant as he parted the small crowd that formed trying ahead, the group tying to convince the guard at the entrance to let them in.

"How do you win?" Stanis asked, trying to mask his temptation with curiosity.

Cole turned and pointed back to where they came from, just as the two cars slammed past below them and smoke and fire blazed from their mufflers.

"Two pricks line their cars up there and whoever can shoot their ten second car down this track fastest…wins". Stanis tried to hide his embarrassment from his lack of knowledge.

"Don't worry, it's a rich person's sport." Cole stated, obviously sensing his discomfort. "All you need to know is that no matter how silly we believe it to be, you can't tell Arabella that."

"Ara?" Stanis asked before he could stop himself. She was here somewhere; he knew that from Grant's intuition on the subject, but he was finding himself lacking any answers.

As they approached the massive tent, soft music greeted them, along with the scent of lust and caviar. Men and women dressed in frocks of color lined the couches and mingled around the private bar. Grant stepped up to the guard, who held a firm grasp on the black velvet rope.

"You're not on the list, buddy," the guard grunted. Stanis caught a glimpse of the private viewing area over Grant's shoulder, as he continued to argue.

"They're with me, Calvin." Abby suddenly appeared in Stanis's eye line. She was smiling widely at Calvin, while he apologized repeatedly. Stanis hardly recognized her, with eyelids painted in glitter, and her lips a dark red, she barely resembled the girl he'd seen a few days ago. She grabbed Grant and Cole's hands and tugged them into the tent, forcing Stanis to follow. Her tight white crop top and bagging tan cargo pants made her stand out from the rest of the patrons in the tent, who were all wearing bright colored ensembles. Her hair was down, and it spilled all around her shoulder. The golden locks curled slightly at the ends as they grazed her hips. She handed them all a shot and pointed to the seats on a large maroon couch at the front of the tent.

"This is the perfect view of the track," she expressed, eagerly, before she plopped herself down next to Grant. Her closeness made him shift slightly.

Stanis let a smile slip onto his lips after he took the shot with ease. He glanced around at the other patrons, his eyes wanting one individual to appear. Tempted to ask Abby about her, but before he could, she leaned forward and placed a roll of cash into a tube that projected out of the floor. The magic of it tallied her count, then after it displayed an even split between the next two racers in a neon glow, ity shot back down.

"You boys are right on time. They're up next," she stated excitedly. She met Stanis's eyes, her smile dimmed. He turned to Cole to ask him another question, but stopped, mesmerized by the two black cars at the starting line.

The pair seemed to be two sides of the same coin, the same black sleek body, but the hoods were painted with two different colored serpents.

The first one, he noticed, a purple python that curled around a thick silver vine. Dark roses, hardly visible against the base paint of the car, sprouted around it rhythmically. Smoke billowed from the edge of the mosaic, mixing with the purple glow emerging from under the chassis, aiding its anticipatory dance. A hiss came from the car, sending the crowd into screams. The driver settled behind the steering wheel, sporting a dark black helmet that was twin to their opponents.

This driver's hood sported a viper dressed in gold spots that covered its entire coiled body. The snake sat in a bed of fog that was so realistic Stanis found it hard to decide where the car separated from the smoke. The snake's fangs snapped in an illusion of magic that made the crowd cheer wildly. More smoke billowed from the back of the car as the driver revved the engine. They nodded towards their opponent, lifting a hand to their helmet and imitating blowing a kiss. Which the other driver caught, midair, before shaking their head.

Realization hit Stanis like a punch to his chest.

Arabella wasn't up here because she was down there. In one of those crazy fast machines. His heart raced rapidly; the urge to put a stop to it pulling him to his feet. Cole's hand grabbed his wrist and pulled him back into his seat.

"Easy, Stannie." Cole forced out through gritted teeth.

"Which one is she in?" Stanis yelled across the small space at Abby, who was laughing at something Grant had whispered into her ear.

Her smile died as she fixed her attention on Stanis. "That's the fun of it." She said as she looked towards the two cars and laughed. "They switch cars every time to confuse us all." She seemed to be amused by her friends.

The two cars purred in unison, while orbs flashed a warning above. On the third blink the cars shook, their tires squealed until forming a ring of smoke around them. Stanis' heart plummeted to his stomach as they shot from the start together, his head hardly grasping the swiftness of their assault, instead feeling the effects of the drugs he smoked. Cole mentioned it was a ten second act but time dripped by slowly.

He had a small nagging to cheer on the viper as they pulled slightly ahead in the last second, before they both shot across the finish line directly in front of them. They all stood, Abby jumping frantically while hugging Grant. She would've had the same reaction no matter which car won, and as Stanis cheered alongside her, the thrill in her eyes became intoxicating.

"I'm so glad to see you also wanted Ritz to win!" She shouted over the cheers of the crowd. Stanis's heart sank into his stomach.

Fuck.

Cole laughed maniacally.

Ara shifted her way out from behind the python, removing her helmet, and flicking her strawberry blonde hair around her shoulders. His breath caught as he watched her strutting in her tight black pants and navy leather jacket. Slight regret budded when pieces of his memory flashed the familiar silver threaded viper, shielding her from the back. He bit the inside of his lip, while she pulled Aritzia in for a large hug. They both laughed, but all he could see was *Ara*, as the two of them pushed each other playfully. Making her way towards the sideline, her gaze found him before she entered a covered tunnel; then she disappeared from his sight.

Chapter 17

The shouting from the crowd dulled, as she and Aritzia pushed further into the tunnel.

"You head up, get your celebratory hugs and then I'll meet you up there." Arabella said, gripping Aritzia's wrist, smiling wildly at her. She felt so much love for both her and Abby, but Ritz had always been her twin flame. They both had a huge addiction to adrenaline, and she knew they shared an admiration for racing.

"Okay," Aritzia said, squeezing her hand back, and laughing, "but you owe me a drink." Aritzia turned to leave but glanced back at her, "Are you sure you are okay after your last vision?"

She had told Aritzia about Hael and Laylah, Abby's parents. Knowing that telling Abby would be an entire ordeal, so she confided in Aritzia first. Arabella hoped she could help her decipher it further, before they tried to explain it to Abby. "Yeah, I'll tell her about it soon." She didn't know when exactly, but she had a nagging feeling in her gut that it should be soon.

Aritzia turned away from her, ascending the stairs in front of them.

Firm arms wrapped around Arabella's waist, as she lost sight of her friend, lifting her off the ground. She released a small squeal of excitement as her adrenaline shot back through her.

"I lost half a grand tonight, babe." A dark voice whispered in her ear.

Arabella laughed maniacally, "You know I can't ruin all the fun by telling you which car I'm in, Killian." He placed her back on solid ground, and she whipped around to face him.

Humorously, Killian looked her up and down with hunger and not a lick of actual anger. As one of the richest Enkrateia in Lafornas, she doubted he was actually angry with the loss.

"You are so hot, you know that?" He said, closing the distance between them, his auburn hair brushing over his eyebrows. Heat rushed to her cheeks, but she had a nagging feeling to keep him at a distance. She usually reveled in the chase that Killian begged for, but looking at him now, something platonic fizzed in the air.

"Of course I know that," she laughed with a smirk on her lips, backing away from him. He followed her steps, dancing her back towards the wall. She admired his large frame as it boxed her in. His massive shoulders curved in perfect mounds, and his shirt had a hard time containing the matching pecks. He was sporting a dark black leather jacket, which did little hold in his strong form. She wasn't sure how far the tattoos decorating his skin ventured exactly, possibly covering all the inches of his hidden skin. Killian was a massive catch, but he also was exactly like her brother, so the appeal dwindled in the wind. Adrenaline found its way creeping back under her skin, when he placed his hands against the wall next to her head, grinding his hips closer to hers.

"Please let me kiss you, babe." He whispered, his breath grazing her cheeks. She looked into his deep blue eyes, avoiding the sight of his tongue wetting his lower lip.

"You know… I am betrothed." She breathed, forcing herself to lean away from his touch, but failing.

His eyes ignited with delight, and his freckles crinkled across his nose while his smile widened. Basking her in the scent of fresh berries and admiration, for a brief moment, before he leaned in to steal a kiss. She found herself not wanting to pull away, but she did.

He released a small laugh as he tipped his head down briefly, while she slipped under his arm and out of his embrace. Her back found the other wall before he turned towards her, his auburn hair reflected in the faint light of the hallway.

"You've let me kiss you before, babe. Why not now?" He asked, slumping against the opposite wall, dramatically.

"We can't always win, It would spoil the taste of victory." She joked back.

He stared at her smile, while dragging his lower lip in with his teeth. Then he let his eyes scan her body. Causing her to shift her legs to try to ease the pressure building between her thighs. He released a long breath, but remained in his spot against the wall opposite her. A few other drivers pressed their way between them as they exited the arena.

Arabella smiled at him across the distance, taunting him slightly. As more people weaved their way through and the tension between them decreased, along with their detachment. "Did you find him?" She asked, after the long silence enveloped them.

He smirked as he reached into his front pocket, pulling out a small tin, then tossed it at her.

She caught it without breaking eye contact, flipping open the small lid to unsheathe a perfect joint and a small rolled parchment. Inhaling the decadence of cannabis and something more familiar mixed with the scent of her leather jacket. She pulled back her collar slightly to reveal her tank top strap underneath. She heard Killian shifting, as she tucked the roll into the strap of her bra, then concealed it again. She fiddled with the small paper, unrolling it briefly to catch its message.

"Thanks, buddy." She smirked, shoving the roll back into the tin, before tossing it back, and heading for the stairs. He grabbed her hand to stop her from escaping, tugging her into his tight embrace, and she let him. His soft fingers, the ones not gripping her wrist, grazed her neck as he pulled her hair over her shoulder. Small breaths threatened to escape her lips as he pressed a delicate kiss to her skin. The touch was gentle, and caused her eyes to flutter closed.

"I'll see you real soon, babe," he whispered, then broke their contact.

She ascended the stairs quickly, hoping her feet wouldn't catch a stair, while his gaze burned into her backside. She forced herself to keep her eyes straight ahead as she increased their distance, allowing the smallest of smiles to pull at her lips.

She emerged from the tunneled staircase and scanned the area that made up the Driver's Circle, weaving her way through the other patrons as they mingled with their glassy eyed friends and family members. Until she spotted Abby's beckoning golden crown. Stopping just behind the couch, her and Aritzia now perched on, Arabella leaned over the back and wrapped them both a hug.

Abby squealed with joy, drawing all the attention to Arabella's arrival. Stanis locked his jade eyes on her and she encouraged herself to keep her mind closed off to him. She didn't know if it would work, but it was worth a try. Before they attended the ball she quickly reviewed her university texts that mentioned mental blocking, but had never used it in action.

Frost emanated from Cole's direction, so she ignored him too. She didn't know if either of them would ever talk about their issues or if they could ever savage their friendship.

"You both did so amazing, and you almost had Ritz…right at the end there." Abby jumped up to allow room for her to sit down. Abby made her way around the space and sat on the floor in front of Grant, allowing her shoulder to rest against his knee. Her hair draped over his dark navy jeans, while she leaned back to say something to him. Grant bent to meet her, quietly, intercepting her secret.

At least they are getting along well, her best friend finally let her guard down around a male figure. A smile painted itself across her face as she sat down next to Aritzia, who watched with a more distressed look in her brown eyes. Arabella ordered a drink from a passing waitperson and removed the joint from her hidden stash, placing it between her teeth. The paper caught on her chapped lips. As she searched her pockets, she noticed Stanis' gaze on her.

"May I?" He folded to present a flame.

She leaned in and sucked deep, "thank you." She took a second long breath and released a billow of smoke. A couple hits and mummers between her friends later she noticed Stanis, again, watching her eagerly. She gently passed the roll to him and as their fingers grazed one another, a small shiver shot down her spine. Unsure where the encouragement had ventured from, she watched his lips curl around where hers had been. He pulled, not one but, two drags, then rested it in the tray on the table.

The distraction of a new pair of cars crossing the finish line, sent the crowd into another round of applause, forcing her gaze away from him. Grant cast a silencing magic around their group, and leaned over Abby. She adjusted closer, as well, drawing the group in tighter. "We need to discuss what happened in the Archives." His deep voice attempted to whisper.

"We weren't able to find anything tangible, but we saw other people snooping around as well." Abby chimed. "They were talking about the Federations efforts to rid all Vacants and capture any Enkrateia who contain magical abilities worthy of their cause."

Arabella checked the faces of the people surrounding them to ensure no one was focusing too much on their group's activities. Aritzia discreetly shook her head as their gazes collided.

"What does this have to do with us finding the treasure?" Stanis said, the sound of his voice jolting her.

"This is important, if tracking it led us to this information. They were obviously looking for it as well." Abby retorted angrily. "Why else would they be in the same place?" She now looked to Arabella, for reassurance.

"Yeah, we should take this seriously because some of us are pretending to be Vacants," Arabella added. "Even our own family members think so, to keep us safe from this exact thing." She stated as she looked towards Cole, hoping to find him returning her stare.

"The Relaggins wouldn't turn me into the Federation, and neither would your father." Cole responded without meeting her gaze. Stanis looked between them, and scowled, seemingly disagreeing with something that was said.

What the hell was his problem?

Stanis's eyes locked onto her, but he didn't open his mouth again. His sudden lack of effort with her was creating a stir in her mind. He was all about bossing her around the other day, when they first met, but now he had nothing to say.

"Why would the Federation want the treasure?" Aritzia pondered aloud .

"And specific Enkrateia magic wielders?" Abby added. "As well as all Vacant's executed?"

Everyone remained silent until they were forced to dis-spell their silencing magic as the waitperson returned with multiple drinks in hand. The silent tension reformed, as soon as they were left alone again.

Arabella finally broke the silence. "I'm not sure, but I know we can't talk about this here." Her tone confirmed it was nonnegotiable. She picked up her drink and slammed it back. The noise of constant eruptions from the crowd and the cars whizzing by were giving her a headache. She leaned in to grab her joint from the tray and dashed it out before it burned away.

"Can we head out, Ritz?" She stood, tugging her jacket collar to influence the group's departure.

"Yeah, let me head down to the lockers and grab my clothes," Aritzia responded as she stood, rounding the couch.

Abby and Grant made their way to the exit, along with Cole, not far off their heels. Arabella was faced with a moment of awkwardness as her and Stanis stepped into the aisle simultaneously, bumping shoulders.

"Go ahead, Beautiful." The purr in his voice made her tremble slightly with anticipation. He wasn't all that annoying after all, he had been nothing but tranquil this evening, and now he was even being polite.

As she stepped across him, aiming towards the exit, his hand found her elbow. Then, before she knew what he was doing, blackness engulfed them. She had an odd sense of falling, no floor sat beneath her feet. She searched the darkness around her, but the pit seemed to consume all the light. She wanted to pry his calloused hand off the soft leather of her jacket. His grip tightened, and her skin lit ablaze at the feeling that pricked the hairs on the back of her neck.

"I thought you enjoyed a good adrenaline rush, Ara?" He whispered in her ear.

She could sense his smirk without even being able to see it, swearing to herself that when he was done messing around, she would not stop herself from punching him until his eye sockets were purple.

Chapter 18

*Sometime in the Past,
then in The Future*

Stanis held onto her arm firmly, pressing back as far as he could remember his brain ever traveling. Once he felt the familiar wall in his mind, he pressed firmly into it with his free hand. The darkness tumbled away. His feet hit the dirt beneath him, sending a bloom of dust flying.

"What the fuck, Stanis!" Arabella stumbled beside him.

He adjusted his grip to catch her around the waist. One could never fully get used to time travel. He had never pulled anyone else through the fabrics of existence, so he imagined it would be shocking for her. Her hand found his chest, and she drilled into him with her sterling gray eyes. Her hair was a curtain of strawberry blonde, veiling her face. He thought about how naturally beautiful she was. Even with the smell of leather and grease coating her, he could still smell coconut and flowers.

"Let me go!" She pushed out of his grip. "Explain, now!" She demanded, brushing the strands from her face and taking in the surrounding landscape.

The vast sea of black desert surrounded them, and the foggy clouds above thrashed viciously. No wind touched their skin, but she scanned the pink sky peeking out of the dramatic storm with perplexity in her eyes. She was acclimating to her surroundings better than he had. He found her eyes again, her determined legs stomping her towards him. Closing the distance between them, he braced for a scolding. She threw her fist back and slammed it into his nose before he could even think of reacting.

"What the fuck, Ara?" He grasped his nose, as blood pooled in his throat. The taste of copper coated his tongue. Her hands rested on her hips, while he spat to the side of them. Her scowl was murderous.

"Explain, asshole!" She demanded through clenched teeth. "Or I'll give you a pair of blackened eyes."

Fuck! Was his eye blackening? He'd been punched before but never by a girl and certainly not that hard by such delicate hands. *Did all girls punch like that?*

"Yes, it is. If you'd rather speak that way, *freak*, we can, but you're going to tell me. Now!"

"You really don't trust me, do you?" He forced out, and stepped back to reassess her, his brow lifting. His heart was thrashing with adrenaline, and all he managed to want was to pin her down and make her pay for the bruising she just delivered. It would have to be later, because now she was arching her brow at him and frowning deeper.

"This is the past." He gestured around them, spitting blood into the ashy sand. "We're exactly where we left from in the present timeline, but nothing existed before."

"How far in the past?" She didn't even flinch at the thought of them crossing timelines.

"As far as I could take us."

"There's no one here. No buildings." Again, she was reacting well despite her acts of violence towards him. Her shoulders softened as she observed the desert surrounding them again. The black sun began setting behind her, haloing her in a pink tinted glow.

"Very astute. I've come here a few times and every time, no one's here." He confirmed. "I have traveled in all directions, and it just goes on endlessly as barren slate desert."

"Another big word, for you," she said.

He sucked his teeth. Then, a long moment of silence swept between them.

"Except for that way," he gestured towards the Ventois Depths. The faint sound of raging waves crashing to the blackened cliff faces rang in the distance.

"Why do you care?" She asked, rolling her eyes. "Why are we here?"

He felt anger coiling in his spine, but he suppressed it. "I needed to talk to you," his teeth clenched tightly, "away from everyone".

"Um, I was helping you," she scoffed, "Along with all my friends, dumbass, but now I change my mind, after you decided to act like a psychopath." He realized she definitely knew how to throw around insults. "Now, take us back to the present, or whatever you call it." She demanded.

"Ara, I need, *you and I*, to go alone to find the treasure," he said, "I can't drag Cole into all this, and your friends won't be able to help us when it counts."

"*What the fuck does that mean?*" She shot telepathically. "My friends have been nothing but dependable to me.... and you if you haven't noticed." She stalked away, aimlessly.

He took chase to stop her. "Where are you going, Ara?"

She whirled on him. "Ugh, that's not my name," she seethed into his face.

"There's nowhere to go here. Look around."

"So, take me back! Or forwards, or…"

He stared down at her, waiting for her to crack her façade, but he had pushed her too far with this approach, so he changed directions.

"Okay, but can we go somewhere else first?" He interrupted.

"Some other time?" She asked, her eyebrows raising.

"Yes, I need to go visit a… *friend*…who I think you might like very much."

"If any of your *friends* are like you, I doubt it will be a fruitful endeavor." She said the word friend like it was a made-up concept. Before he could respond, she asked, "What do I get out of all this?"

"What do you want?" His heart bubbled, slightly. He was enjoying the fact that she agreed to this, knowing he'd do anything for her regardless of what she asked.

"I'm not sure yet," She paced, "but I want three separate favors"

"Three?" His scowl resurfaced.

"I haven't decided on them yet, but when I do, I'll clarify that it's one of my favors." Her tone lightened. "That way, you aren't saying I used one before I actually am," she explained.

He did not know what she was rambling on about, but he wanted it all to stop.

"Again, you don't trust me do you?" He ground out.

Her jaw ticked, but she didn't respond.

"Three favors it is, anything else, Beautiful?" He asked.

"Yes." She was back to murdering him with her stare. "And no more nicknames."

"Is that it?" He said. Pushing the fact that she had called him about twelve different names by that point to the back of his mind.

"And," her stalling was killing his patience, "tell me before we jump through time again."

"Is that all, now?" Irritation laced his veins.

"Why did you bring me here?" Her façade softened and his heart beat out of rhythm.

"I told you, I needed to talk to you." She didn't interrupt him. "I have been afforded the opportunity to meet other Visionaries, in my time traveling. Mostly when I jump, I can't interact with anyone. There have been a few circumstances that have differed but..."

"Like in the present timeline?" She interrupted.

"No, in my," he hesitated. "In our present timeline of existence, I am free to be a normal human, but in others, I'm an insect on the wall, watching and collecting information with almost no recognition of my presence.

"Most of the time?"

He hadn't realized they were close enough to touch again. The scent of coconut and devotion drifted to his nostrils, forcing him to almost forget what he was doing.

Focus.

"Yes," he breathed. "Well, there have been a few people who have interacted with me." With great effort, he framed his words correctly. He didn't want her questioning him about the time he slept with a girl in the future. That was a regret he wanted to keep buried.

She was observing him with a blank expression, waiting for him to continue. "One of those people is a Visionary, like yourself, and I want you to meet him." He waited a moment for her to process. Watching her brows furrow and her breath even out. "He's in the future, so I needed to explain some things before we jumped there. It's nothing like the present and I wanted you to be prepared because it can be…*jarring*."

She stared at him with a *no fucks given* attitude, for a moment, then stepped away. Digging her figure tips into her eye sockets, and releasing a small groan. Moving her fingers to her temples, her eyes fluttered to him again.

Stanis watched intently, hoping she'd agree, realizing how much he needed her acceptance. *"Please, I need you to meet him."*

"Ugh, also you need to explain that!" She demanded, throwing her hands back down, before crossing them over her chest.

"Explain what? The telepathy? I thought that was *your* mind trick"

"My mind tricks!" She scoffed, "that's really rich, Stanis."

He waited for her to explain further. Of course, she had decided to blame her for their connection. Their connection?

Realization hit him rapidly, causing him to step back, and turn his back to her.

I should tell her?

"Tell me what?" He could tell that irritation was seeping from her, she squared up again anticipating a fight.

"It doesn't matter" he dragged a hand over his face and through his stubble. His mind wandered again, to the fact that he hadn't shaved in a few days. Maybe he should do that. "We need to go." His abrupt command struck her into action again.

"What?" You haven't explained much." She flailed her arms and shook her head.

"What else is there to explain?" He demanded through gritted teeth.

She sucked in a large breath through her nose, "yes, or no's?"

"Fine." He felt like he was arguing with his brother. A new set of questions filtered into his head. She was a mirror image of Cole at that moment. How much time had they spent together?

"Are you really looking for some lost treasure?"

"Yes," irritation was knocking again.

"Is time bending your only magic?

"Yes, apart from a few spells I picked up along my way." She was staring at him now, exposing him to more than just the dry heat. He straightened, trying not to sweat under her gaze.

"Okay," she said, reaching out her hand.

"That's it?" He said, a bit taken aback.

"Yes, that's all the yes or no questions… I have at the moment." She smiled at him, with a heart palpitating grin, but her eyes said she was full of shit. He didn't want to fight with her any longer, so he reached out and yanked her into him. Spinning her so that her backside pressed to his chest, forcing a small breath to leave her lungs. He wrapped his arms around tightly, and willed his magic around them before she could argue with him. Tilting backwards onto his heels, he encouraged them to free fall into blackness as it enclosed around them. He summoned a brown glow to surround them, mostly to help prepare for their destination. He had a feeling the amount of sunlight would set her more off kilter than anything else.

After minutes of falling through the abyss, he forced himself to look down at her and noticed that she was staring at him over her shoulder, the expression painted on her face was unlike any he had seen prior. His heart swelled slightly, as he considered it might be admiration. Their moment was abruptly interrupted by a blinding bright light and a heat that knocked the breath out of him.

"What the fuck?" Arabella gasped as she rebalanced herself and pushed out of his arms. Their skin peeling apart, making his heart fall on the concrete. They had landed on top of a lofty high rise building in the center of Limos. He stepped forward to survey the landscape, hoping to quickly determine which building they stood atop. Arabella was already at the edge, pressed against the chain link fence and scanning the street below.

"Shit," she gasped, "how are we this high off the ground?"

"Limos grew to be an even larger city than you could imagine in the present time. Infrastructure and technology have surpassed even my understanding." He headed towards the rooftop door behind him. Sensing Arabella following him as he yanked on the door that didn't budge.

"Fuck," he muttered. The scorching heat was going to burn them alive if they didn't get off the fucking roof. With all the technology advancements, it still alluded him how the world could've gotten so fucking hot.

"How far in the future are we?" She was knelt in front of him. It was a dream, nothing else could explain her sudden need to bow at his feet.

"What?" He breathed, clearly frazzled. Until she pulled a device out of her jacket pocket, then with a flick of her wrist the lock on the door clicked open. She stood and without acknowledging him swept over the threshold. The door swung back at him forcefully, but he grasped the edge of it before it hit him.

"Do we exist in this timeline?" Her voice echoed through the stairwell.

His eyes took a second to adjust. The cool air circled them as they descended the stairs. He vaulted over the railing, jumping in front of her as she reached the landing. He didn't much like being a shadow.

"I'm not sure actually," his brows furrowed, "I haven't seen us on Orcus Haven."

"Great!" She squeaked. "That must mean I will finally see another Isle."

"We have to walk multiple blocks, is that okay?" He asked, his brows furrowing.

"No one can see us, right?" She asked.

"Yes." His mouth was in a tight line. They descended flight after flight of stairs and his breaths strained. Beads of sweat on Arabella's eyebrows intrigued him. While her chest heaved slightly to bring air into her lungs, he wished different circumstances brought her straining on, imagining her naked beneath him, strawberry blond hair fanned, and moaning his name.

When he shook himself out of his daydream, he realized she was gone. Adrenaline rushed him out the stairwell after her, almost trampling her as she observed the rows of cars that lined the parking garage laid in front of them.

"Come on!" He demanded, shoving around her as he aimed at the opening on the far side of the ramp.

He was almost back out into the heat of the day, when he heard the purr of a vehicle come alive behind him, then the squealing of tires rushed towards him. A car slammed on the brakes just behind him, he leaned to peek through the silver framed window, his eyes finding her. His favorite wicked grin beckoning him to get in.

As they sped through traffic, weaving manically, Stanis watched her shift gears, all while she continued to smile madly. She was following his short directions, around corners, and through side streets. Intentionally, he misled her multiple times to increase the duration of their trip. His shoulders settled into the leather seats, while she leaned back and rested the thumb at the base of the steering wheel as they waited at a red orb indicating a traffic stop. She had picked up the futuristic regulations of driving quickly, but he noticed the few times she intentionally forgot to stop when it was required.

"Who taught you how to drive?" Stanis asked, hesitantly.

"My brother," she smiled, "he was a Fen's racer before he left." Her smile dimmed faster than it arrived.

"Where is he, now?" He asked.

"I'm not exactly sure." The air in the car thinned, the sound of her voice was heartbreaking.

The car ride was silent for multiple blocks. "This was his jacket." She said softly.

So much relief washed through him. "It's this building." he pointed to a brown three-story unit, with a small staircase leading up to a tiny red door. She stopped the car directly in front of it, and as Stanis pushed his way out, he noticed her lean down under the dashboard and unfasten some wires to cut the engine off.

Arabella stepped up to the small entry behind him, he made a clear effort to always be in front of her. It wasn't until she reached the landing and pressed into the space he left for her, that the door hummed to life. He could sense the familiar magic dripping from the glowing gold metal six that hung slightly off centered, contrasting with the unmarred crimson metal.

"He's a bit…." He struggled to find the right word for a minute, "eccentric."

She stared at him for a long moment while he knocked. Minutes went by and their efforts continued to cease any reward. Silence stretched between them again, the urge to hear her voice nagged at him. He hadn't meant to make the ride awkward, Stanis was unaware she had a brother.

"That's another big word," she stated plainly, now leaning back on the railing that caged them on the landing.

"What?" He gaped at her, before pounding his fist on the door again.

This time, the door swung open. As his fist was still hanging in the air, a fragile man emerged, with milky hair and a matching beard that swept the floor. He ducked instantly at the way Stanis held his fist.

"Fuck!" Stanis leaned down to brace the man, pulling him back up to his full height, which still only reached Stanis hips. "Lumen, I wasn't attacking you."

"Oh…oh…of course Stan…please come in. Your room is as you left it."

"Thank you, but I won't be staying long. I'm here to introduce you to someone." Stanis shifted revealing her to the house's keeper. His fluffy white brows perked up followed by the end of his glistening gold cane, which now pointed at her.

"Oh, oh, yes, yes" Lumen scrambled to find words before he ushered them to enter, his cane never touching the ground as he scrambled down the galley hall.

"I thought you said this man was a Visionary?" She whispered.

The interior of the town home contrasted heavily with the exterior. Softwoods dampened the light flooding through the windows. Filtered to decrease the intense rays, but still allowing enough light to feed the cumbersome number of potted plants clinging to the ceiling and budding against each other on the shelves. In between some pots sat books of all sizes and colors, they were accompanied by small glass vial bottles corked tight with tri-colored stoppers. He could see some still had full brims of shimmering liquids, while others were half filled. The glittering powders resting at the bottoms, catching his attention. Warm brown couches and green leather chairs shoved together in the small entry room, much like the small cabin he had grown up in before his parents' massacre. Lumen most likely enjoyed the clutter, having come from nothing himself.

"He is the greatest of his time," Stanis announced. "Isn't that right, Lumen?" The old man had made his way deep into the core of the house already, disappearing from sight.

"You have a room here?" She asked, picking up a small foil lined book on the side table before tucking herself into the center couch.

"Stan lives here. Of course, he would have a room." Lumen said, reemerging from the passageway leading into the kitchen, carrying a large tray of tea and sweets.

"And you always greet him with tea?" Arabella asked, with a small giggle. Stanis wanted to bottle that laugh, so he could listen to it anytime he wanted.

"No dear, this tea is for you. I have a feeling that jasmine is a favorite of yours," Lumen smiled before sitting in his olive armed chair, across from her. He passed her a cup, and she inhaled deeply.

"Lumen Auger, at your service." He stated, bowing his head. Stanis watched the pair of them intently, unsure if it was a huge mistake to bring her here. She'd be safe with him, but the old man wasn't much for company. Lumen kept to himself, locking the doors of his study while he worked. Often stating it was the easiest way to prevent unwanted visions from intruding on the ones that held importance.

"Well, Mr. Auger..." Arabella started.

"Oh no, no, just Lumen is fine," he chuckled. "No formal manners needed here."

"Okay," she accepted his request, "Lumen." She sipped a small amount of tea. "*Stan*, here, told me you are a Visionary?"

Unsure of the new nickname that touched her lips, Stanis felt the urge to sit as well but decide against it.

"Yes, dear." Lumen nodded and regarded his collection of sweets.

"I'm going to head upstairs and shower," Stanis interrupted. Gaining nods from the two of them, then he shot up the stairs, taking two at a time. He stopped at the landing and listened to the conversation below, a smile pulling at his lips as more joint laughter flooded to his ears.

He didn't stride any further towards his room, or the shower. Instead he called upon his magic, ripping himself through time's gates.

Chapter 19

Cole pushed any and all panic from his mind as he continued to search the crowd for Arabella and his brother. He wasn't surprised that Stanis had fled, but now Arabella seemed to have gone with him. Aritzia's tight lip scowl matched his own, while she too craned her neck over the bustling market flooding the street.

"Are you sure she didn't follow you down to the lockers?" He pressed.

"Yes!" She hissed at him. Her voice is thick with venom. "She would've told me."

He knew she was being honest, Arabella was nothing if not loyal to her friends, and the trust between the three of them was unbreakable. No magic was needed to sense it.

Apprehension forged into annoyance, when another person bumped his shoulder to reach a stall, as the crowded market grew. Every weekend the stalls remained the same but people flooded the small side street to be first in line for the vendors. It didn't matter if they sold trinkets or hot food fresh off the rolling grills. Cole had been tempted like the rest of them, the first few years he attended, but the appeal faded eventually. Aritzia didn't seem to care either, as they stumbled through the growing lines and crowds of glossy eyed people. Vendors shouted under their otherworldly ornate tents, their beige flaps, and colorful swinging flags scribbled with names beckoning their attention, but failing. The smokey scent of grilled meats wafting over their heads, attempting to snag his food loving heart. But Cole's mind was stuck on their mission, finding Arabella and Stanis.

It wasn't uncharacteristic of Stanis to disappear, but it was for Arabella. Cole had pounded his fists endlessly on the large wooden doors of her family's mansion. The Lord and his wife hadn't been home, so he was forced to take the butler's word. And note. He handed Cole a single slip of unenclosed paper. He recognized the Lord's hand writing immediately, and even though it was addressed to his daughter, Cole couldn't help himself not to read it.

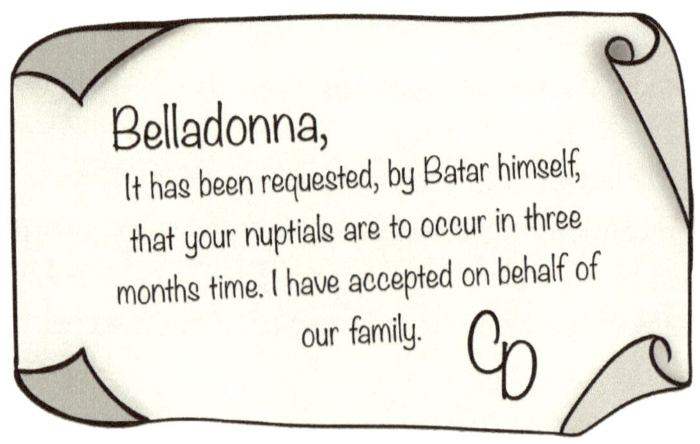

Cole reflected on the time he'd spent with her fiancé, Lukas, he sure had a loose mouth. That being said, Cole would've also moved up the wedding date, if his position were like Lukas's, because being stabbed was hard to forget.

"Does she tell you everything?" Cole pressed, unsure if he wanted the answer now that he uttered it allowed.

"Yes."

"Okay." An awkward silence pooled between them as the market around them buzzed with its strange sense of life. It was the fourth location they had searched in the past three days.

He pulled the small device from his pocket and typed out a message to Grant.

He didn't wait for a reply, before sheathing it in his jacket pocket.

"Let's go, then," she said.

Following Aritzia, as she aimed for the store across the street, his sight was tugged to the dark rumbling clouds billowing above. She guided them into a small store hidden behind a market booth, its sign barely legible. The bell twinkled rapidly as the door opened then closed again firmly behind him, announcing their entry.

"Welcome to Lucifer Metal Works!" The bug eyed shop owner bounced around them. "How can I assist you?" His wildly long hair flew around his head.

"We need this order sent to this address, please." Aritzia gently handed the energized man a slip of paper.

"Of course." The man stretched out his words, wriggling his eyes at her. "Just a moment," he clucked before running off to the back storage rooms.

Cole didn't care about Artizia's business, the cool air in the shop was enticingly sweet enough for him to stay at her side. The shop owner returned with her receipt and then firmly shook both their hands, telling them the swords would be one of a kind, and repeating his gratitude to them both, until Cole forcefully pulled his grip off. Unwelcome sweat beat down on his spine when they exited the shop and landed in the chaos of the market again.

"There you both are!" Abby pushed her way through the masses, reaching her arms around Aritzia.

Abby beamed with warmth towards Grant and him now, and he was grateful for her interruption, hoping she came bearing good news. She had initially blamed Cole for the entire mess, insisting he brought Stanis into their lives, but after a few late night conversations with Grant she'd changed her perspective.

"Grant's asked us to meet him back at the apartment, he said he's found more information, regarding the maps that Stanis left. He thinks they went after the treasure."

"Why would he think that?" Cole pressed.

They had made it a few blocks concealed by silencing magic, but Aritzia disabled the spell before she became too drained. He contemplated invading on her mind to see why, but he'd stopped doing that recently. Finding his blood felt fueled by the restraint, but also because he was helping them learn to block his intrusions. Stanis had managed to figure it out, so it didn't take them long either. Most likely, faster even with their combined expertise. Also he was finding it too hard to keep up with Abby's endless inner monologue.

They had been searching for days, with little rest. When they weren't out scouring the rain soaked crimson streets, they scanned the many journals his father had left them seemed to be the answer. All of them had been heavily enticed to find Arabella and his brother. Mostly to find Arabella, but a small feeling of dread was building inside him. Cole hoped Arabella wanted to be found, because he was unsure how he'd react to the idea of them simply *running away* together.

With the click of his key they gained access to the apartment, or as he and Grant now called it, their base camp. Since Stanis and Arabella disappeared, they had turned their apartment upside down. Displaying all pages of the journals, that indicated any hints to the location of the treasure, along the walls. Red strings connected the pages of clues spanning the entire room, for them to analyze and decipher. The massive web spanned from a singular wall, and all the furniture was rearranged to face.

Grant's hands frantically scribbled notes all over a huge black board, at the back of the room, as they entered. The chemistry between him and Abby pulled his concentration to her. The two of them had become very fond of one another, she'd even spent the nights at their apartment. Cole imagined it was on the couch, but he had a feeling Grant was never far from her.

"What have you found?" Cole removed his pine jacket, looping it on the hook by the door. His feet sang when he finally fell into the chair closest to the webbed wall.

Grant lunged for the open journal on the table in front of Cole, glasses clicked together as he brushed their rims. "This journal details the key to this map over here." He swung his body excitedly. "It indicates more patterns and routes of entry."

Cole rubbed his temples as his hands searched the varying sized glasses for any remaining liquor. His intelligence had never matched his roommates, so he often let his head bob in an agreement.

He tracked Grant around the room as he pointed to maps on the wall, removing one and striding across the space to another. "If my thoughts are correct and the clues Abby has deciphered using that journal over there." Grant swirled around. "Then I may have found the door... to the location of Itia's resting place."

"Grant, shorter sentences." Cole pleaded as he shot back a half empty glass of brown liquor that had been hiding behind a stack of journals. "So many damn journals," he grumbled, before catching Aritzia's stare.

Grant continued overlaying the makeshift maps, but Cole only managed to see pages taped together at the edges, creating a large grid. Then removing both from the wall, Grant held them up in front of Cole's face. "See?" He said.

"See what exactly?" Cole responded dryly as he stared at the maze of lines painted on the page hanging from Grant's fingertips.

"Abby, help me out?" Grant's smile was the softest Cole had ever seen him wear.

Abby ducked behind the page and illuminated the back side with an orb, revealing the overlapping lines from the maps. Cole leaned in closer, squinting and hoping it would magically make sense. He could see that the maps almost lined up, so he traced the clearest route with his finger.

A grumble pulled his attention to Aritzia briefly, shifting her eyes towards the top of the page, and encouraging him to follow.

Abyss Catacombs

He stared at Grant perplexed. "How?" He said, breathlessly. His heart began to beat rapidly, forcing him to his feet. The burial site was right beneath the city they tracked every day.

"The catacombs have been here for longer than the actual city of Limos, the infrastructure has been built right over them. The maps in your dads journals point directly to them. All I had to do was confirm it." Grant's bright smile seeped gratitude. "Luckily for us Aritzia works in the city planners office and swiped these maps for us."

"They're a little outdated," Aritzia added.

"You think he went into them?" Cole asked fanatically. "And took Arabella?"

"Not for sure, but if Stanis knew where to start looking he may have taken her in there," Abby responded, in an animated tone.

Chapter 20

The Past

Stanis had spent the days leading up to the ball in a panic. His nerves were so on edge as he dressed in the suit that Grant had gotten him. Instead of letting the moment affect him he tucked away the event in his mental library, noting he needed to return to uncover more answers. Grant seemed to always be around; he understood that it was his apartment, as well as his brothers, but damn. They hardly ever included him in any of the conversations, stating he wouldn't understand. Stanis remembered that he had debated on multiple occasions going back to his own place. He didn't want to leave Ara behind though, not seeing her those few days had been torture.

The sight of his reflection in the mirror had been the domino that fell, beginning the events they now found themselves in. He'd introduce her to Lumen, she'd want to hear him out, want to be with him. She was a breathtaking amount of light in his darkness, an abandoned Mount Isle cave would be brighter then he was, but she had led him back to solid ground. Without even realizing she did it, she had changed something chemically within him. At the time he should have recognized the mating bond, but it hadn't been an all consuming burning moment for her when they finally spoke, like it was for him. He would have to help her see this was their future, that he was her future. His past had been tainted with darkness but his future was seemingly brighter, something he hadn't thought possible for him. He would have to truly make the effort with her, something he'd never done but that didn't matter, he'd do anything for her.

The hands of his watch spun furiously, he flicked the glass, but they didn't cease their dance. He now crouched on the roof parallel to Cole's apartment building, watching the few patrons who dared exposing themselves to the acid rain. Catching sight of a single elderly woman hurrying to the door of her small home, cradled between highrises. She had been the perfect indicator for his timing, she had walked slow enough for him to track her every move, the second she gripped the stair rail he found the window to watch the show.

He had needed to drink something to set his nerves into a better frequency. Which was why, as his old self left the bedroom and aimed for the kitchen he ran right into Grant.

"Looking sharp, man," Grant's voice was thick.

Stanis tried to remove any indifference from his face. Forcing a smile in acknowledgment. He inched past him, trying to avoid pushing shoulders with him, but both their frames spanned the length of the small kitchen.

Grant forced a shoulder into him, at the last moment, knocking Stanis off his footing. He slammed into the fridge and his hand gripped the handle.

"Fuck! Do we have a problem?" Stanis shot back towards Grant, pressing himself into his space.

Grant shifted to gain height over him, but he squared up just as high in retaliation. Stanis felt the fury all over again, at himself, for not considering Grant would take the first opportunity, where Cole had left the two of them alone, to attack him. But that hadn't been enough to motivate his return.

"I'm starting to think we might!" Grant was baiting him and his blood was boiling up to meet the challenge.

"What the fuck does that mean?" Stanis wondered what would've happened if he hadn't backed down from Grant's challenge. Despite being provoked, he knew Cole wouldn't side with him over Grant. The two of them had been close, no magic was needed to see that fact.

The hands on his watch vibrated to life again, spinning faster and faster. He grumbled a breath, he needed to hear the signal.

"I'm not going to fight you, but if you hurt him again, I might reconsider."

Stanis laughed at his words, as he reached over, flinging the fridge door open. The air in the apartment had been so thick he was surprised neither one of them had fully lunged at each other. No, they just danced around, puffing their chests, until Grant cracked again.

"Cole doesn't need you." He could see now Grant was flustered. "So when you go back to wherever you came from, I hope you remember that."

"Because he has you, right?"

"Exactly," Grant's posture softened momentarily. He shifted again to frame up for a fight, before Stanis could pay it too much attention.

"Grant, I don't want to get into this with you, I don't trust you to have my back in a fight, so our hatred is mutual."

Grant had stared at him for a long while after that, he didn't need to rewitness him sitting on the couch ignoring the brutes presence. The rain had begun to pour heavily but the drops didn't hit his skin. He'd never liked this time of year, when the acid from the rest of the seasons finally fell in sheets, being built up too long. No one stepped into the streets when it rained like this, the pain from the drops lasted days, it wasn't worth it letting it touch your skin. Fortunately for Stanis the weather couldn't graze him when he drifted back in time, usually he was a ghost amongst the living.

Stanis made it to the base of the apartment building, in record time, slipping in through the door he had intentionally left wedged with a small pebble. He vaulted the stairs in a few swift jumps. Three cracks of lightning cast the stairwell in bright light in flashes, then the second signal came. Thunder clapped the sky directly above their heads, shaking the building like a transit train.

He pressed his ear to the wood, next to the B6 draped on the door. "Can I ask you a question?" Stanis remembered Grant's change in subject to be a bit jarring.

"When you confronted Arabella at Filly's, the night of the bombing, did you instantly feel different?"

Silence was the only reminder that he hadn't trusted Grant enough to refrain from pondering the question. He'd gotten lost contemplating the extent of information his brother had confided in Grant. So much anger towards Cole that night made him descend into his darkness.

Cole had been the first branch Ara had grasped for in her moment of need. Stanis hated letting regret seep in, but he felt it repeatedly when he considered if he hadn't left would she have latched to him. Would he have been enough for her to hold herself up against? He doubted his younger self would've been strong enough for her.

A new thought gripped him, maybe Grant had seen him at the club? If so, that would mean he had to have been there too. Stanis hadn't seen anyone resembling him that night, but he certainly had a way to find out.

"No." He said firmly, "I need to do something before we go out tonight."

The third signal.

Stanis quickly ripped the paper out of his pocket and folded it, until it was discrete. He then tucked it behind the metal six of the door. Footsteps headed his way from the other side, so he quickly stumbled back, tipping to fall through time.

As soon as Stanis stepped back onto the landing in the hallway, he wanted to urge his magic to encase him in shadows but the hairs on his neck stood on end. Something was calling to him, he searched the hallway for any signs.

Nothing.

That was until, his eyes found it, tucked by its corner was a small piece of paper waving at him from behind the metal B6 on the door. A grin flushed across his face, it was exactly where he would've hid something akin to that.

Gripping firmly and pulling it from its clip, he noticed the hands on his wrist watch begin to spin faster. Unfolding the note briefly he scanned the ridged words before ripping it and tossing it to the pale ground.

Stanis leaned back to free fall over his heels, landing himself exactly three days in the past. It wasn't that far to travel, so it only took seconds to get there. He pressed his ear to the door just as he heard footsteps headed his way. He stepped further down the hall out of the way, hiding in the shadows. He never was sure when he'd encounter someone with the power to see him, so he remained cautious.

Holding his breath, he watched the apartment door fly open, Cole emerged in his green jacket, he scanned the hallway before firmly locking it behind him.

Stanis watched him go.

His watch hands spun quickly for a few seconds, then slowed to a more leisurely pace. "Always in such a hurry," he muttered to himself.

Now, he just needed to wait for Grant. How long would he have to stay there before his brother's *bestie* emerged? As if Stanis had summoned him with the thought, the door flung open, and out stepped Grant. He began glancing around the hall suspiciously, just as Cole had, then with a flick of his wrist his facial features changed.

Stanis watched with a wild grin on his face, and followed Grant on his midday stroll. He was fueled by exhilaration and the thought of his future selfs predictions aiding this moment. The first time he tried he'd missed his window by a day. He knew this fucker was hiding something, and he loved when he was right.

Grant walked for multiple blocks, constantly checking his surroundings, as Stanis followed him like a tight shadow.

Stanis checked his watch again, his timing had definitely been off, the bombing still wasn't going to happen for three more hours. He'd assumed he needed to see if he was there, but obviously that wasn't true.

Grant shoved past a thick line leading into the street that led into a small bakery. He ignored the few people cursing at him, one of which glared more heavily at him than the others in his tan suit, but Grant didn't stop. No one even glanced Stanis's way, allowing his shoulders to loosen. Grant ducked through the main area and into the back kitchen.

"Hey Eros! He's in his office," a baker called out as they passed.

Grant nodded and grabbed a pastry from a nearby tray, so Stanis did the same.

"Fuck it."

Just as Grant entered a small office and closed the door behind him, Stanis slipped between the opening, shoving the entire flakey treat in his mouth.

"Finally, I was thinking you wouldn't show," said a small man seated behind a large desk. The wooden masterpiece filling up the entire width of the closet-sized office.

Stanis watched the interaction like an act at the theater, leaning back against the far wall as Grant sat in a tiny chair adjacent to the man. He couldn't help but laugh at the humorous sight.

"Have you gotten any more information about her?" Grant's voice was stern.

"She is a member of a family high up in the Federation, that's all I could find."

"I asked you to get a name!" Grant demanded slamming his fists on the desk. The man jolted and scrambled to apologize.

"I told you all the information last time, she is almost thirty and she definitely lives on Orcus Haven." The man whimpered.

"I've known that for years, why do you think I am here?" Grant shoved out of his chair, sending it flying backwards, clattering it to the ground.

Maybe he and Grant could be close someday, he seemed to be handling the situation at hand similar to how he would have approached it. Maybe he'd been wrong about Grant's secrets? He brushed the thought aside, he'd prove or deny that later.

He followed Grant back out the door and weaved to the shop's entrance, as fast as they arrived. Grant headed down the street but Stanis's attention caught the man in the tan suit, who now held a bag of pastries and intentionally headed in the same direction as his tail. Stanis waited to see if Grant would notice as the blocks went by. That's odd, Stanis thought, catching a third glimpse of the man as they trekked back to the apartment.

Then a fourth, fifth, and sixth.

"Come on Grant, are you that naive?"

Grant finally looked back over his shoulder, and as Stanis followed his gaze to catch their predator, but the man evaporated into a cloud of black shadows.

Odd.

Grant seemed to have missed it as he trudged on, Stanis quickly caught back up to him as they entered the apartment building again, and ascended the stairs. Stanis followed Grant back into the apartment, and sat on the couch. Unfortunately, Grant spent the remaining hours with his ear pressed to a machine in his room. Stanis sat and waited until he heard his voice floating to his ears from the hallway and his familiar loud knock rang through the room.

He willed his magic to form around him and pushed back into his seat, free falling back into the vacancy of space.

Well that was a waste of his fucking time.

Chapter 21

The Future

Lumen Auger sat, patiently, waiting for her to summon a vision. The feeling of his stare burning through her eyelids, as they remained sealed tight, making it hard to focus.

It had been three days since Stanis had left her in the future, and over those three days, she had spent most of her time talking to Lumen. He guided her through one vision already. It wasn't much help to their impending quest. It had been a flash back of a childhood game. A fond memory set in the gardens out behind her family's old estate. She'd laughed maniacally, as her brother found Cole within seconds, revealing her hiding place immediately after.

"Found you, little shadow." Her brother's smile was always rigid, but with her, it crumpled up around the edges.

She thought about Cole often in her absence from him. Nothing but darkness welcomed her when she slept. Not even her familiar dream of her mate kept her company. The urge to stay in the guest bedroom all day and rot in her sheets was overpowering, but she welcomed the small knock that appeared at her door every morning. Lumen was never there, just a tray of tea and a small breakfast. The tea was appreciated gift, but she never ate. The longer she remained trapped here the easier it was to ignore the need.

"That's enough," Lumen's voice pierced through the air.

She sat facing him on the opposing olive couch, but her eyes found the window immediately, anticipating the rain that hadn't come since they arrived. Every day was the same. Her morning jasmine tea and pastries in her room, then her lessons in the afternoons with Lumen in the main living area. Over an extra gapping array of other snacks. Mostly delicate sandwiches which she wondered if he had made or brought in. Large bowls of fresh fruits and oddly shaped nuts and crackers splattered across large trays rimmed with edges for easy transport. It wasn't long before she realized Lumen was an admirable host. She also recognized the expense of his buffets, the extravagance of importing items like the funky natured cheeses of the illustrious White Horn-tipped Mountain Goat from the far reaches of Mount Isle illuminated her. Along with the exotic oval berries from the Desert Red Feathered Palms; ones that only produced their fruits in the peak winter months on the Rutmeuses Isles.

She would spend the evenings, during Lumen's rest period, scanning the texts and observing the glistening vials. Many of the jars glistened when she'd lift them, shaky hands indicating her fear of dropping them. She had heard of medications formed of magic but they seemed to be masters of science that were hidden from her. She'd hoped she'd recognize some as forms of alcohol or tranquil drugs. Anything to take the edge off, but the ones that didn't sparkle smelled putrid and nothing like the cannabis she favored or the vodka she used to drink with Abby and Aritzia. Titles scribbled in old ink, along the book spines, were often the most intriguing. Their depictions of myths and monsters keeping her company as she waited for Stanis to return.

"How did you meet Stanis?" Her feet urged her to walk to the window, but she refrained.

"We met in prison," Lumen stated before piling a few finger sandwiches onto his plate.

Shock pulled her gaze back to him. He never seemed to be the fibbing type, but she was sure this was his attempt at a jest. "Truly?"

"Lying is a weak man's tactic." Lumen chopped a small sandwich in a few bites before shoving it whole into his fragile mouth. His beard wriggled as he finished it off. "I know too much of what is to come to muddle it with lies."

Unsure how to respond she searched the room again for anything else to discuss, she had hoped his lessons would have provided her with clearer visions. "What truths do you know about mates?"

"Two halves of one soul," he leaned forward to observe the other treats on the table between them. "Would you like to eat?" He tipped his plate towards the elaborate array.

"No, I'm not hungry." She untwisted her ankles out from under her. Leaning forward into her palms as her elbows rested in her knees. "Why was Stanis in prison?"

"Most likely the same reasons anyone goes to Murr, I suppose." Lumen added some cubes of cheese, along with a handful of octagonal crackers to his plate.

"Meaning?" She wrinkled her nose at the scent of the cheese. Grasping for her tea instead to ease her grumbling stomach.

"Meaning because the Federation deemed it so," Lumen gruffed.

"Can they do that?" The taste of the tea had turned bitter from over-steeping, so she placed it down on the small side table. "Send someone away because they deem it justice?"

"Seemingly so." She noted how Lumen spoke in half truths to elude any lies.

"Why did you get sent there?" Unsure why she asked, but hoping to expand her lessons on attempting not to lie.

"I needed to fulfill a purpose, which ended in a lot of misery before it got better." Lumen placed his now empty plate on the hard wood surface of the table, next to the tray. "And for Matilda."

"Matilda?" Suddenly Lumen became more interesting, she never thought of him with another person, especially his mate. He was declared powerful, according to Stanis, so it was to be presumed he had a mate, at some point.

"My mate," his gaze softened, most likely recalling the emotions she elicited in him. "She was murdered and I was blamed."

"You had a mate?"

"Every human with a complete soul has a mate," Lumen smiled, "or two."

She recalled the lesson she was taught as a child. The rehearsed phase dancing in her mind. *Batar, their ultimate ruler over all humanity, was so angry with his betrothed, Itia. Who he had deemed responsible for the curse thrust upon all humans, that she cracked them down the center. Forcing humanity to spend forever trying to find the other half of their power, specifically, their mates.*

"But you didn't..." She began.

"Kill her?" Lumen's small laugh eased her shoulders. "No."

"Do you know who killed her?" Arabella knew she should say something else, nicer. Something a kin to "I'm sorry" or "my condolences", but Lumen didn't seem to want fake pleasantries.

"A story for another time." He shoved more food into his mouth. "Have you seen yours again?" He fiddled with his tea cup, the porcelain clashing together in a tiny symphony.

"I don't think of him anymore." She wasn't sure if that was the truth. She didn't want to lie to Lumen, he had been so open with her. It wasn't all that simple though, lies formed on her tongue as easy as the salvia that coated it. She truly hadn't dreamed of her mate again, her magic drawing them together had been severed since she was thrust into the future.

"Hmmm," Lumen leaned back and observed the ceiling above them. "And is he in your visions?"

"I'm not sure, my memories are all that has come to me as of late." She had been able to pull something deep from the past but it seemed of little help to the impending tasks ahead. How was she to be a true Visionary if all she could pull at were the strings tying her to her brother.

"Early development of any magic can be tricky business, I'd hoped we found their amplifier as of late…"

"My magic has amplified." She stated defensively. Forcing her magic wasn't an easy task, she needed assistance, she knew that. She had always believed Cole to be her emotional tether to her visions, or so she had thought. "It happens more often when someone is in danger, or when I'm making physical contact." She explained as Lumen poured more tea between their cups.

"Stanis!" Lumen bellowed, causing her skin to jump, never having heard his voice raised before.

Her shoulders stiffened.

"Yes,   sir?" Stanis appeared seconds after Lumen's summoning, his eyes finding her immediately. She felt her jaw tick, as she yanked her gaze back to the darkening windows.

"Arabella needs some assistance," he gestured Stanis towards her couch. She definitely didn't think he could help her with anything.

"No, I don't!" The words flew out before she could stop them.

Stanis crossed the room, acting like nothing laid ill between them, sitting down next to her. Her knee touched his when he adjusted into the seat further, the contact making her skin tingle with fury. She shifted away from his touch quickly. Rapidly, Lumen began collecting the saucers and cups, to clear the tea away and leave.

"Wait, aren't you staying?" She asks eagerly.

Lumen regarded the two of them and shook his head before leaving them to the awkward silence.

"What do you need help with, Beautiful?"

She peered into his soul, searching for something uncertain. The past few days, he had forced her to remain in the town house, alone. She wasn't sure why he cared so much, he had been to prison, making him an ex-con. He should have understood what creating a cage meant to her.

Every so often her gray race car out front would taunt her, with its white stripes and sleek wheels, it beckoned her to run away. Unsure of where she would go, the heart of Limos had become unrecognizable. Stanis had confused her more, telling her to make multiple detours with his obvious wrong directions, before they located the townhouse. Limos had also grown to twice its height, so she could no longer see the outskirts that lead to Drafthaven from the third story. Not that she could go there. The few times she had tried to leave, Lumen had conveniently needed something from her.

Stanis was no doubt the arbitrator of that, keeping her in this prison.

This hadn't felt a kin to imprisonment though. A set of her shampoo and conditioner, along with a bag of new clothes, had been set out for her after the first day. Her favorite coconut scented shampoo had to be imported from the lush Rutmeuse Isles. The expense alone to do so should've been enough to deter them from getting it for her, but many things in the future alluded to her logic.

"When can we go back?" She asked.

"Tomorrow."

Unlike before he left, Stanis seemed more inclined to answer her directly. She knew prodding him might send him back to his old ways, but she didn't seem to care. He was almost unrecognizable. She did, however, miss the feeling he gave her before. It was a complex one, but it was far from boring, which is exactly how she'd explain the last few days.

Boring.

"Where did you go?"

"It doesn't matter." He huffed.

She'd pushed too hard. Or had she not pushed enough.

"It does matter," she spat, "to me".

His jade eyes searched her face, something new flashed in his irises causing her gut to flex. His brow scar drawing her attention. Her brother had a similar marking through his left, and curiosity made her stare a moment too long. Her brother had always told her to listen to her gut, but what was it trying to say?

"You left me," her voice cracked.

The lump of his throat bobbed. They remained staring at one another for a long drawn out silence. "It was important that you worked with Lumen…undistracted."

Her brows formed a line, then her expression dropped. Guilt rushed into her veins like glacial sea water. "Lumen has been helping me summon my *visions*…um…so I can better prepare for them, or even pinpoint specific ones," she stated.

"So we can find the treasure?" Some deep seated urge always bringing him back to that. Maybe he owed people money. It wasn't a feeble concept in Lafornas. It would explain his fixation on getting rich quickly. She never understood men's insatiable greed and fixation on violence to gain money or more power.

She knew how to obtain her ultimate power, and finding her mate would help bring balance back to her soul. After tiresome lessons in her schooling she'd learned finding a mate was the main goal in life. Unsure if she still agreed with that concept anymore.

She mostly wanted to avoid her own current life crisis, so she'd agreed to help Stanis. Her impending nuptials, her father's constant berating, and her life as a "vacant" Aristoi member currently resulted in nothing but animosity between her and her parents. Maybe finding this treasure could renew her sense of purpose in life, and she could finally have a reason to not marry Lukas. Her father was most likely struggling with money too. Especially if he needed to use his vacant daughter as a payment. Desperation was one of the only reasons for owing another person in this existence.

"What can I do to help you have a vision?" Stanis's voice dragged back from her inner monologue.

"I have a theory that if I'm making physical contact…or if someone is in danger." Her hands shifted together in her lap. "I can summon it that way."

"Okay, so we should hold hands."

"Or I could punch you again," she had a hard time holding back the small laugh that left her mouth.

"Maybe another time," he said calmly. She did, however, notice the smirk and slight twinkle in his eyes. She shifted in her seat, heat warming her cheeks, before she cast magic over her face to wash it away.

Another silence stretched between them.

In an effort to distract herself from the discomfort, she reached for Stanis's hands. He flinched at her sudden movement, sending another smile to her face.

His throat cleared, then his large calloused hands were on hers. The warmth of them washing tingles into her fingertips. They both stared at their connecting limbs speechlessly, as minutes dripped by.

"Are you feeling anything?"

"Yes," she said, breathlessly. "I mean no, not yet," she corrected, realizing he meant a vision. She closed her eyes and pushed her magic to the surface of the skin. Trying to focus on the man in front of her, but struggling to commit. She thought of her friends and Cole, hoping they were doing well, wondering if they feared for her safety.

Shadows formed around the corner of her eyes, a tingle ran from the fingers connecting to Stanis, before shooting up her arms. She felt her head fall slightly limp, but she kept her posture firm, forcing the vision to follow her lead instead. This time, she jumped into the smoke head first.

The black fog cleared away, and she found herself standing in a musty cavern covered in skulls, dimly lit at one end. She willed her feet to move towards the glow down the corridor, but they remained in place. She looked down at her body, examining her hands, finding a set of male palms. Large, muscular, and decorated with a sheet of tattoos trailing up the arms, tracing the long veins out of sight under the sleeves. Before she could continue her self-examination, she heard an esoteric voice speaking through her mind. His inner monologue rang out to her, and she was dropped into a familiar feeling.

"Three sisters in the eye, a drop of two pure fates intertwined with six snakes, awakens her from a sleepless state."

Her vessel hid around a corner, attention fixed on the glowing tunnel that fluttered with whispers. The glow grew, and the drum of footsteps indicated multiple people also inhabited the tunnels. She eyed the caverns, they seemed to branch off in many directions, all disappearing from sight. Fear rose, and the breaths escaping her became a forced rhythm.

Her vessel peaked around the corner, giving her a glimpse of two individuals racing into view.

"Where's Grant and Abby?" Cole's voice shattered her heart, then she noticed who he was speaking to.

Ritz! Her heart sank as it begged to call out to them, but she couldn't. The vision continued, forcing her to watch in hiding, unmarred by her desires.

"An insect on the wall." Stanis' words rang in her head.

"They were right behind me." Aritzia responded to Cole as she reached down, pressing her palm to the ground. "Let me see if I can sense their presence."

The feet attached to her soul began to run into the depths of the tunnel, driven by fear, away from her friends. She begged the limbs to stop their retreat, forgetting she was just a passenger in this vessel.

"Stop!" She screamed. "Please, wait!" She pleaded as reality set back in and she faced Stanis. His face thick with concern as he lunged for her, wrapping her in his arms as she shook and her heart pounded in her chest cavity.

She hadn't realized she was firmly planted in his lap. Blanked by his unyielding grip. She didn't pull away, instead she focused on her vision, trying to dissect all the information that had been thrown at her, before it faded. Who was the man? Where were they? Why did he run from her friends? Thousands of questions berated her mind, and she forced herself to pin down one in particular.

"Three sisters in the eye, a drop of two pure fates intertwined with six snakes, awakens her from a sleepless state."

Something deep in her gut forced her to repeat it, demanding it was important.

"Was it something you saw?" Stanis's voice was soft in her ear. Quickly, she pulled herself out of his arms, adjusting into the cushion next to him, and pressing her fingers into her eyes. Needles stabbed under her skin where her legs brushed the couch.

"Can we smoke here?" She asked eagerly. "My heart's still beating out of my chest." It had been a few days since she had a hit, and she was scrambling to swallow the large amount of information she had just taken a bite of.

Chapter 22

Stanis grabbed her wrist, pulling her upright, then led her up the deep wood stairs. Her feet were sensitive with every step. Plants kissed her skin as they passed, the sensation guiding her further back into her own body.

They emerged at the top of the landing and he led her down the hall and into his room. She hadn't ventured to spy on his lodgings the past few days, so she didn't know what to expect.

Curiously, she observed his quarters. It was simple, consisting of a large wood posted bed covered with dark linens, a small desk, and a round window overlooking the street below. The state of it was like the one she had been assigned down the hall. The grandest difference circled the entire room. Lining all the walls was the collection of bookshelves, filled with tomes and small mechanical devices.

He made his way to a desk that sat angled in one of the corners, rummaging through the drawers, until he removed a small box. As she made her way around the room running her fingers along the book spines, no titles jumped out to her, but she suddenly felt she was in a recognizable space.

"Have you read all of these?"

"Most of them."

She sat on the side of his bed, flipping through the few open pages of the book resting on the nightstand, while waiting for him to finish rolling a fresh joint. Watching him lick the paper, imagining how warm it would be on her lips, before his fingers were sealing it tightly.

She surveyed him, surprised by the comfort he brought upon her. That this room did.

He obviously had lived there, collecting all the books and devices, from his travels through time. She didn't have items that she felt needed to be collected. Never having found the need to hold onto materials in an effort to remember someone, or something. But she had, she'd kept her brother's jacket, she wore it everyday, and when it wasn't around her shoulders holding her tight, she knew exactly where it was.

She looked up at him through her long lashes as he approached. The sight of his fingers trembling, as he brought the bone white roll to his lips, and softened her discomfort further.

"I thought you'd hate me," he said.

She smiled. "I did," she breathed, before adjusting herself deeper into the sheets.

"Did?"

Arabella knew he hungered for her, she wasn't naïve to the attractions of men. The way he watched her, always finding her across the room. The way his gaze slid down her body.

The need to touch him was becoming overwhelming. Her leg crossed over the other, clenching herself tight. She knew once their skin touched again he would lose all self control. He was short tempered, impatient, and yet, something deep in her wanted him to lose himself, become feral.

"I don't hate you," she smirked.

As smoke billowed around him from the exhale, he lowered the joint to her, placing it on her lips.

"Do you *want* me to hate you?" A giddiness coated her voice.

The sight of his cock hardening pulled her eyes to his inseam. She pulled in a deep breath, and gilded herself back onto the bed, melting in dark sheets. She swore to herself that she could feel his eyes trace her form as she lay out, tempting him.

"You can hate me," he growled, "as long as you also let me fill you with pleasure, while you do it."

"I don't know how to respond to that." She hadn't opened her eyes yet. Indecision hit her harder than expected. She was used to being a temptress to men, but this felt different. Something primal inside her needed him. More than any other man she'd ever been with. More than Cole. She forced herself not to remember his name, instead uttering the one of the man in front of her.

"Stanis," she breathed looking upon him again.

She was teasing him as she made a point to slowly sit back up, bending at the hips to reseat herself directly in front of him. She placed the joint in the tray on his night stand.

He reached out to brush the hair from her cheek. *"You're so beautiful."*

"Stanis, wait," she gripped his wrists, and her voice thinned. "I have to tell you something first."

She brushed her thumbs over his palms, swirling them delicately.

"I think Cole would be upset by the two of us...um...together," she finally let the words pass her lips.

"He understands my feelings for you." His words were quick and breathful.

"How do you know?"

"It just," His words failed him suddenly. "It's…a feeling I have."

Her eyes fell to her lap. "I imagine they are the same feelings I have for Cole." Shame revealed itself in that moment. It was a new and odd feeling she didn't know she harbored in her soul. She rebelled a lot, at any opportunity, but she'd never felt shame for doing so, until now.

"You're telling me you have the same feelings for him as you do for me?" He cupped her jaw, searching her face for any shed of her lie.

"No." She felt the truth inching from her chest but she feared what would happen if she dared to reveal even a hint of her relationship with Cole to his brother. She'd let Cole inside her, into her heart. She swore countless times that she wasn't weak, but Cole had made her believe in that feeling. She had convinced herself that mates weren't the goal. Of course they were.

"I don't feel anything for you."

Stanis's face flashed with something dark before he fixed his scowl back into place and stepped away from her. For a moment he had almost revealed something that looked solemnly close to…pain. Or was it her pain she felt? Because what she said wasn't true, like a lot of words out of her mouth. In honesty, she had felt the rolling of her stomach when he was near. She had been led to believe that discovering her mates identity would be overwhelming, but what if it wasn't always obvious. Maybe it was a choice too, along with a fated destiny.

How could she explain this to Cole, she wouldn't be able to face him after she had let Stanis touch her. She had never felt bad about her other sexual partners aside from Cole but they weren't *his brother.* But why did she care? Cole made it obvious they weren't fated.

Her heart pounded against her chest as she stood, observing Stanis, who was now on the opposite side of the room. His head ticked down and his broad shoulders flexed as he gripped the door frame with an outstretched hand.

"What do you feel for me?" The question flew from her mouth faster than she could even comprehend why she feared his answer.

"Nothing," he seethed.

Her heart fell to her stomach. She forced herself not to move, she tilted her chin high, even as he stalked towards her. With a few steps, he was inches from her. Her hands instinctively landed on his chest. His breathing was rabid and the heat from his skin would've been scolding if it wasn't also so inviting. Her breathing hitched. She prayed he wouldn't see how he truly affected her. His fingers reached to her face and caressed her cheek, trailing over her features then down to grip her chin.

This certainly didn't seem like nothing.

"Again," his throat bobbed, "*nothing* in this world has felt whole since I first laid eyes on you," he whispered. "Before you I was a shell, still being filled. Only to be torn apart, then forced to walk this earth with no emotions at all. Empty. Is how I felt the moment I left your side that day in the club. I wandered this world for years driven to forget the idea of you, Ara." His words felt like razor blades across her heart. "Nothing, but pain has laced my heart since that day in my brother's apartment… seeing you lay your hands on him." He couldn't peel his eyes from hers, their sterling green hue shifted from resentment to something softer.

"Don't stop," she ordered, vibrating directly into his soul.

"Nothing has been as beautiful as your laugh or as soft as your skin against my fingertips." His fingers trailed her collar bone. "Nothing has been this clear to me since my obsession with the treasure began. Nothing but the idea of your kiss alone has ever made me question myself. Now I wonder if you truly have been the treasure all along. Nothing but you truly matters anymore."

A tear rolled down her cheek, the feeling of it sparking something in him. He reached out to stop it from wetting her face further. She pressed her cheek into his touch, letting him brush the tear away. He gripped her face between his hands and searched her expression with his gleaming jade eyes.

Then she kissed him, lifting onto her toes she pressed so tightly into his lips with hers. Unsure why this time felt less risky than any other, but also more so tenfold. He pressed back into her kiss, as she swept her tongue along the seam of his mouth. He tasted like cannabis and boarded up angst, everything she needed wrapped up in one moment for her to cherish forever.

He pulled back from her suddenly, the panting between them pounding in tune with his heart. She searched his features for a hint of what was wrong, but all she could seem to find was wide jade irises. His scarred eyebrow raised slightly forcing her to realize she hadn't said anything back after he had poured his entire soul into the space between them.

"Stanis," her voice was breathless, sounding unlike her own. "I....lied before." She needed to tell him all her secrets, but fear tickled the back of her mind when she thought of Cole again. She couldn't betray him like that, it was his secret as well. He should be given a warning before she told Stanis.

Her heart broke as her eyes searched the man in front of her for a hint of a façade. She waited for the punch to the gut but as she thought deeper about her mate, she couldn't remember who she saw anymore. She realized she hadn't had the dream since she met Stanis. She didn't truly believe he was here now, because her mate was always leaving. This man wasn't doing that. No, he was stepping into her space and demanding her attention.

The gut rolling, that she trusted less than anything else in her life at the moment, crept back in. She felt the pressure in her eyes building and the press of tears forming. She forced herself to push them away, her throat thick from holding back her emotions.

"I feel completely different with you than I do with Cole." She waited for the insinuating words to land but Stanis remained unfazed. "I feel so much for you. I feel like I'm being driven mad," she breathed. "I feel like if I give into it, it'll be torn away from me like it never existed in the first place. I'm terrified to give myself fully to someone who isn't my mate, but I am more terrified that I could, and won't regret it for a single second of it."

Stanis lips slammed back on hers, sucking up her breath with it. Her stomach lurched and her hands gripped his arms. She'd meant to push him back; to make sure she wasn't actually going mad, but her finger tips dug deeper into his skin.

She released a moan of surprise. His kiss was bruising, branding her with his desire, and she was engulfed in it. She kissed him back, opening her mouth to him until his tongue made its way inside. Poisoning her mind with desire like she'd never felt before. Stanis's hands drove into her hair, caressing her scalp, then fisting the roots. He urged her to move backwards until her legs hit the mattress. Their lips parted temporarily, and the look in his eyes became overwhelming.

Shattered by the lack of contact, she reached out, grabbing his cheeks and pulled their foreheads together. Then wrapping her arms around his neck. They guided one another to lay in the rumpled sheets. She forced her fingers through his golden flecked brown hair, amazed at its softness. She curled the locks around her fingers, fisting them tightly. He was crushing her with his weight, making her more breathless and famished for more.

"Gods, kissing you is better than I imagined." His voice caressed her mind.

A smile grazed her lips; causing him to pull back, instead he traced his kisses down her neck to her chest. His hands roamed up and underneath her shirt with burning touches. He groaned into her neck as he found her bra and pushed underneath it, finding her nipple hard and aching for him. She pulled at his clothes, begging him to remove them. Pushing off the bed in a swift movement, he flung his shirt over his head.

Arabella sat up on her knees, pulling her shirt overhead, feeling his hands on her again before it was even off. His burning touches pushed along the edge of her bra strap, sending tingles through her spine. He unclipped her bra, throwing it across the room.

Her head spun, while she panted. His fist palmed her breast while he kissed her with ferocity. Without breaking their attached lips, he removed his hands, and she heard him opening up the drawer of the nightstand. She reached for his waistband, finding the belt and tugging to loosen it. He yanked from her grasp entirely. The sensation on her lips along with the smile on his face, knocked the air out of her. She hadn't even considered what she was doing. She'd been with men before, but never spent this much time teasing into the main event.

"Unbutton your pants, Beautiful."

To her surprise she was finding this new level of control he was instituting utterly thrilling. She bit her lower lip at the sight of his hard cock pressing against the inside of his jeans.

Moisture coated her inner thighs, as her gaze trailed the muscles bared before her. Over the abdominals that encouraged her eyes to find his crotch, then back up over his pecks. His chest was marred with tiny scars, peaking out from dark scruff lining his chest. Slightly embarrassed by her staring, she found his handsome face, and unsurprisingly it sported his infamous smirk. But this one was different. She hadn't seen it before. Paired with the shimmering jade eyes and heaving chest, his smirk became something she wanted to remember forever.

"Like what you see?"

Stanis's eyes flicked to her bare skin and trailed down to her pants. His hands twitched at the sight of them still buttoned. Speechless and panting with anticipation, she removed them.

Slowly.

"Do you like what you see?" She mocked.

Before she could register the words fully, he rushed forward, his kiss murdering her again. He lifted her to straddle him, but once her legs were firmly wrapped around his torso, he was pressing her back into the mattress with his full weight, opening her thighs.

"Fuck, Ara." He shifted his weight, but before she could argue, his hands made their way between her thighs and he pressed two fingers to her wet core. She gasped, letting her eyes roll back and sending her head craning. *"I could watch you do that all day."*

The telepathy between them was proving useful, because his voice was massaging her soul while his fingers worked in a steady rhythm.

"Don't stop then."

"Do you like when I touch you here?" Her hips bucked at the sensation of the pressure he applied inside her. *"What about when I also kiss you here?"* He shifted again, trailing kisses down her chest, then further, until his lips wrapped around the bundle of nerves surrounding her clit. *"What about here?"*

"Yes." She gasped, her hips lifting off the bed.

"I have something I think you'll like."

Arabella didn't have time to let her mind register before she heard a faint buzzing, and a cool object pressed onto her clit. She gasped with the instant shock of ecstasy that shot through her core. She reached down to grab at his fingers, finding a small mechanical device vibrating between them.

"Trust me," he whispered in her ear, while pressing into a nerve ending. So much pleasure pulsed through her, at the realization that she did in fact trust him. Or maybe it was the fact that whatever this device was doing to her was otherworldly.

He laid himself next to her, pressing delicate kisses to her skin. Continuing to thrust his fingers deeper into her core as she danced with her pleasure, refraining from holding in her moans. His need grinding on her thigh as he drove her to climax.

She closed her eyes, visualizing *him* staring down at her with his insatiable appetite, *him* filling her, *his hands* in her hair again, then she tipped over the edge. Gripping the surrounding sheets in tight fists and squeezing his hand tightly with her inner muscles, as he kissed her neck and chest. Her body went weak, as he slowly removed his fingers, lifting them to his mouth before sucking them dry. The sight of him devouring the taste of her desire scolded into her memory.

Stanis grasped the vibrating device and shut it off, placing it back on the nightstand, exchanging it for the joint that still barely burned in the tray. He handed it to her, and she pulled a deep breath of it, encouraging reality to set back in. He was already pulling his clothes back on when she wedged herself up on her elbows to watch him.

"You don't want a turn?" She asked him with a smile.

His smiled was short, before pulling his shirt over head. "You seemed like you needed it more, Beautiful."

She was used to men leaving after sex, but they had always found their release too. She couldn't help her brows from furrowing. *"Had she done something he didn't like?"*

His smile was heartbreaking. But her irritation towards him began building back up.

"You're perfect. I wanted to take my time with you, so.. um next time I will remove any doubt." Stanis stuttered as his eyes found the floor.

A long silence stretched over the space, while Arabella searched for her missing garments.

"I have something for you. I hadn't intended for you to seduce me, so I got distracted." His new smirk remained, dampening her irritation, which was driven away in light of her curiosity. Arabella fully intended to redress and hide in her room, but now she found her shirt and underwear, and the fact that he wanted her there, more comforting.

He pulled a book from the shelf, and a hole appeared between the pages. Crumpled within was a gold chain. With delicate fingers he removed it from its nest. She grasped it in her palms and studied the pendent staring back up at her. Her breath caught as she realized it was the symbol she had seen in her vision a week ago. Metal formed a two dimensional diamond shape, with an infinite swirl inside it. A black gem crested in the middle, leading the swirl in its expansion from the center.

"My father made this for my mother," Stanis's jade eyes glowed. "He said it reminded him of life's treasures."

Arabella had a hard time believing that if his father had given his mother any sort of gift, that meant he also treasured her as well. But pushing the negative thought aside, she reached out to hand it back to him.

"No, keep it," he stated firmly.

She hesitated before she stood and turned her back towards him. *"Help me?"*

His fingers traced her shoulders, guiding her hair to one side. Slipping the chain around her neck, he fastened the clasp. She closed her eyes as blackness seeped around her, a familiar wave of magic coiled around her fingers. Shooting up her arms and into her neck, sending her into darkness.

Surrounded by skulls, deep in the caverns again, so stood over a large gash in the earth. The black abyss sunk further than her eyes could see. Looking down at the masculine hands, she found the knuckles locked with Aritzia's.

Aritzia's other hand was outstretched as she summoned earth and stone to move from the other side of the canyon towards them, attempting to form a bridge.

Yelling came from behind.

"Hurry!" Cole's frantic demand slipped from her lips.

"I'm trying. It's not as simple as you think. The catacombs are coated in Norilekcin rock. It is draining my magic reserves faster than normal."

The yelling became louder and a dim light filled the tunnel behind them.

"Maybe it's Abby and Grant?" Ritz said hopefully, but she continued to wield her magic. The bridge was almost complete, but the voices were getting closer.

"It's not!" Cole snarled. "We are going to have to jump the rest of the way."

Arabella felt the heart within Cole's vessel beating frantically, and her fear for her friends rose to greet it.

Cole pulled Aritzia back from the edge, her magic forcing the bridge to stretch as far as she could before chestnut eyes locked onto him. So much fear laced Aritzia's face, making Arabella want to scream at them to reconsider. Before she could argue, they ran for the edge, propelling themselves across the open canyon and slamming their guts into the end of the free standing bridge edge.

Arabella didn't discern the impact, but she witnessed as his hands scrambled to get a grip on the flat stone. Aritzia, also struggling to get up; as she attempted to swing her leg up onto the edge, but was slipped.

Cole's hand reached out to help shove her the last few inches as she rolled herself up and onto the bridge. As Cole reached to grab the bridge again, his remaining hand dropped from the edge.

He was free falling.

A scream begged to be released from Arabella's throat but darkness engulfed her as she watched one of her best friends reaching down over the bridge's edge to save the only man she ever loved as he fell into darkness.

Stanis had his lips on the back of her neck and his arms around her waist. She realized the vision must have been only a momentary occurrence. Not even noticing she had left the room temporarily, his face tangled in her hair.

She pulled from his grip, frantically, to face him. His expression was tight as his jade eyes fixed on hers. Considering her next words carefully, her heart constricted, while panic rose in her spine. She took a deep breath and prepared for their world to shatter again.

"Cole's in the Catacombs."

Chapter 23

"We need to go to him!" Arabella yelled. Stanis had felt the urgency the first time she had said it, but she was frantic now.

He was frozen as he watched her throwing things into a backpack, including some of the small mechanical devices around his room. How she knew what they were, he wasn't sure.

Finally, his body regained control. He lunged as she threw a copy of Gorgons 101 towards the pile of supplies she was gathering. He placed it back on the shelf, then grabbed her hands, forcing her to turn towards him. She released herself from his grip immediately.

"Ara, please, can we just think about this for a moment? Maybe, tell me what you saw." Stanis had felt the cold drift through her body as he leaned forward to kiss her neck. He hadn't seen her face, but the sensation was familiar.

"We don't have time. He could already be dead!" The crack in her voice shattered his heart.

He felt his soul drop out of his body. "What?…Dead?" He struggled to ease his shaking hands along with his trembling thoughts.

Anger gripped him as he cleared the contents of his desk with one slash of his arm. Sending books and artifacts soaring to the wall and floor. His arms pumped with adrenaline as he panted heavily. The urge to flip the desk vanished, once he felt soft hands on his shoulders.

"I'm sorry," Arabella's voice was hollow, "I don't know for certain."

She pulled him back to sit with her on the edge of his bed. The same bed he had finally gotten to claim her. He slowed his breathing at the thought of her moaning beneath him, visualizing her panting; *his* name on *her* lips.

"I know he is in the Catacombs under Limos with Aritzia right now." She said definitively.

He searched her eyes for the truth, finding her undeniable belief in that thought. She lied a lot, but she wasn't now. Forcing himself to be silent while she continued explaining her two visions and her connections between them. *Of course, the Catacombs were the answer. How had he not seen it?*

"Are you going to listen to what I have to say or not?" She attempted to stand. He gripped her hips and pulled her back down onto his lap. She let out a breath of frustration.

"Of course, I'm listening to you, Beautiful. You just have to be patient with me. I'm not used to deciphering clues with another person, especially one who is smarter than I am."

She bit her bottom lip and stared into his eyes, searching for his integrity. He knew the connection he felt was deepening, but he couldn't focus on that.

"Tell me why you think my brother is dead."

Her façade dropped, her brows crunching as she lifted herself off him and looked down at him.

He was straining not to push her, as she was obviously contemplating how to respond. His fingertips trailed the skin on the back of her thighs. His need for her starting to reform.

"He's not dead, I would know that."

"You'd know that?" A bit of humor laced his tone. Which he regretted once he saw the seriousness in her eyes.

"Yes," she stated, refusing to elaborate as she stepped away from his grasp and loaded more contents on the bed into the backpack. A tear rolled down her cheek, but she whipped it away quickly. Without hesitation he jumped up to comfort her, but she backed away. Placing her hands up between them, barricading him.

"We need to go back, Stanis." She pleaded, casting magic to her face to hide her sparkling eyes from him.

"We will, but this is the first time we have been together and I have so much to tell you," He paused his little speech but remained pacing. He took a deep breath and forced himself to spill as much of him as he could at her feet, before she could interrupt. "You don't know what I've had to do for us. How much time I've spent jumping through time to get the answers I needed before we could.."

She moved towards him, and he stopped, suddenly at a loss for words. "What do you mean for us?" She mused.

"Ara," he paused, unsure if he was ready to crack himself open to her. He had spent years pushing himself away from her to conceal her from him. Her ability to assimilate into his life so well was alarming. Within this moment of time, their existence was hidden and no one kept them apart. He knew not even the gods could touch them. "We're mates," he breathed. He reached to pull her close, but she didn't budge.

She pushed her fingers into her eyes and turned from him, cracking his heart open slightly.

"That's not possible," she said, driving that crack deeper. He willed his anger to remain caged, but it was fighting frantically.

"I already have a mate."

Shaking his head was the only reaction he could form. How was she not understanding that he was reaching out for her now? Yes, he had disappeared, but she hadn't seen him that day, so she wouldn't know of her other half.

"Who?" He jabbed. Anger building to the surface, as he stood to face off with her.

"It's not that simple," she said, throwing her hands around. "Also, none of this matters because Cole needs us right now."

Her tone was fueling his burning pit of anger, and he couldn't grasp her reasoning. "Fuck that! This is more important and if I'm saying that you should know, it's true."

"I know nothing about you, let alone, if you can be trusted. I'm not sure what game you're playing with the mind control and nice acts, but at the end of the day, you've kept me here against my will!" Her voice was laced with so much poison.

He lashed back at her in spite. "Against your will? I've told you we would go back, multiple times. I haven't been controlling your mind. We have a fated connection, because we are mates! I am finally Enkrateia too." He felt like he was fighting for his existence with no lifeline. A sinking ship set a blaze as he was forced to watch it burn.

"Mates?" She laughed mildly, searching his face for the matched humor. "Enkrateia?" She shook her head. He had waited years to tell her, and now she thought it was all a huge joke.

"Take me back then." She stated, folding her arms across the front of her chest, after he didn't continue. He gritted his teeth at the sight. He needed to attack this issue of her ignorance differently.

"Yes or no's?"

"Then you'll take us back? You owe me one."

He hesitated, feeling like he was making a deal with Batar himself. "I promise."

She stared at him, her face unreadable as she waited for him to continue. Fear, outside of Cole's safety, didn't seem to be a factor for her, and he realized in that moment he dreaded any answer she could give him. He'd decide to start off with an easy one then.

"Is Cole looking for the treasure?"

"I don't know."

He could tell she wasn't lying, unsure how he deduced that, but at least he had that to hold on to. "Are you sure he's going to die?"

"Yes, I saw him falling from a cliff's edge and I felt his fear." Her eyes pooled with tears, but she didn't let them fall.

His heart cracked further, he knew his next question. It was one that haunted him for days. He stared at her as she waited for the next question to be fired off, realizing she would never pick him. Even if he could convince her they were mates, even if he became Enkrateia. He painfully built up his mental walls between them, protecting himself from hearing the answer too soon. She was so firmly set in her decision, and he wouldn't be able to be the person to convince her otherwise. She truly believed they weren't mates. She was choosing someone else despite everything between them. Had she chosen not to accept the things he had been, since they first touched? Could someone do that?

"Do you love him?" He bit out.

"I don't know."

He watched as her eyes shifted to the floor. He reached up to grip his hair in his fist, tugging to make sure he could still feel anything outside of the immediate pain that was consuming him. He needed her to choose him, so he hesitated again. Turning from her and sucking in a deep breath. His face swelled with tension that he hadn't felt since his parents had passed. He pushed down the feeling as it burned his inner nostrils.

He had two more questions queued up, but he had to make sure his anger didn't burst from his skin when she answered them. Being strategic was the best course now, but he felt his heart almost completely broken in half. Wondering if he slit his wrists right then if it would even be enough sensation to bypass this current misery. He knew he was fated for death anyways, with or without her.

"Do you really believe Cole's your mate?"

"Maybe," she breathed.

He was shaking as he tried to wrangle in his darkest fears coming to light. His fists squeezed so tight, but he hardly felt the warmth of his blood pooling between his fingers.

"Have you two had sex?"

"Yes," she said as a tear ran down her cheek.

Any doubt that his heart was now completely in two was washed away, because he felt it completely fall from his chest. He stared, panting, trying to will himself not to sense any of the pain that was wrapped around his entire body. He needed to get out of there. Nothing prepared him for this. Not wanting any of what she had said to be fact, but the thought of his brother's hands on her was making bile rise in his throat. He wanted to run, but he didn't know where he could go. This was his sanctuary, and now it was burning around them, never to be seen the same again. He shook his head as he waited for her to burst out laughing, explaining that it was a humorous way of punishing him, but she didn't.

"I need to shower before we go," he said tightly, sucking in a breath through his nose. He'd shut out everyone before, this wouldn't be any different. It would be easy, after he washed off the scent of coconut that clung to his skin. He'd pulled himself back from the edge multiple times in his life. He wasn't sure why he'd never jumped, just that he knew she must have been the one pulling him back. Now, he doubted that the illusion would save him next time, if there was one.

"Wait, is that all you have to say?" She said.

He turned away from her, aiming for the hallway. "I'm not sure what else you're looking for, Ara, but I do know if I was Cole, and I found out you did those things with me," he said gesturing to the bed trying to remain calm. She was so close to him he couldn't breathe, but he needed to lash out somehow. So he tightened his shoulders and leaned towards her, lowering his voice, "then I'd never forgive you."

The room chilled around her as she stood staring after him. He had forced her to admit things she had never uttered aloud to anyone. She didn't know what the concept of love entailed. The emotion she could understand was desperation, and she desperately feared for Cole's life and his mix of adrenaline with hers had made her frantic.

She waited for Stanis to come back, and she didn't understand the urge she had to follow him. instead, she was planted in place, reviewing everything in her head. They had been having so much fun one moment, then they crashed and burned the next. It didn't matter, she didn't deserve to love. She also couldn't, she was betrothed. Her eyes rolled.

Stanis had seemed so hurt by her admissions, even though she hadn't revealed all her secrets. His sudden and desperate plea to be hers was hunting her. She had dreamed of the day she finally met her mate, wouldn't she have felt something differently? She had always believed it would be something she instantly knew. Something that changed her life's corse. A kin to the way men looked at Abby, but a mutual understanding between them. She never had a man look at her like that the first time they met.

She would've known.

It would've been like when Abby met…realization trampled her.

Like when Abby met Grant.

How could she not have seen it? Abby never looked at men in return, not seriously any ways. She was her best friend. Why hadn't Abby told her? She felt her heart breaking for the second time that evening.

She pushed the thought aside, not wanting to focus on that now. She needed to think about Cole, her feelings ran so deeply for him ever since they first met, but she was a child then. Had her infatuation shadowed her ideals of mates?

Too much pain filled her chest as she thought about all her woes. All she could manage to do was keep herself busy, so she gripped the backpack full of supplies and headed for her room. Seizing all the clothes Stanis had gotten her from the drawers, not thinking she'd ever come back to get them. She was unsure why, but they seemed important to her. She had thousands of dresses back home, but these matched her style and she appreciated when he noticed how comfortable she was in pants and her black boots. Snatching her brother's soft navy and white pin striped jacket from the wardrobe, and forcing her arms into the oversized holes, she let it wrap around and shield her blind spot. No rain had fallen since they arrived, but it was better to have it, just in case.

The only explanation that could come to her was that because Cole and Stanis were brothers, it must mean they were all connected somehow; and she would have to determine which one she wanted later. There wasn't time for this confusing triad, at the moment. She needed to shield herself from any thoughts of Stanis. He would inevitably try to speak to her telepathically again. So she imagined herself pulling a shade around her mind and hoped it could block him out, until she was ready to face this issue again.

A knocking sounded at her door and in the open frame stood Stanis, as composed as the day they met. His wet hair pushed back from his face, his mouth formed a tight line and his eyes appeared darker than the pine trees sleeping in the Weeping Forest. But he held firm.

He was gorgeous, his dirty blonde hair darkened by the moisture, but his soul glowed, reaching for her. She always thought he was attractive, with all the pain she had just put them through, he'd become damn heart breaking to look at. She felt her smirk forming as she realized they were wearing similar outfits.

"Let's go," he demanded, but didn't reach a hand out to her.

"Don't you need anything?" She said hesitantly as the air between them thickened with unspoken words.

"No," he said, turning and heading down the stairs. Arabella raced after him to keep up but he seemed to quicken his pace, then he was out the front door before she could think to find Lumen to thank him. Quickly gripping a paper from the table by the door, she scribbled out her gratitude. Hoping it would be enough to portray how she truly felt.

Her pause caused her to lose sight of Stanis as he strode down the street. She finally caught a glimpse of his brown leather jacket and raced after him. Nipping at his heels, as he guided them through the city. Wine colored streets stretched out around them, battered and trodden by swarms of glassy eyed citizens. More transit train rails had been built, drifting between the buildings like vines.

They didn't exchange any words, she noticed the silencing sphere he had surrounded himself with. Thankful for that, fearing any more words between them would cause more animosity. In Stanis's hastily escaped, she had, unfortunately, left the pack she'd prepared.

Expansion hadn't been limited to just the architecture, more people than Arabella had ever seen in a single place flooded the streets, commuting around the city by foot. Every once and a while a car would slam by, reeking of wealth. Is that what she looked like to these people? The sight unsettled her briefly, not having long to dwell because they'd arrived at their destination.

Stanis entered a small shop, labeled as **The Devil's Opium Den**, striding past the front desk without a word. The small blue and purple haired teenager didn't even glance his way, distracted by a mechanical device squeezed into her hands. The scent of poor choices and lavender drifted through the air.

Arabella quickly followed close behind him as he marched past the cabana booths packed with sun baked customers. Interest to join them nudged her, no clubs like this existed yet in her timeline.

Pushing firmly through at the back of the den, Stanis never slowed his pace, even as he descended a staircase leading deep underground. A cocktail of adrenaline and fear sank with her as they made their way further and further down into the heart of Limos. Her legs were burning until they finally made it to a landing at the bottom.

Simultaneously, her and Stanis lit orbs in front of them. A familiar sense of competitiveness rose from her chest. She smirked, but as their eyes met she was faced with his infamous scowl.

Recognizable tunnels reached out in front of them. Skulls wedged between all crevasses of the walls within the large opening they now found themselves within. As six tunnels extended in all directions around them. Each ending in blackness. Her soul was being pulled down by one of them, and she stepped forward to follow her gut.

Stanis grabbed her suddenly, then his deep voice seeped into her skin. "We're jumping back in time now," he said.

She hadn't realized she was craving his attention and starving for the sound of his voice. Shadows engulfed them and she tilted back, free falling. The stomach rolling was lighter, now that she had been able to more accurately predict its onset. They emerged from the darkness but remained in the same tunnel.

"Did it not work?"

"What do you mean? No, we're in the present," he said, irritation seeping off him.

"How can you tell? Everything looks exactly the same?"

"I know what I'm doing." A touch of hurt slipped into his voice. There was no intention of insult. She was simply confused by her inability to differentiate their timelines without visible clues.

"Do you know where we are?"

He looked around her, then scoffed, seeming to wait for a punchline.

"Ugh, do you know what part of the city we are under?" She pelted at him. He was obviously back to pissing her off.

"Yes, the location will be the same building we came in through up above, just in the past," he said the last part slowly to condensed her.

"Okay, thanks." She stormed off into the tunnel beckoning her, slightly hoping he would choose a different one.

He didn't.

He followed her as they walked slowly, listening for any sign of danger ahead. His presence created the recognition of deep-seated comfort, which wasn't so surprising now. Slowing her pace until she was at his side, she reached out to grip his palm in hers. He didn't stop her or pull away, but his arm went rigid.

Their orbs casting shadows across his face revealed little emotion, as they continued deeper into the Catacombs. Another skull lined room opened up in front of them, this time with three other tunnels. The floor vanished, forcing her to catch Stanis's arm as he stepped, dangling one foot out over the crater below. He stumbled back, and they gripped each other tighter.

He released a large breath and grinned wildly. "Wow, if this is the adrenaline high you're constantly chasing, Beautiful, then I understand the appeal."

"You're a psychopath," She said with a laugh escaping her lips. He gaped at her for a long moment, then turned his attention back to the hurdle awaiting them.

"How do you think we get across?"

"Elemental magic." She said dryly, as a thought budded her brain.

Stanis stared at the expanse of space quizzically, making a smile tug at the corner of her mouth. Was he truly enjoying this crazy adventure they found themselves in?

"We need to use our magic," she spit out, unsure what she actually meant.

"Are you saying we ride one of your visions over there?" He nodded, letting out a small laugh.

"Why not?" She asked, folding her arms in frustration. She drilled him with a furious look as he scoffed at her. "I'll try to summon a vision of you and I, over there while you jump us through time." She pointed across the canyon towards a small landing entering another passage. "We can see the space we need to get to."

"No." He said, shaking his head. "Only a mated pair would have enough power to do something like that." His face held a small amount of regret once the words left his mouth.

"Well," she hesitated. She wasn't a fan of his lack of support. "What's the worst that could happen?" She straightened her spine.

"I don't know, we fall to our fucking deaths, Ara!" His voice echoed down into the darkness.

"The worst that could happen is we end up right back here a moment later. Just focus on moving us a few minutes forward in time, and I'll imagine us on the other ledge through your perspective."

"My perspective? Why not your own?" He said, the humor in his voice was lightening her heart, and she haltered her laugh as well.

"That's not how it works… I don't know, it just is that way."

"Oh yes, very convincing," he said, mocking her. "No. Let's head back and we can go a different route."

"Stanis!" She grinned wildly as she grabbed his wrist, pulling him to turn back. "I'm serious, let's just try to see what happens. We have to go this way. I can sense the pull, can't you?"

"No, I can't," he said, scrunching his nose up.

She willed herself to be firm, but his fear was weakening her. She tried to hold in her laugh. "Are you scared?" She asked, smirking at him.

"No." He said in a shallow voice. "Fine, just do it and I'll know when you summon the vision."

"How?"

"Your power is stronger than you know." He gripped her lower arms tightly, and warmth spread between them.

She forced them closer with a tug on his lapels, diving under his jacket and fisting the back of his shirt. Closing her eyes and concentrating her magic to her finger tips, then pushing it up her arms. The powers fought at first, which was unsurprising, but as she tugged harder, its stiffness slipped away. Throwing her head back, she welcomed the dark to flood in. She tried to imagine herself standing in his arms across the canyon. An image formed in the center of the shadows and slowly came into focus. Darker brown flecks fogged in from the corners of her eyes and she felt a tug of magic latching on to hers. She accepted it, encouraging her shadows to mix with them.

Reality washed over her, her soul feeling the after effects deeper than ever before, as the shadows danced in her peripheral resistance to fade.

"Ara?" His voice was soft.

"Yes?" She breathed.

"You did it," his jade eyes twinkled with pride.

She let a smile crack across her face as she formed a mirrored smile. He reached out and grazed her cheek, then brushed his thumb along her bottom lip. She inhaled, preparing for him to lean in to kiss her. Her adrenaline from the jump pushed her to lean into his touch. Slowly, he pulled his finger down to the pendent that lay on her chest. Brushing his knuckles along her skin and lightly her ablaze. She squeezed her thighs together as the tension between them thickened.

He dropped his fingers lower and dipped two into the opening of her black v-line tee shirt, right into the space between her cleavage.

Whirling her around him, she fell backwards, dangling over the cliff's edge. Air whipped her hair across her face, blinding her briefly before her heart forced her to latch onto Stanis smirk. Her stomach contents jumped to the base of her throat as gravity hit her.

She jerked, stopping her plummet into the canyon. Her heels remained tilted back over the edge as Stanis gripped the bra strap between her breasts.

She dangled from his outstretched grip. Adrenaline throbbed frantically through her veins as her high reached a new peak.

"Are you scared?" Stanis asked, smirking down and raising an eyebrow at her as his arm muscles flexed, he had no issue holding the weight of her at the end of his anchor.

"Fuck you, Stanis," she said, as he pulled her back to him. Placing her firmly back on two solid feet. It wasn't until she pushed past him, forcing herself deep into the tunnel and out of sight, that she let her smile slip across her mouth.

Chapter 24

Cold air washed over her skin again.

Abby poured her magic through her veins to warm her bones. Having forgone her jacket when they exited the apartment because the heat was record breaking that day; but now that they wandered the clammy Catacombs, she regretted wearing a small back crop top.

She reached for Grant's elbow, warming his skin as well. Bumps never seemed to line his glorious brown skin, but the smile he gave her when she did it was worth it.

"Thank you," he looked down, smiling wildly at her as they continued to walk through the maze.

Her blush crept onto her face, and she soaked up the sensation it brought, she hadn't felt like this around any other man in her entire life. She knew they were mates immediately. Cliché as it was, to say that. She had grown up idealizing her parents, as they often told tales of their love. They never stated they were mates directly, but they knew deep down their connection was stronger than a fated one. That their love was equal to the Enkrateia. The thought of them weighed heavily on her heart.

She often felt more than anyone else around her. Even her friends; Arabella always seemed to be so depressed until they were all together, and Aritzia was always so reserved, she could never tell what was going on with her.

"That's simply how it is here, Darling. It's also why *you* are so special." Her mother, Laylah, had told her anytime Abby faced adversity within herself. The Celestial's always felt joy in their hearts.

Grant was like that too, she realized the moment they spoke. He had a firm muscular shell but it guarded a truly large heart. Her smile stretched when he gripped her hand, intertwining their fingers.

"Tell me more about your parents?" She asked him, wanting to distract herself. She could feel his emotions changing to something dark and painful. Ever since she met Grant her magic had grown into something spectacular.

She had first felt it at the ball, when she gripped Arabella's hand in comfort. She never expected to be pulled into a vision. Arabella's unfamiliar panic had fought her at first, the idea of being discovered was overwhelming, until Abby had suddenly made it all stop.

Since that day, she often found herself using her magic amplified to help people ease their anxiety, especially Grant. A sigh escaped him, and his solid shoulders softened. She didn't like that she had been given the power to manipulate emotions, but she sensed he was scared to reveal things to her. He hid deep secrets that he couldn't manage to share yet.

They had spent hours communicating through a small device that Grant had gifted her on the day they met. He had designed it based on old models his dad had created, insisting that he was the only one who would receive her words of correspondence.

The device now laid unused in her pocket. She wished she'd given it to Aritzia, before they all got separated.

Grant had pulled her out of the way as the cave walls had shifted around them, seemingly having a mind of their own, separating them for Aritzia and Cole. She knew Grant had regretted his actions. Being separated from Cole broke his heart, as deeply as hers did being separated from her best friends.

A day or so went by, at least she felt like it was a day. Time didn't exist the same in the Catacombs. They had only stopped once to try to sleep but the ground made it impossible for her to find comfort. His presence had made it easier. He held her in his arms as he sat to keep watch, allowing her to find a few moments of peace.

"They aren't here," he said calmly. He was dialed in on the tunnel in front of them as they walked, she held another device he had given her, and shown the light ahead of them. The nagging feeling of shame weighed on her, she could've mastered an orb of light that would've been stronger but insulting him didn't seem smart.

He took care of her, and she admired that he would do anything to protect her. He sensed when they were in danger.

The first time, they had been quietly strolling through the darkness when he pulled her tight to his chest, thrusting their bodies tightly together. As he squeezed them into a crack of the wall, he was forced to throw his mechanical bow to the floor. She could hardly breath as her heart raced and she sensed his own fear trying to escape his chest. He killed the light, blanketing them in darkness.

Closing her eyes, despite being blinded, she forced them to become calm. His hand covered her mouth, his calloused fingers trembling. His breaths eased as they remained shoved together next to the skulls in the wall, but deep snarling sent shivers down her spine. The rustle of something dragging caused lumps to form in their throats. She prayed to the god's above that the monsters couldn't see in the dark, or dare to look in their direction.

Grant held her long after the creatures passed and she remained frozen in his arms for a while. He removed his hand from her mouth, pulling back and reaching down for his weapon, but she grabbed his arm.

Their hearts pounded furiously again. Then, she was kissing him like it was the last kiss she would ever taste. He let her and eventually he had his tongue dancing along hers. He pushed his groin into her further and the compaction of them being in the small space and his body crushing her was invigorating. Her legs gave up trying to keep her standing, but it didn't matter, because he held her up with his large form. The kisses grew frantic despite the movements being limited. Their height difference allowed him to only place kisses across her face like he intended to form constellations across her skin.

Unsure if it was adrenaline or his domination of their situation, she sprung to meet his every action, the taste of him was like sunshine and honey. Having witnessed addiction, but never experiencing it herself, she could only fathom that that was what falling into the sweet embrace of a vice felt like.

Sweat lined her palms, even after she had brushed her hands on the dark brown cargo pants, incessantly. "What do you mean? Where are they?" She asked him while attempting to match every giant step of his, with two of her own. He never really expanded on his thoughts without her pushing him. He didn't seem to notice though.

"They," he paused, stopping them and turning her towards him with a firm grasp on her shoulders. "It's harder to explain, but I promise it will all make sense soon."

She wasn't sure what he meant but an overwhelming amount of trust shadowed her doubt. She didn't want to press the topic further, in an effort to keep him talking.

"Okay, well at least tell me about them. Do you have any siblings?"

"Yes, she's younger, but we didn't spend much time together. I left home when I was fourteen," he said mildly.

She felt her brows furrow. "Why did you leave?"

"It's complicated," he paused again, and she mentally begged him to continue hanging on every word. "My father sent me away to find something…something that will help all of Lafornas. He told me that I was responsible for returning th.." The urge to interrupt him almost seeped through. "He said I was the only one who could bring it back, I'd be the only one who would seek it out, and be able to know when I found it."

She wasn't sure what that all meant but she had known other men who were sent on quests by their father's. Not much unlike Arabella's brother, or even Cole's.

"Did you find it?" She asked, jokingly, finding it obvious he still hadn't returned home; so that was most likely impossible.

An angelic smile beamed across his face. "Yes," he said as joy filled his heart and flowed to her.

"Good, I am happy to hear that," she said truthfully. Until she realized what that would mean. That he would go home. Would he want her to go with him? Would she want to go?

She couldn't imagine leaving her parents to go live somewhere else. Yes, she had discussed living with her friends but that was still in Limos. She could see her parents as often as she wanted. She had tried to tell her mother about Grant the day they met, but she had arrived home too late, she had already been asleep. Then the next day her father had been insistent on her mother visiting an old friend; telling Abby it was in preparation for something big.

She wasn't sure what that had meant either. Her father, Hael, had always been a bit eccentric and was rambling on about a better world often. He wasn't insane by any means. He just seemed to think living close to an emerging war, with the bombing numbers rising everyday, was a bad idea. They were protected by their status in the Federation, but how long could that last? She constantly feared he would make her leave her friends, but he never seemed serious.

Before now.

Before Grant.

The ground had shifted under her feet when his dark eyes finally found her.

"How far away is your home?" She said.

He looked at her with a furrowed brow. "Why do you ask?" He seemed to be guarding himself again, but she wasn't going to let him back away now. She never liked when a room was quiet and unless she pestered him with questions, she was the only one talking.

"I hope to meet your family. I mean…I hope for you to meet mine as well, once we find everyone and go back. My parents will be thrilled to meet you." She said, as excitement of the idea came to fruition, and lit up her soul.

He didn't say anything at first and she started to ponder if she had even asked him a question or not. "I'd like that someday," he said.

Her stomach dropped at his words, unsure what that meant, but before she could question it, his grip tensed. She felt a wave of worry surrounding them. Their adrenaline embraced her tightly, preparing them for whatever he was sensing.

The cave opened up in front of them, and the sudden increase in light was blinding. Blinking rapidly to allow her eyes to adjust, she finally saw they had emerged into the grand dome. Filled with a massive collection of vegetation, unlike anything Abby had ever been afforded to see. Her eyes widened, as she took into the lush green jungle of vines. The overgrowth of greenery draping, then expanding to engulf the entire path ahead. Sunlight fell down from the ceiling in cracks in an atypical fashion. The air around them was warm with humidity dancing on her skin. Releasing Grant's hand gently, she reached forward. Palms turned out, petting the leaves of the underbrush as they stepped further into the jungle.

He lunged at her, surprising her, and pulled her to his chest.

"Don't!" He gasped in a low voice. She tilted her head, frowning up at him, trying to read his expression, fear washing into her where they touched.

"What's wrong?" She said, scanning the thick wall of green spanning in front of them.

"Something's not right, I don't see a clear path forward." He stated methodically. He spoke in that manner often and she wondered if he was raised in a *Hoplite family* as her father called it, similar to Aritzia. As she pocketed the question away for later, a rustling came from deep within the foliage.

"Let's find a different way," he stated, attempting to turn them around.

"What?" She said pushing from his grip. The fear in his eyes blazed brighter as he scanned her face and then the jungle at her back. "We've walked for like forever, and this is where it led us, we can't just go back. We need to find a way through," she said fearlessly.

"Do you hear that?" Grant asked through tight lips. "That's some beast that will kill us."

"You don't know that," she said, but doubt curled in her stomach.

"I do know that anything in Abyss will kill us if it gets the chance." He said firmly, grabbing for her hand, "we can find another way."

"If all the beasts down here are meant to kill us, then we will face a different one, eventually. Let's just decide to face whoever is in here, while we can at least do it in the light."

Something she had stated triggered him, his façade softened before he gazed around her head. "Fine," he ground out, "but stay close to me."

"Okay," she said breathlessly, of course she was going to do that, she wasn't stupid enough to leave his side. She also didn't want to leave him, she had the ability to heal them, which she hoped held the same weight for him. "You stay close to me too, then."

His beautiful smile stunned her, making her blush and a small laugh escaped her lips. His grip on her hand was firm but surprisingly tender while he led them into the fortress of verdure. She pondered why they hadn't followed the perimeter of the dome until they found another door, but it was too late for that now. There were little indications of their location within the dome, even as she scanned the ceiling, all she found were pockets of glow. The tree coverage opened up sporadically, allowing her only a brief view, as a huge shadow flew over them.

Instinctually, they both ducked, finding shelter under a large twining tree. Grant snuck over the voluptuous roots budding from the black dirt, aiming his bow towards the glass sky.

Wings beat rhythmically above them, alluding to some species of large bird that circled above. With a second glance, it was more apparent the creature had humanoid appendages.

"What the fuck?" Grant whispered and she found herself mirroring his sentiment.

A stench of death coated them, making bile rise to her throat. They cupped their palms to their faces, masking them from the stench but it wasn't enough. Saliva coated her mouth, making the attempt to hold down her vomit harder, but not impossible. She reached for Grant's arm, forcefully pushing her magic out to ease their growing nausea.

The wave passed as the creature dove into the tree line, disappearing somewhere in front of them.

"We should go back and follow the perimeter of the dome." She whispered.

He shook his head and pointed in the direction the creature landed, Abby had a horrible feeling it was towards the beasts nest.

"No." She whispered, trying not to raise her voice, her face in disgust as she tugged on his elbow. The trees shifted around them, closing off the path they had come from, encasing them within the foliage.

She released a breath of frustration, realizing he wasn't likely to blame, but he still had managed to win this small fight between them by default.

"Fine." She said as she stomped out in front of them, towards the middle of the curtains of vegetation.

Grant aimed his bow over her shoulder while they stalked forward. The creature's scent of death and rotting flesh rose up to greet them the closer they crept towards its lair.

Abby shifted between holding her breath and taking air through her mouth, instead of her nostrils. Every crunch underfoot spawned an increase in their heart rates, until the clearing came into view and her heart ceased its drumming.

Checking for her pulse, she stopped at the mossy edge. Grant pressed a firm hand on her shoulder, urging them to kneel and conceal themselves in the underbrush. A solid finger split his lips, to encourage her to remain silent. For the first time in a while, she didn't need the reminder.

Observing the space in front of them, she glimpsed a table piled high with a buffet of foods displayed in the middle of a small velvety field. Glittery chargers, sparkling metal challises, and decorative bowls all piled high with mounds of what she could only imagine, were types of food she wasn't accustomed to. Her stomach rolled, until she managed to dampen her hunger. A whole hog the size of a car glistened in the center of a grand arrangement of fresh produce. The table scape looked like it had been painted from a dream, with varying sized candlesticks dripping hardened wax onto the wooden surface below them. A rainbow of food spilled onto the floor, and as her gaze traveled over the pile in the short grass. She noticed other objects too.

Instruments.

Broken chairs.

Even weapons of different size, shapes, and names.

Then the most terrifying sight, carpeting the floor around the objects, were thousands of opal bones. Scattered around like spilled puzzle pieces. A few intact skeletons remained, dripping with flesh and sinew, beneath layers of rusted bronze chest plates and greaves.

Her stomach dropped to the floor as she sucked in a harsh breath, she had seen death before in her work at the Regglin's House, but nothing to this level of decomposition.

Searching Grant's dark features for any hint of reassurance, she only found his russet brown eyes focused on the scene in front of them. He was glorious in his black tee shirt, with his tattoos peaking out. The sight of them and his raven black hair always astonished her.

His sight on the winged women was unmoving, jealousy began to creep across her skin like an insect. An abusing groan flooded Abby's ears, as the woman scraped her claws along the black stone floor, ripping the grass. Tossing shards of bones and armor around aimlessly. Avoiding the instruments peeking out from under the table, she swept around the food, sniffing, but never touching.

When suddenly his form began to rise, before tucking her gently behind him. Then honing in on every step, as they crept around the edge of the nest.

"I can smell you, Gorgeous," rang out a woman's voice, drawing their attention back to the winged-creature. "no man enters my home without me knowing it." She shifted her wings, sprawling them out to their full length and the stench washed over their noses again. Abby gagged but refrained from making a noise. Her gentle fingers caressed Grant's forearm, sending relief to coat his flesh.

"Why don't you come join my feast?" She whispered as she scanned the edge of the jungle. Before it was too late, he gripped Abby's waist, hoisting her through the air and out of the monster's sight behind a tree.

"I knew I'd find you," her raspy voice forced him to act.

He sprinted, diving amongst the vegetation, away from the women who held all his devotion. So much for not leaving each other.

Her ass landed in the dirt, and her eyes rolled. She scrambled to her feet, then dashed towards the weapons strewn amongst the floor at the base of the table. She slid across the ground, straight through an opening in the scattered corpses, her thick soled boots hitting the pole on the underside of the table with a thud. Frantically, she reached up to the table top grabbing a napkin roll, tied in a bright green ribbon. She untied it, then fastened her hair up and out of her face before testing the knife's point with her finger tip. The blade's edge was too dull to break skin, becoming useless, so she tossed it aside.

She lunged for the closet sword, finding it to be heavier than she expected, and ditched it, in search of a smaller one. Her eyes caught sight of a needle point dagger glittering in the sunlight. As her fingertips grazed the hilt, a claw adorned with long talons shot from above, snapping at her wrist. Luckily the claw caught the edge of the table and only clipped the back of her hand. A hiss escaped her as the nails met her flesh, briefly. The gash burned her, while blood met the ground. Tucking back under the table, she attempted to close up the wound, but to her surprise she was met with failure. She touched the stone in the grooves on the floor where her boot had scuffed the grass.

"Norilekcin Rock," she breathed, realizing why her magic was absent.

The vulture screeched as an arrow sliced through the jungle, piercing her between the wings, lodging into her spine. Grant bounded towards them, knocking back another arrow. The creature struggled to recover, engulfed in her fury. The monster unaware of Grant, while he circled around the table scape, keeping his weapon locked on her.

"I didn't realize you brought dessert with you." Her voice called out, in a hollowed tone, her threats weakened by the assault. Abby searched for another answer, her eyes falling to the instrument perched across from her. Intuition forced her to dive onto her knees, her hand grasping the cold metal of the trumpet that summoned her. She brushed her thumb over the smudges along its bell, debris fell away, uncovering a message etched in the bronze metal.

The brazen song will set you free.

The winged-women's cackling drew her attention back to Grant, who continued to side step around her, Abby watched their dance and when his back was firmly to the jungle opening she saw a wooden door cut into the perimeter wall. Abby waited for him to fire another arrow, her feet scrambling to pull her out from under the table. Then she raced towards him, thrusting her entire body into his. Attempting to force his large frame to run. The trumpet sang against her thigh, humming along with the beat, in an attempt to seduce her into using it.

"Go," she screamed, her voice breaking.

Her feet lifted from the ground, Grant was hoisting her over his shoulder. Her eyes instantly tracked the siren, who launched into the sky, breaking tree branches in her pursuit. Abby's gut plummeted at the sight of the vulture swooping down towards them. With outstretched claws, her talons locked in on them.

The trumpet warmed in her hand and the woman's flat retina eyes blared larger, as she realized Abby was clutching it.

In an instant, her hair whipped her in the face. Grant threw her to her feet, shielding her with his large frame. Her back pushed against the wood of the door. Before she gripped the handle, falling back through the threshold as the door flung open, Grant's firm body forced her to safety.

A scream latched onto her throat at the sight of talons ripping into his shoulder. Her knees bore into harsh rock at the horrid realization of her mate being gripped by the beast. Tears blinded her vision and her heart threatened to escape from her chest.

The horn burned with a fire so strong that she almost dropped it. Grant scrambled to get his footing, tugging at the claw embedded in his shoulder. His beautiful dark eyes burning with pain, the agony of it all spawning her destruction.

She needed to free him from the monster's grasp. Forcing a large breath into her lungs, then pressing the instrument to her lips, she boldly rang out its song. The sound shook the leaves around them, and reverberating across the dome.

Vulturous screams muffled with the music of the horn. Grant's back hit the ground with a thunderous clap. The siren shot into the air, clutching her ears, as her wings propelled her into the ceiling of the dome. Her body tumbled lifelessly, cascading through the tree canopy in the distance.

Desperately Abby's hands gripped his wounds, applying magic to every surface of his skin, in an attempt to heal him. His groans cracked her heart open, as she hoisted him to his feet. They scrambled through the open door, then forcefully shut it behind them.

Darkness welcomed them, as they melted to the floor, panting, clutching one another. Her legs folded around his torso, as he pulled her further into his lap. She didn't know how long they sat there. Neither of them seemed ready to let go of the other, so they remained, intertwining their souls further, until they felt whole again.

Chapter 25

Cole's heart was beating out of his chest, the agony in his wrist was beyond any pain he'd ever felt before. Aritzia had lashed a vine around it as he free fell into the canyon below. The force of his body falling, only to be stopped abruptly, caused most of the bones in his wrist and hand to snap.

He heard the cracking as he was thrashed to a stop, and felt the pain incinerate his entire arm. He bellowed in agony, continued to sense moisture from his eyes rolling down his face as he dangled over the opening. Somehow managing to grip the tendrils twinning around, consistently bearing his weight. Then with his other hand he hoisted himself up. Aritzia tugged her magic simultaneously, so after only a few minutes of torture, he was laying flat on his back gripping his wrist to his chest.

He was grateful she had saved his life, but he desperately wished she could've wrapped the rope around his waist instead. The pain shooting burned through the rest of his body. Another cry of pain escaped his lips, as Aritzia assisted him up into a sitting position atop the bridge.

"Fuck," she said in astonishment, his wrist already black around the base of his thumb.

The throbbing causing his stomach to roll. Attempting to distract himself from the pain he sucked in a deep breath through his nose and wiped the perspiration from his face with the unbroken palm. Revealing his pain was nonnegotiable, he had been raised to be grateful. Nothing else mattered, except for the debt he owed her now.

He clutched his wrist to his chest, biting his lip so hard he drew blood, not that he'd felt it. The taste of copper was the only indication. He held firm in his notion not to let her see him sweat…or bleed. She watched him with such kind chestnut eyes, her presence in the chaos was becoming his only sense of reality.

"Here. Let me help." More vines braided from her fingertips, twisting and knotting until it formed a sling. He adjusted the twin swords he had strapped to his back, moving them around his new accessory. Only to be confronted with cursed frustration. Aritzia helped him undo the straps and slung them over her shoulders instead. The grace she held when attaching the scabbard, moving her deep caramel locks to the side, imitated a glorious warrior. Standing before him, was a goddess walking amongst men.

"Thank you," he said breathlessly as he stood. Glancing across the gaping hole together, until footsteps trampled towards them. His non-mangled hand scrambled to pull Aritzia away from the edge and into the dark tunnel.

"God's, I hope this treasure is worth it," he whispered. If it wasn't, he was going to kill Stanis himself.

Once hidden in the darkness deeper into the Catacombs, he glanced over his shoulder, noting the three figures who were now slowing their hunt to confront the canyon, and half built bridge. Recognizing only the tallest member of their clan.

Lukas Hik.

Cole had hoped he wasn't recognizable as Stanis's accomplice at the ball, but with Lukas father's power and influence it was inevitable they would be identified. Especially, after Stanis had stabbed him in the leg. No one forgot something like that, and after the embarrassment Stanis had caused him, he didn't blame Lukas for wanting to go after them. Lukas most likely wanted to kill Stanis, but there was probably a line to join.

Their chorus of hollering they conducted had set him and Aritzia into a run. A sour taste coated his mouth, the darkness whispered to the memory of the rest of their group. They had ventured into the Catacombs together, but separated by its forever changing routes.

Reuniting their group was the priority, and somehow they managed to divide it further. Aritzia insisted once they got back to Abby, she could help heal his wrist. He wasn't entirely listening to her, as she guided them through the darkness. She had ignited a small device that Grant had given her, shining a light ahead as they weaved through the tunnels. The humid air grew thick, as they began to descend deeper into the tunnels. Hot air coated his throat, refusing his lungs to take in full breaths. The temperature increased, as they ventured deeper into Catacombs. Cole lost track of the tunnels, the maps hadn't indicated they would change. The entire journey would be, and forever remain, uncharted.

Aritzia waved her hand around in front of them, dissipating some of the moisture suffocating them, but he could tell she was straining her magic reserves. She would worked silently, until he would question her about certain actions. She responded stoically every time.

He scanned her form as she walked in front of him, admiring their swords on her back, trying hard not to stare at her ass tucked in her tight gray jeans. She made that difficult, as she continued to sway her hips with determination. To his surprise, he enjoyed her company, and she was proving to be a very competent ally, saving his ass on multiple occasions, as well as extending him kindness. She most likely heard about his worst character traits from Arabella, but she didn't treat him unfairly.

He hadn't been with someone since Arabella, and he missed her lust for his touch. He enjoyed his time with her, but she always faded away in her thoughts when she reached for her climax. Invading her mind proved to be a mistake countless times, finding himself feeling self conscious for not being her ideal fantasy. He understood, though. He wasn't fucking her because he wanted to be with her either. She simply liked the attention, and somewhere deep within him he liked the idea of betraying Stanis.

But now, seeing Stanis with Arabella broke something in Cole's heart. How was he supposed to tell his brother he had messed around with The Fates? He worried about him and Arabella, though. Hoping Stanis hadn't forced her to go somewhere against her will. Finding the idea absurd, but he still wondered if it was true. Hopefully she had given him a good beating in the nose for them all. A small laugh escaped his lips.

The floor evened out again, and his calves burned furiously. The scent of ammonia and death engulfed his nostrils. He covered his face, noting Aritzia doing the same as he caught up to her. They emerged into a large cavern the size of three city blocks, the ceiling opened up at a small hole, letting the stars pour their faint light over the area. A small gag escaped him as his arm brushed the moisture that licked the wall of skulls, coating him in a mucus textured glob. He could make out the holes of twelve tunnels opposite them on the far end of the space. How the fuck were they supposed to decide which tunnel to pick?

He admired the view as Aritzia bent down to press her free hand to the dirt at their feet.

"That one," she said definitively, pointing to the sixth entrance near the middle.

Cole stepped into the opening and began leading them through the desolate landscape, attempting to breathe through his mouth as the stench grew around them.

"Wait!" Aritzia gasped, stopping in her tracks.

"What?"

Aritizia dropped the light she was holding, letting it clatter to the dirt. Darkness blanketed them, the stars boarded up at the ceiling's opening. A large thud rang through the air and the ground shook. Sounds of gravel scrapping and waves of rocks moving bounced off the walls of the surrounding cavern. Cole's heartbeat picked up, realizing they were no longer alone in the space. Something very large now joined them and a new test was upon them.

The wall at their sides began to slide, generating a soft grinding noise, as it pulled across the gravel. Aritzia scrambled to grasp the device again. Quickly relighting it and turning the beam towards the sound. Frozen in place, she illuminated the reflective ruby scales covering the wall. Cole's limbs seized, as well, at the sight of the creature encroaching on her. The wall ended, revealing a serpent's tail the size of a transit train, coming to a sharp point, then disappearing into the darkness. Thick air formed around them again, causing the hairs on his arm to stand. They were prey in a very large snake den.

Hissing surrounded the cave, ringing out from every direction. Cole was only a few steps from her, soft glow of the light danced on her features, urging him to remain unmoving. Slowly, she reached over her shoulder and grasped the hilt of one of the swords. Unsheathing it slowly, as her eyes lit with a deep raging fire.

Bile rose in Cole's throat as they listened for any other sign of the beast surrounding them. He lunged forward, gripping Aritzia's arm, turning their backs towards one another. He squinted in the darkness, waiting for the creature to reveal itself when the ground shook.

The cavern silenced, refilling with bright star light. Revealing a gigantic scarlet serpent's head resting next to them in the dirt. The creature's eye remained closed as it slept, breathing a steady rhythm that shook the floor beneath them.

The breath in Cole's chest released slowly as his fear rose to escape. He encouraged his heart to slow, but he was struggling to rein it in. Aritzia's panic matched his through the tight grip on his wrist. Her breaths eventually steadied. He slowly observed the space as more ruby scaled snake heads rested around them on the ground, creating a maze of coiled serpents. They could no longer see the tunnel entrances. Now stuck deep within the resting place of, not one, but what looked to be six or more enormous snakes.

Slowly, Cole tugged on Aritzia's wrist, forcing her to follow his ascent into the surrounding maze. Keeping his steps quiet, and allowing for space between them and the snake heads dozing around them. He hadn't realized getting eaten by a huge snake was one of his biggest fears, but in that moment, it sure made the top spot on his list.

Aritzia kept her hand firmly in his, the sword in the other, as they weaved around, finding themselves following the length of one of the massive creatures. The snakes shifted every so often, forcing them to freeze. Locked within the others embrace.

Aritzia didn't seem to fear their situation. He scanned her features as they stalked through the maze of scales. Courage seeped through her skin, absorbing into him where their palms touched. She was obviously trained in the art of composure because he had struggled to keep his head throughout multiple of their trials thus far. Whilst she carried their small team. He hoped that once Abby could heal him back to his full strength, that he could reach the bar Aritzia was setting. Her chestnut eyes found his again, a small curve pulling at her maroon lips. She was a woman of few words, so her smile was becoming something he craved to see. His heart was rising again, washing away the fear as he felt the warmth of her grip strengthen.

Then it dropped to the dirt again, as they reached a dead end, scarlet snake bodies blocking them in all directions. He looked back and followed the direction they had trekked, revealing two walls of flesh leading away from them ending in two heads. A lump lodged in his throat at the sound of gravel scrapping. Aritzia released a small gasp, as she gripped his fingers tighter.

They watched in horror.

The serpents rose high above their heads, revealing the base of all their necks connected into a long singular being. Their tongues flicked rapidly. Cole's met Aritzia's gaze as she mimicked their tongues and covered her eyes with her palm. They hadn't seen them yet. Instead they were using their tongues to sense who had wandered into their trap. Cole never thought a beast such as this could actually exist. Snakes were a myth in Lafornas, since… well, he couldn't remember. Searching the depths of his brain, he knew it was a while ago, and it definitely wasn't a gargantuan one with multiple heads. His fear pushed up again, and he began loathing the sensation it brought to his skin.

The snake's tail flicked around its body, revealing the wall of twelve tunnels. Cole gripped Aritzia, pushing her towards the openings, hoping they could make it if they ran fast enough.

"I can smell your fear, little human," a mystical voice echoed around them, but they kept to their escape.

"I can smell your weak male magic running through your half filled veins," the snake hissed again, followed by multiple other hisses that were reminiscent of laughs.

One of the small snakes, toward the base of the creature's body, lunged for Aritzia's back. Only to be sliced off in one fell swish of her sword. Three heads grew back in its place, hissing aggressively. The young serpents fought in confusion, distracted enough for her to reach Cole again. Gripping her tightly with his free hand, he tried to run and ignore the pain in his other wrist as it slammed against his chest. Another snake lunged out next to them, missing them by a few steps.

Cole's palm fell from Aritzia to shove her ahead of him, in an effort to reach the tunnel faster. He kept right on her heels, craning his head back to see their predator. Nine snake heads loomed high in the cavern, all facing different directions. Aritizia was right. They couldn't actually see anything at all. Their eyes appeared glossed over and tongues flicked about, attempting to latch on to something in the air. The center snake was larger than the rest and her head fanned out like a sail.

"There you are," she hissed with determination.

The beast's tail slammed into their sides, knocking them from their path. They tumbled across the cavern, as it pushed them towards the wall.

Aritzia stabbed at the creature with her sword, causing the snakes to release a symphony of high-pitched squeals. All nine heads pinned their attention to where she had caused their pain.

Cole scrambled to grab the protruding scales atop the tail as it continued to hurl them towards the far wall. Managing to get a good grip with his free hand, but he struggled to push away the pain his other wrist felt, as he rolled on top of the creature to straddle its body. Balancing himself enough to grab Aritzia's arm, he hoisted her up. Placing her to face him. The fear in her eyes mirrored his, and he watched in slow motion, as the snake's tail slammed into the wall a second later. Propelling them both into it with head cracking force. Pain licked the back of his scalp, but adrenaline battled it at the sight of Aritzia struggling to remove her wedged ankle. She thrusted her magic at the wall to free herself, but the black stone didn't budge.

"Fuck this place is covered in Norilekcin rock!" She said.

The tail shifted away from the wall, throwing them both into the dirt. The snake's tail slithered away from them but the heads were zigzagging wilding towards them from across the cavern in a deathly pursuit.

"We have to go?" Cole forced out, trying to find the breath that was knocked from his chest. He was convinced his wrist had fallen off at this point, realizing he couldn't feel it any longer. The sling still gripped it to his chest, but in the repeated blows his hand had lost all feeling. Adrenaline forced him to ignore any of it.

They scrambled to their feet, Aritzia lunged for the sword that lay in the dirt, steps away from them. He waited for her to run, then followed close behind. Green smoke flowed from the snakes's mouths. Cole wasn't sure why, but he had a deep-seated feeling that smoke would lead to a painful death, so he pressed his feet to pick up their pace. The tunnels grew larger in front of them, but the sixth tunnel was too far. Aritzia aimed for the third one, and he was determined that was a good enough choice for him.

Three snake heads skidded past behind them, hissing loudly as they realized their prey had moved. One hissing wildly, as they slammed into the wall. Green fog billowed at Cole's back. He felt the burning sensation through the soles of his boots, a scream of pure agony ripped from his chest, as his flesh was seared with the poisonous shadow. He refused to stop running, despite the agony he was feeling as each foot hit needles.

Aritzia dove into the tunnel ahead of him, he pushed himself to his physical limit to follow her into the darkness. Her light guided them deeper into the dark tunnel and away from the stench of the snake's den.

He refused to stop, even as she did, to look back.

Passing her, as all nine snakeheads fought to enter the tunnel after them. Gouging in one another and hissing wildly. Cole still didn't stop, forcing Aritzia to follow him now, their feet thrusting them into the darkness. His adrenaline refusing to let him stop running until he was sure the snakes couldn't reach them. He followed the walls with his finger tips, as they turned and spilled out in front of him in all differing directions. Only stopping enough for Aritzia to catch up with him.

Then he dove into another tunnel opening, his fear driving him that direction. He heard Aritzia call out from behind for him to stop, but it was too late, he slammed into the dirt wall that appeared in the darkness.

Chapter 26

Their footsteps crunched beneath them as they descended deeper into the Catacombs. Stanis had refused to let his anger for Arabella dissipate. She desperately tried to act like nothing happened between them, causing his frustration to elevate. Being in her presence loosened the air in his chest, but memories of her words crashed like abrupt waves.

Forcing him to relive the pain.

Maybe that's why he'd pretended to throw her over the cliff's edge. He released a small scoff at the memory of her wide eyed gasp. She cursed at him, but her smile revealed the opposite of fear. He wasn't sure if that excited or terrified him. It was obvious now the idea he'd painted in his head was wrong. Had she truly betrayed their bond? He'd never seen her around Cole enough for them to have formed an attachment strong enough to reflect the idea of love.

Love, the intangible concept he had thrown at Ara, expecting she understood it, even though he'd hardly met a person in Lafornas who had. A mating bond, yes, but love, absolutely fucking not. But Stanis did love her, even though she loved *him*.

Or was it Cole who betrayed him?

His nostrils flared. It would be both their faults, because Cole knew Ara was his mate. He had tried to get Stanis to admit the fact aloud many times before. Was he trying to get Stanis to deny it, to justify his obvious crush on Ara?

He huffed in frustration, gaining him Ara's attention. Fortunately, she remained silent. The sound of their steps in the barely lit tunnels were a welcomed grace. He followed the soft glow of their orbs, winding deeper into underground ruins. Arabella had stated, at multiple forks in the road, which way was best, but he wasn't seeing how she came to this conclusion.

"Cole and I slept together before we met," she said.

A grunt was the only reaction he could find deep in his soul. His emotions were knotting in his stomach at the thought of them together. He hoped she would drop the topic, but she didn't seem like the type to let this go.

"Are you telling me you've never had sex with anyone?" She stopped, pinning him with a glare.

He pushed forward silently, ignoring her interrogation. The last thing he wanted was to discuss their previous sexual endeavors. He didn't mind sharing the few illicit encounters that he had had. They meant nothing, and he hardly remembered their faces.

"You don't have to give me a number, I most certainly don't want to give you mine…"

His growl interrupted her. "Drop it, Ara." He forced himself to turn from her. His anger was budding at the base of his chest and his arms tingled with anticipation, knowing they would be through one of the cave walls soon.

"Do you hear that?"

Unsure of her game play, he didn't dare respond. A roar built around the cave, growing as they pushed forward. The air thickened with humidity, coating his skin in apprehension. A faint glow greeted them as they approached. Each one of his steps was cautious, in preparation for another free fall. As his eyes adjusted, the realization set in; they had found an opening in the catacombs. A huge body of cobalt water appeared in front of their eyes as it poured viciously down, into the awaiting river below.

"Water!" Arabella exclaimed.

He was awestruck at the sight. Water this shade of blue didn't exist in Lafornas anymore. He had seen small ponds when he was a child, but those were long dried up. Arabella reached down to inspect the foamy waves washing onto the black sand shore at their feet.

"Don't!" He flew forward, gripping her shoulder.

"What the fuck?" She ripped out of his grip. "Why not?"

"Look!"

She followed his gaze back to the water's edge, the glinting of the falls around them casting a haze of perspiration in the air. Where the water finally eased and flowed into the river away from the falls, petite violet orbs were swirling and smashing into each other, fighting in the current.

"What are those things?" She asked him, like he had all the answers.

He pushed off the sarcastic comment melting on his tongue. "I don't know."

"They look like they have eyes," disgust wrinkled her features as she bent down to observe them closer.

The insistent urge to pull her away from any danger budded, but lessened when a familiar chill rolled through her neck and into his arm where they made contact. He held firm to her. She was seeing a vision. Sweeping around beside her, adjusting his grip, but never breaking their contact. He surveyed the area around them and the tunnel, hoping she would return to him quickly. They were prey waiting to be seen.

She gasped suddenly, her knees hitting the soft beads of ashen sand, turning to face him.

"What?" He searched her eyes.

"We need to follow the river. That's how we find them." She said, like it was the clearest answer.

"How do you suppose we do that?"

As if he had summoned the answer, the streams parted down the middle, pushing the water into two columns with a symphony of burbles. Through the passage emerged a sleek black vessel the size of a small car. The high-speed machines Arabella raced down the tracks at Fen's bore an uncanny resemblance. Her sterling irises shone bright, as it approached them. The vessel pulled close to the river's edge, beckoning them to climb aboard. The waterfall folded back into one magnificent stream.

It was then, that Stanis saw the person standing at the back of the boat, their features slightly hidden by a dark black hooded cloak. The hood tilted ominously slow, revealing the lower half of a masculine face. His skin flickered from unmarked into drapes of sinew with a flash of the lights from their orbs, but returned immediately as he stretched a cloak-covered hand towards Arabella.

Thrill danced along Stanis's skin, his scowl had resurfaced at the sight of the onyx vessel before them. "Fuck that!" he exclaimed, his anger finally directed away from her and clinging to something else. "I am not getting into that thing."

"Are you scared?" She asked with a devious grin.

"Absolutely not." He lied, trudging through the water, sending the phosphorescent orbs scattering with tiny screams. His hand outstretched to aid her, which was a relief because the boat's captain had done the same, but it wasn't as inviting. The contact their palms made sent a chorus of desire into his head. She pushed past him, shattering the moment, as she found the intricate black leather seats awaiting them. Four empty ones sat beside them.

His jaded eyes bore into her soul as the boat pulled away from the shore and thrusted back towards the dark tunnel that engulfed the rest of the river. The sickness deep in his stomach lurched with every wave. Or was it how she was watching him that unsettled him?

She dragged her gaze away, observing the creepy shadow figure, who began guiding them and the boat at a more rapid pace. Moisture hit Stanis's face, as he leaned forward, their knuckles brushed and she welcomed his touch.

"Did you know," he whispered, "that you are absolutely glorious?"

He smirked and leaned back, catching the slight sigh that left her lips. His feet tingled in his sopping boots. He wasn't sure which sensation felt worse. The itching of the crusted salt or the rattling his heart felt now that he had claimed her as his.

"What do you think those orbs are?" Arabella asked him as she leaned over the edge of the boat. He remained rigid, refusing to let the water near him again.

"They are the souls," a mystic male voice said behind them. Stunned, Stanis faced the shadow at the rear. Noticing that the man's mouth didn't move as he spoke to them. "I am guiding them to salvation." His ascent was thick and Stanis had a sense he was much older than he had imagined.

"Who are you?" Arabella said.

"I am many things, I am no one, I am a guide, a pawn..."

"Don't you have a name?" Stanis interrupted. He didn't like riddles.

"Yes, Akrasia," he replied coldly, "my name is Charon."

"Akrasia?" Stanis mumbled

"Where do they come from?" Arabella was acting like they were in a classroom, not floating on a river of souls.

"That is not answered in a simple manner. For the souls of the living have been divided between planes. Once they find their way to me, I help bind their souls with those capsules." Charon's flickering hand lifted, revealing flawless flesh, that then flashed with wrinkles as he pointed to a pile of glass spheres scattered at their feet. Not wanting to get sucked into one yet, Stanis shifted his boots towards the center on the boat.

"How do they find you?" Arabella asked, her brows furrowing as she looked towards Stanis. His stomach was feeling queasy again, and he had a feeling she wasn't so sure of their voyager either.

"The depraved souls wandering Abyss eventually decide their gloomy existence is done." He was speaking in riddles. Stanis rolled his eyes at the nonsense, but Ara seemed to believe this shit.

"They find me more easily than others. Now I must travel further to seek the souls trapped in Abeyance, since the divide. Very few souls are forced to come to Abyss from Idyll, but the ones that do are damned to fight their way through Abeyance."

"Wait." Stanis said with a humor filled expression, "you're telling us you find souls from other worlds and bring them to this river *Abyss*?"

"No, this is The River of the Dead." Charon retorted dryly, a hint of arrogance washing behind it. "You are ignorant for an Akrasia born."

"Where's Abyss?" Arabella asked, somehow following the tale Charon was spinning.

"It doesn't matter, Ara," Stanis said through gritted teeth. "We're just here to find Itia's treasure." He looked towards Charon again, surely he could lead them to it, if he chose to.

"Abyss is all around us, Lafornas, once a great world united…is now *divided*. Souls from Idyll destined to head above but some head down… to me."

Stanis huffed a laugh, shocked at how he saw that being a clear answer and not one that was more confusing.

"Divided?" Ara whispered.

"Ara, you can't seriously believe any of this shit." He grabbed her hands to make her focus on him. She was stuck in a state of pondering as she searched the floor around her.

"Have you been to Idyll?" She faced Charon, grabbing for Stanis's hands, he didn't resist.

"No, only the living dwell amongst the Valleys of Idyll. The dead do not get to explore its beauty. Feel it's love." Charon started with slight irritation in his voice. He was staring at her directly now with his glossy eyes.

She really did have an interesting addiction to getting them in shitty situations. Why was she trying to upset this stranger?

"Are you dead?" She asked.

"Ara," Stanis tried to pull her attention back but she just pinned Charon with an intense stare. Charon was obviously craze driven, living in the Catacombs, he was talking about love like it was real. Why had that concept been so prevalent the past few days, more often than ever in his life?

"I exist to guide the souls, life and death are an intangible concept to me. The blood running through your veins is hot and flowing. We are not the same."

Well, at least they weren't dead yet, Stanis had let that thought occur to him many times. But if this were all true then there were other planes of existence.

"When was Lafornas divided?" he asked, grasping for something real to hold onto.

Lapping waves and silence answered him initially.

"I can not say for certain, Akrasia." Charon lifted his brittle arm slowly, pointing to a shore line that came into view, as they exited the tunnel into another opening cavern. "The end of your journey is here."

Light poured in from the ceiling, stars sparkling the black sand beach at the side of the river. Without hesitation, Stanis flew from the boat, his boots sinking into the soft billows of sand. Ara gracefully leapt from the boat, before striding for the wall encasing the cavern with gigantic black basalt columns.

"A debt is owed, Akrasia." Charon reached his translucent limb towards Stanis. "If coin isn't available, a day off your life if acceptable."

"Fine." Stanis huffed. Charon sliced Stanis's palm, he winced, attempting to pull away. Charon's grip only tightened. His clammy lips found the open wound and sucked. Stanis finally managed to yank his hand free, suprise washed over his disgust as the cut sealed itself as fast as it opened.

Charon scoffed. "Wasteful."

The boat took off at high speed, out of sight, shooting into another tunnel. He didn't care that he had managed to get out of the deal with the upper hand. Charon hadn't specified, so he wasn't to blame if his number of days alive amounted to nothing. Ara sat atop a short column, her back to the wall, as she dug her palms to her eye sockets. The scent of fresh ideas and heavy minerals encircled him with every step.

"Ara?" Stanis pushed any anger away as he looked down at her. She didn't budge. He knelt in front of her tugging at her wrists to reveal her eyes to him.

"Don't fixate on all that shit he said."

"How can we not, Stanis? Her voice cracked, making his heart drop. "You've never questioned our world, all the violence the gangs bring, the constant fear we live in for our friends lives? You've never felt like you've been trudging through Hell?"

Stanis watched her as he thought about his own tragic life, everyone around them had seemed to live a similar fate, that's just how it was.

"What are you saying?"

"I've seen it," she said her eyes were filled with moisture. She watched him search his features. He was too stunned to respond, so she continued. "I've seen valleys of grass flowing in the breeze, overlooking a huge body of water, real bright blue water. The pink sunrise's rejuvenation of the land. Not the pounding of acid rain that defecates everything in its path. I always thought it had to be a different Isle…but everywhere seems to be either coated in fog or a scalding heat."

"You're thinking too much about this," he said frowning, he wasn't able to follow Charon's strange thoughts, and now he had confused Ara as well. Maybe he'd transfixed her with magic and was trying to drive her to madness.

"No I've been to Idyll, in a vision, I know it. Abby's parents ran from some evil there, her father Hael mentioned it, and I felt their love". She drilled into him with a furious look, jumping up and throwing his arms off her. He stepped forward to comfort her, not knowing where the urge came from, but her denial set a fire in his soul.

"We don't have time for this!" He bellowed, the cavern echoing his voice back to them. He followed the sound around the giant space, his eyes bouncing back to find her staring at him with a softer look.

"Stanis, this is bigger than us, bigger than finding treasure. I need to find Abby, her parents are going to leave. I think they are trying to go back to Idyll."

"Ara," he said.

"Divided!" She interrupted him, "you said it yourself, your father told you Lafornas was divided."

He stared at her trying to remember his own words. "The magic is divided," he failed to see the connection, "that's why finding mates is important, to connect the power."

"What if it's more than that?"

"I don't know," he said as he began to believe that idea, slightly. He gripped the back of his neck, then paced through the thick sand.

"What if Lafornas was divided into two planes of existence, Abyss and Idyll." She was trying to lay it out for him.

She spoke with her hands and he couldn't help but noticed how bewitching she was as she worked out the issue facing them. He watched her mesmerized, finding himself believing her wisdom. Hoping they had the time for all that as well.

"In my vision.. um, the one in the Archives…I saw Abby's parents, her dad Hael said something about leaving through a doorway, and returning to Idyll once it was safe. But they didn't have a lot of time."

"Ara, I believe you, and we will reunite with Abby, after we find the treasure." He said optimistically.

"Is that all you care about?" She said, her attitude bordered on irritation again. "Abby could be with them now, being dragged back there. I have to go to her, I can't live without her," her voice cracked and tears cascaded down her cheek.

His body reacted instinctively driving him forward, wrapping her in his arms. She let him hold her for a moment, then pulled back to look up at his face. She was so beautiful and every molecule within him wanted to pull all pain from her body. She deserved to know all that he had discovered.

"Ara, the gods chose him." Stanis fought the urge to bring his lips to hers, he needed to tell her. "The only way to unseat Batar is to become more powerful, and…"

"Oh my god's!" A high pitched voice rang out behind them from the entrance of the tunnel leading onto the beach. Ara scrambled from his arms, shooting towards the call. Tripping over the sand, his boots attempted to chase her.

To stop her.

A flash of golden hair sprinkled from the tunnel, revealing Abby gliding towards them. She collided with Arabella, before they both fell to their knees, hugging; their tears washing between them. Grant emerged covered in dry blood and a shirt ripped to shreds. He had a large mechanical device resembling a bow strapped to his back. They were all companions of disgusting and dirty, but Stanis felt no relief that they had arrived.

Chapter 27

The pounding in his ears begged for him to wake. He pushed the feeling away, wanting to remain asleep for a little longer. The pounding persisted and his entire head throbbed, mercilessly. His mouth coated in gravel as he tried to shallow the pain in his throat, making his entire body flex. That's when he felt the real pain, his breath caught in his lungs as he begged his body to stop the aggravating torture. His eyes cracked open, finding the cave ceiling staring back at him, a dim brown glow illuminating the space. He clutched his arm to his chest, biting down the pain his wrist was emanating. He slowly breathed through his nose before pushing himself into the sitting position.

Slanting his body up against the corner of the space next to him, he glanced around, noting that he was alone at the dead end of the tunnel. He shifted again as the pain in his back from laying on the floor added to his body's stress. A sword leaned against the wall across from him. The sight stumped him, as he struggled to remember where he was. Or who he was, for that matter.

Footsteps sounded, announcing the arrival of a woman. He stared at her with immense curiosity, but she didn't seem to be a threat to him. He glanced at the sword as she sat herself down next to the orb and flung off her scabbard that carried its twin blade, displaying black tank top straps as her dark blonde hair shifted around her shoulders. Intricate lines painted her skin forming a flower that bloomed on her shoulder.

"Good. You're up," she said, glancing at him. He hardly noticed her deep brown eyes, but something caught his attention as their faint glow bounced off the orb. He swallowed again, trying to coat his throat in preparation to respond.

"I've been scouting the tunnels and I think I could find the route we were following before you... ran off."

He shifted, feeling anger rise in his stomach, but not sure why it was triggered. Had he run off? That seemed like a cowardly thing to do. He stared at her as apprehension crept in. After a brief moment he attempted to stand,then realized his legs were fine, but the agony in his feet and his wrist were the issue. He wasn't strong enough to escape, or move much at all.

"I'm sorry, Cole. I didn't mean that," she said, stunning him, as she shifted towards him to inspect his wrist. "Here, let me help you."

"Cole," he whispered to himself, as a flash of a memory familiar to the one in front of him struck. "You saved my life," he breathed as he looked down at her. She weaved a small vine of magic through her fingers. His breath hitched, her big brown eyes pulling the gratitude from his body.

"Well, technically, I have saved your life a few times, so you're in a pretty large pile of debt."

He scoffed a laugh, "yeah, let's add it to my already growing pile of debt up above." He wasn't sure what triggered him to say that. He was struggling to remember much else, but he knew she was not a threat. No, in fact, she was obviously very important to him. He watched intrigued, while she shuffled closer to him, her closeness sending electricity through his skin. Reaching beyond his shoulders she fitted a vine around him and his chest. Eliciting a sigh of relief when she pulled away, some of the pressure lifting.

She smiled at him, and he dropped his eyes to her lips. Mesmerized by their lusciousness, the urge to lean in and steal a kiss from her overriding him. He could blame it on being thankful for her help, but he knew this desire was completely selfish.

A squeal rang through the surrounding caves, and she jumped up instantly. Cole grunted in annoyance, mostly at himself for falling prey to his weakness again.

"Abby?" She gasped.

She lunged for him to help pull him to his feet. Adrenaline forced him to match her. She grabbed the scabbard and swords, holstering them firmly in a cross on her back. Glancing back at him for a brief moment, before she ran into the dark, her orb uprooted from the ground and flew past his head.

With a painful grunt, he followed her glow into the darkness.

Chapter 28

"You killed a Harpy?" Arabella asked again, with so much excitement in her eyes, as Abby retold the tales of her and Grant's adventures through the Catacombs. Stanis watched her intently, as he leaned back against a column, his ass in the sand. Amused that she actually read some of the books in Lumen's townhome. He hadn't felt this relaxed in a while. They were almost to the treasure, he got to see Arabella smiling wildly after being reunited with her best friend, and he didn't feel closer to death. He had tried to be jealous about their connection, but it wasn't possible. Something in their mating bond, forced him to like Abby too, as part of the deal with Itia herself.

Grant lowered himself down next to him, and he grimaced at the thought of having to play nice. He still didn't trust the man as far as he could toss him, or whatever the dumb saying was. He had fought next to him through the night at the ball, and by the sounds of it, he had helped to protect Abby. Stanis decided that was enough, since it made Ara light up with so much joy when she embraced her friend.

Abby had healed all their bruises and as she retold the story for the sixth time, he considered maybe Abby had actually saved Grant, but the way she told it made him sound like the hero.

"Well, we aren't certain if she is dead, but we escaped her and she fell from the sky, crashing hard. I doubt her wounds will heal easily." Abby's grin lightened a little, but she smiled again as she looked down between her and Ara. They sat basically in each other's laps, hands locked in each other's grips.

"Um…" Abby said, glancing at Stanis's direction, "I need a second with Grant if you don't mind?" The question was obviously directed at Arabella.

"Of course." She exclaimed as she got up.

"Oh no, stay," Abby exclaimed, pushing Arabella's hands back as she stood, "Stanis can take my place." She shifted her gaze to him, "right Stanis?"

He jumped up before she even finished speaking, situating into the vacant position in the sand. He pulled Arabella between his legs, trying not to get too excited by her ass grazing the crotch of his pants. She hadn't protested, and when she leaned back into his chest, his heart melted slightly. He wrapped her in his arms and nestled into their cacoon.

"I can't believe she's here," Ara whispered, tilting her head back towards him. Then returning to watch as Grant and Abby, weaved arm in arm, strolling along the river's edge. He didn't respond, letting her get her emotions off her chest. Her body shifted against him. To his surprise she twisted to face him, wrapping her legs around his torso. He grunted, adjusting his legs, and situating her into his lap further. He leaned forward so that they were breathing the same air, when her forehead rested on his, his hand gripped her ass.

"I didn't really realize she was also in the catacombs when I saw the vision of Ritz and Cole," she whispered. Her voice cracked, as she closed her eyes.

Stanis tried to ignore the sound of his brother's name, as it fell from her lips. She sucked in a deep breath and pulled back away from him. He caught her elbows to keep her in his hold. A strawberry blonde strand fell into her face and he tucked it behind her ear.

"She's so lucky to have you, Ara," he said as her sterling eyes scanned his features.

"No," she said firmly, "I'm the lucky one. Without her light, I would've drowned long ago."

His brows furrowed. She truly believed that she was only alive because of one human holding her steady. Then he realized she was that for him. He had been forcing it away for so long to protect her when he should've been there for her.

"I think I know what you mean," he said.

He grasped her chin in his hands and pulled her in for a tender kiss. She leaned into him and the passion swept deep into his skin, sending his lips ablaze, and his cock stirring. She tasted like hope and sweet victory. He felt the need to open himself before her, but he couldn't do that without being honest.

Breaking their kiss he started to say, "Ara, I have to tell you something…"

Footsteps clouded his judgment, cutting off the sounds leaving his lips. She stood, knocking him off his axis, throwing herself across the beach after Abby's golden locks, towards the Catacombs tunnels.

Arabella's heart pounded furiously as she caught up to Abby's side, gripping her arm tightly. A sense of ease flew through the point of contact, but her heart still beat uncontrollably. It persisted until she watched Aritzia shoot from the darkness, and tumble through the sand, her arms beckoning the both of them towards her.

"Ritz," Arabella breathed as the three of them collided into a swarm of hugs. Abby's tears wetting her arms, before pulling them all apart to access Aritzia for injury. Reaching out to heal a few small cuts and bruises.

"I'm fine," Aritzia pulled from Abby's grip.

"Thank you, though," she smiled at her gently, "it's Cole actually… who needs help."

"Cole?" Arabella's heart sank as she ran towards the cave opening. She knew Stanis was close behind, but her heart sank as she watched Cole emerge in front of her, falling to his knees then his face planted into the sand in a heap of muscle.

"Fuck!" Multiple of their voices crashed together.

Arabella threw herself onto the sand in front of him, pushing at him to roll over, but his weight made him immovable. Seconds later, Grant and Abby were at his side, helping to hoist him up and carry him over to their makeshift camp. She pushed past them as Grant settled him against a rock and Abby went to work on healing his wounds.

"I don't have enough magic to heal everything right now." Abby's voice was strong, and Arabella felt her tension ease a bit.

Cole mumbled something inaudible. Arabella turned to Stanis, who stood far behind them, observing the scene. His brows furrowed.

She tugged Aritzia away from the rest of the group. "What the hell happened?"

Aritzia's eyes shifted around the cave and across the floor. So much pain pooled in her face. She didn't answer, and Arabella realized it was because she didn't know what to say. Arabella pulled her into a tight embrace, allowing both their tension to fade slightly. Neither one of them was as fond of hugging as Abby was, but she felt the same bond with her. Always so grateful to be near Aritzia strength, lifting others up with her. She didn't need an answer, because she knew her sister had fought tirelessly to get back to her, like she had for them.

"Thank you," she whispered, and Aritzia's face regarded her in question. "For saving him."

"You're welcome." Aritzia smiled wildly and punched her arm. "I didn't want you to think I had killed him."

Arabella released a heavy laugh, and her stress melted away. Finally, she was reunited with all the people she held on the highest of pedestals. She scanned the group as they made their way back.

Stanis leaned against the rock wall, watching Abby care for his brother. She gripped Arizia's arm one last time, then strode towards him. As her eyes found his jaded facade, her brain began to fog over and she fought to keep it at bay, willing herself to be in this moment.

"What's wrong?" She asked, leaning back on the columned wall next to him. Her head spinning again, and causing her to struggle to stay upright. Her limbs wobbled, his calloused hands grasped her, to keep her upright.

"What the fuck, Ara." He pulled her face in, his jade eyes scanning hers, but they fogged over with the vision she refused to let consume her, unsure why she was fighting it. She gasped, turning to rest her hands on the wall. Stanis swept her hair over her shoulder, but she couldn't hear what he was screaming at her, as she stared at the wall.

She ran her fingers over the ridges of the wall, tracing the tiny diamond symbol and infinite swirl with her index finger. She gripped the pendant around her neck. Her body regained its strength, forcing her to crane her neck up, scanning the expanse of the pillars for more answers. "It's right here," she breathed.

Stanis's palms slapped the wall next to her. "You did it, beautiful! You found it." The whites of his teeth brighting his face unlike ever before.

"Three sisters in the eye, a drop of two pure fates intertwined with six snakes, awakens her from a sleepless state."

"What?" Arabella whirled on Abby, who now stood behind her, her head tilted back as her eyes scanned the basalt column wall above them.

"Don't you guys see it?" Abby said.

Arabella drilled her focus on the wall again, searching for the text, not finding any. She frowned and looked towards Stanis, but he was obviously just as lost. She stepped back to search the columns from a different perspective.

Cole groaned, and she ran to him, falling to her knees beside him.

"Cole, are you okay?" His eyes filled with concern as he looked between her and the rest of the group. Stanis chaotically swiped at the wall, and Arabella's concern eased, noting his attentions were fully on the treasure. Cole's eyes found Aritzia's as she helped Arabella pull him to his feet.

Grant was side by side with Abby, looking at the same spot on the wall.

"Two fates?" A smile tugged on his lips. He looked down at Arabella as the rest of them watched Stanis running his hand along the wall in search of a door.

"Does that mean something to you?" Arabella asked Grant as her brows furrowed, still unsure why she couldn't see the prophecy.

"Mates." Grant said pointedly. "Their blood, specifically."

"And the snakes?" Abby asked, gripping his hand. Arabella's heart warmed as she watched her friends' eyes glow.

Before she could utter another word, Aritzia interrupted her. "Cole and I fought off a snake with lots of heads…But it wasn't six."

Arabella glanced to the other side of her, bouncing between Cole and Aritzia. His face wasn't showing anything, and she wondered what he'd been through to make him so…empty.

"What does it say again?" Stanis asked frantically as he aimed for Abby. Arabella's feet shot into action, throwing herself between his fiery gaze and her best friend. The group circled around to face one another, observing Stanis as a monster budded inside him.

"Stanis, calm down. We will figure this out. Just give us a moment." She said. His chest pressed into her palms, fighting against her.

"Three sisters in the eye, a drop of two pure fates intertwined with six snakes, awakens her from a sleepless state." Abby repeated, smiling as she read it from the wall again. "Grant thinks it means the blood of two mates."

Grant nodded in agreement and pulled Abby further from Stanis, who stood rigid again, preparing to fight something…or some one.

"Okay." Stanis grumbled, removing a concealed knife from his waistband and slashed it across his hand. He held it out towards Arabella, sending her heart tumbling to the floor, realizing what he was insinuating again.

"What the fuck?" Aritzia exclaimed.

"Stanis," she said, glancing towards Cole.

"Ara," he growled, stepping closer to her, separating him from her friends. "He's not your mate, I am, and I will prove that right now."

"Wait, you are her mate?" Aritzia pointed her fingers at him as she let out a small laugh. He scowled back at her and Arabella shifted to block her, as well.

"Stanis, I don't know that. I am still confused," she pleaded with him, trying to refocus his attention on her, "but if Cole admits it, then I will share my blood and try."

Stanis's shoulders released their tension, and he turned to Cole. Who was watching the group with frantic eyes, shooting them between each of them, finding Aritzia's more often than others.

"You need me to admit what?" Cole looked like a baby deer in the hunter's snare.

"Tell the dickhead you aren't Arabella's mate," Aritzia pleaded, "so that he stops being a psychopath".

Stanis growled from behind Arabella, but she kept her eyes on Cole. Cole had said it before. He had told her repeatedly that they weren't mates, but never with as much hesitation. It was breaking her heart, and she began questioning everything all over again. She tried to remember her times with him, but they seemed so far away. Has it really been that long? Had her feelings changed? Her heart raced as she realized either answer he gave would crush her.

She felt Stanis hand on her wrist as his blood dripped down her fingertips. She palmed his leg, forcing him to hold firm behind her, afraid he would lunge for Cole, if he didn't answer soon.

"Stanis."

"I don't know," Cole whispered, his eyes tracing the sand.

Stanis slammed past her before she could stop him, and the men both flew into the blacked dunes. Stanis straddled his brother, as his fists plummeted into Cole's face; while Cole tried to block each hit, but struggled with his strength absent.

"How could you betray me, Cole?" Stanis bellowed.

"You left!" Cole panted through punches. "Not just me! You also left her."

Stanis growled, continuing his assault.

"You made your choice!" Cole squawked.

Aritzia was screaming at them as she tried to pull Stanis off his brother. Time froze as Arabella watched the two men fighting over her. Her arms tingled and her vision flattered, her shock consuming her and messing with her magic, forcing her to bathe in all the pain her heart was feeling. She did not know what to do, but Stanis wouldn't stop until she told him to.

"Stanis, stop!" She begged.

"So you decided she would be yours then?" Stanis spat at Cole, straddling over him the sand. His hands to Cole's throat.

"She belongs to no one! You said it yourself! You can't own a woman, especially not one as powerful as her!" Cole forced out in shallow breaths.

Stanis eased his grip for a moment, and with his halt of attack, Aritzia jumped at the opening, using vines to restrain Stanis's arms behind his back and he fell into the sand next to Cole, who scrambled to get to his feet.

"I'm not your mate," Cole panted, "I'm having some gaps in my memory at the moment but I know that Stanis is your mate. He's known since we first came to Orcus Haven as children."

Her confused look matched the rest of theirs now. She whirled on Stanis, while he was tied and stuck on his knees in the sand. Punching him square in the nose. He scowled wildly as he looked up at her, blood dripping from his nostrils.

"You knew?" Her throat hurt, trying to bring on the tears she so often forced down.

"I had just lost them, Ara, you have to understand. I wasn't good enough," he gasped out, "I'm still not, but I promise, I'll never leave you again, until the day I die."

Tears pooled in her eyes, but she refused to let them fall.

"Good, because you owe me one remember," she said, fury lining her veins as she stared into his eyes. The scent of disappointment and cannabis seeped from him and she inhaled deeply as she leaned down to his face. He was merciless and she couldn't help but be encouraged to forgive him. She gripped his chin, tilting it up to examine the deep lines and jaded eyes blazing back at her. The small sob that left his throat rattled to her core. She'd finally found him after years of yearning, but if this was the person who was destined to be hers, she was sure as hell going to make him earn the title.

He was truly kneeling before her. Infuriating her. But choosing to never leave her.

"Of course, Beautiful." His eyes widened as he looked up at her.

His face filled with shock, he began pulling his chin from her grip and throwing himself forward to attempt to stand, struggling against his restraints. She swiveled on her heels to see what had his attention. Abby and Grant had their hands pressed to the wall, blood dripping down the basalt stone. Their other hands linked in firm white knuckles.

The cave's columns shifted and cracked. Opening up in front of them, and sending the sand vibrating at all their feet. A dark silver peaked through the expanding spires, as the crack widened enough to create a passage. The darkness shot to the ceiling and Arabella stood awestruck, as she followed the sight up, then back down to the ground. Something dark radiated through her veins, as she took in the abeyance of existence on the other side.

She inhaled a deep breath, noticing how close her friend was to that evil. Grant tugged on Abby's hand, pulling her forward with him into the darkness. When Arabella exhaled the breath, the blackness enveloped Abby. Only allowing a brief moment for their sterling and sapphire eyes to bid each other farewell. Then, as if it never existed, the crack sealed up, sending a huge gust of air and knocking everyone to the sand.

"Abby!"

Desperate to piece together what had just happened, Arabella scrambled to her feet before sprinting towards the wall where the crack had formed. Her hands found the two prints in scarlet blood, twinkling with flecks of gold. The etched symbol vanished with the rest of the portal.

Taking her best friend with it.

A sob broke from her chest as she sunk to the sand, pressing her forehead to the wall, she hardly felt anything. She didn't sense the warm arms wrapping around her, the pain her heart felt overpowered everything else. All rational left her, as shouts cascaded around her. Her own sobs inaudible to her ears. Numbness engulfed her as tears sopped the sand at her feet.

She couldn't feel anything but the vacant feeling in her chest, the hole where her heart was supposed to be. The abyss it left now that her best friend was gone.

Chapter 29

Everything happened in a blur.

One moment Aritzia was at Cole's side, watching with a deep complexion of uncertainty as Arabella and Stanis fought, then made up, but then fought again. The next, she was at Arabella's side begging her to retreat from the wall.

Abby was gone. Every instinct inside Aritzia told her to crumble, but her father's voice whispered across her soul. *"The best soldiers don't break under pressure. If you can remain strong while others falter, then you will succeed as a great leader."*

"Release me!" Stanis had demanded.

"Where did they go?!" Arabella had screamed.

She pulled her power off of Stanis, releasing him. She had anticipated he'd lunge for Cole again but he didn't. He was lifting Arabella up into his arms. Pulling her away from the wall as she fought to reach what was no longer there.

Abby.

A lump formed in her throat as Cole reached her. The pair of them watching Stanis drag Arabella further away. Planting her in the sand on her knees, forcing her to talk to him.

"We should give them a moment," she said.

"Are you alright?" Cole reached for her, then flinched, as she backed away.

"I'll be fine," she stomped closer to Arabella, who now sobbed into Stanis shoulder while he whispered into her ear. She wanted to help her, but wasn't sure how. Arabella already struggled with her inner demons, and Aritzia was unsure if this would break her too. They needed to find Abby immediately, but she was failing to see the direction to do that.

"Stanis…where did they go?" Aritzia interpreted them.

"I don't know," he growled.

"Get down!" Cole's voice alerted.

She didn't see the group of men who had entered the dark cavern. She didn't see the arrow until it implanted into Stanis back, and until it was too late.

She did, however, see his slight shock and the blood that started to dampen the corners of his mouth.

Aritzia drew her sword and Cole immediately pulled the other from her scabbard, guarding their friends. Arabella held Stanis firm, clinging to him as shimmering blood pooled between them as his form fell. Crashing to the sand. Sobs echoed off the columns at their backs. A thud told her Stanis had hit the sand.

"I wouldn't do that, unless you want to end up like your friend *Stanis.*" A dark voice echoed as the figures prowled towards them.

"Lukas." Cole spat.

Lukas was the devil reincarnated, a dark haired predator prowling towards them. An angel of the underworld, that reeked of death and burning flesh. Aritzia didn't need to know much about him, only that his slim figure and feline smile didn't fool her. He probably thought all women would fall at his feet, but he had decided to shoot at the wrong people.

Unfortunately, for her and her friends, she did know of Lukas. The favored son of Batar, and the heir to the hypothetical throne of Lafornas. He was considered to be just as vengeful as his father was. She expected he'd come for Arabella soon, but Aritzia anticipated they had months to prepare for that.

Aritzia tried to hold firm, but the exchange between Arabella and Stanis was clenching her heart firmly. Her best friend was now hollow, and her voice accentuated it.

"No, no, no, no Stanis, you're not allowed to die," Arabella choked out between sobs. The hole in Aritzia's chest grew larger as more blood flooded into her friend's palms. Arabella hauled Stanis's torso onto her lap. The sound of the arrow, puncturing his spine, and snapping under the pressure of his body embedded itself into Aritzia's memory.

With a groan, Stanis whispered, "I don't think your stubbornness can save me".

"You don't need me to save you, you just need to not die," Arabella begged, wiping the tears away with delicate fingers. "That's my third request. Go back in time and do something," she demanded.

Aritzia bit back her empathetic sorrow, the overbearing question of why Arabella didn't use her magic to foresee this event catching her attention instead.

Arabella definitely should known, that they didn't have any time left, he was crumpling in her arms. If her friend were raised the same as her, she would know what the scent of fresh blood smelled like. She'd be pained at the sight of all emotion washing from his soul slowly, like every person looked while dying. If Arabella had been raised the same as her, the soulmate's bond wouldn't be something she constantly pushed for. No she'd know exactly what it felt like, to be burdened by another faction of her soul. She would notice as a crimson puddle settled beneath them, that her heart was breaking too. Because having someone who completes you, dwindle from your hands, it wouldn't be so hard to make the silver linings fade. Stanis slipped his watch off of his wrist, pressing it to Arabella's palm, as the three hands spun slowly.

A gargled cough made Cole flinch beside Aritzia, refocusing her attention on the assailants, she hoisted her sword up again despite Lukas accomplices no longer poising arrows at them.

"Fix it," Arabella begged, and it was almost Aritzia's undoing.

"I can't fix it this time, so I need you to...." Stanis breathed.

"Don't you dare give up!" Arabella sobbed.

"I need you to know, you were the treasure, Ara. I should've known that from the second I saw you. I shouldn't have left." Stanis breathed. "We could've had so much time together, but I messed it up. I'm sorry for that. But I know you'll find someone to love one day"

Aritzia hadn't realized that her friends had found their mates, it didn't matter truly. It wasn't like finding a mate wasn't hard in Abyss, but she thought they had exchanged all of each other's secrets. She was overcome by the words coming from Stanis, he had seemed so brutish and overbearing. Initially, she believed Arabella must have been dragged along with him, but now, Aritzia felt like she had missed something completely.

Cole shifted again. Stanis was dying, and they all sensed it.

"Treasure?" Lukas's hoarse laugh echoed through the cavern, "only a mortal fool would believe in such a thing."

"But I could've loved you," Arabella choked out.

"You did love me, just like I loved you," Stanis's breaths grew more ragged, "and now you know for next time, that you can't waste it. Not even for a second."

Aritzia didn't dare look back, she held firm in guarding her friend and her mate. Even when the sob from Arabella's throat begged her attention. She needed her goodbye, before the assailants were on them. If Stanis didn't die within the next few minutes, they would definitely finish the job.

"It doesn't matter if he's your mate or not, I know you think that that's what matters. I should've listened to Lumen. Choosing to love a person, that's what matters more. You love so deeply, Ara, I just wish we had time for you to realize that you are worthy." Stanis struggled over every word.

No one in Abyss loved anyone, her father had told her that. Everything was a power grab and love was a poison that hindered real elevation to true power. Aritzia's mother had left them days after she was born, explaining the reasoning behind his thoughts. Her father hated her mother enough to stop loving her, and over the years and through the torture, that concept of love had died in Aritzia's subconscious. But hearing Arabella, and Stanis of all people, utter the words, it scrapped very deep inside her.

"Stanis there is no one else, you promised that you wouldn't leave me. You said we're mates." Arabella sobbed.

Lukas was only a few strides away, but he stopped. The embellishments on his jacket clinked as he shifted impatiently. The two men who followed his charge flanked his sides. Obviously intrigued to hear Stanis take a final breath. A shield of power formed around Aritzia, forcing her muscles to lock. Cole's sword wavered in an attempt to move as well but failed. Heat radiated across their skin like a threat.

"If you love him, tell him before it's too late." Stanis whispered with a final breath.

"No, Stanis!" Arabella's voice was soft and empty. "You can't leave me."

Aritzia could've skewered Lukas for what he did next. He clapped like the sadist he obviously was. She wanted to lift her sword but her arms remained locked in place.

"Again, I wouldn't do that if I were you." Lukas jaw twitched in sync with his wrists. Fire danced along his black irises, as they watched Arabella's form hidden behind Aritzia's legs.

"Why not?" Cole's voice cracked.

"You!" Arabella pushed through them and stormed towards Lukas before they could grab her. She aimed to deliver a, much needed, fist to his smirking face but before it landed Lukas hand gripped her wrist with his black gloves. Pinning her to his chest.

"Murderer!" she spat into his face.

"I've been called much worse, Ara."

She struggled against his hold, but failed. "Don't fucking call me that, you have no right," she growled through gritted teeth.

"What would you like me to call you then, since we're gonna be married? Wife?" His devilish grin made Aritzia's teeth clench. "I need to call you something."

"How about you call me the person who is going to stab you to death." Arabella's tone was not vacant. Not only had they lost Abby, she had also lost her mate. The agony was most likely overpowering her.

"Bit of a mouthful," Lukas said letting his eyes trail her body like a predator.

"Don't think I won't do it," Arabella snarled.

"Me too," Aritzia managed to bite out, but Lukas didn't even seem to hear her.

"Oh, seeing who Itia chose for you as a mate, I don't doubt it." His devious laugh was becoming unbearable, scrapping along her skin like a steel sword. She should've known they would out smart them. Even though they were matched in numbers, Lukas's brutes seemed to have as much experience as she did, but they were out weaponed, with steel and magic.

"Don't you fucking dare talk about him," Arabella seethed.

"You have a lot of rules..." Lukas yanked on wrists, "let's go." He dragged her across the sand, as she fought against him. His friends remained unmoving as they forced Aritzia and Cole to remain still.

"I'm not going anywhere with you!"

"Right," Lukas scoffed.

"Wait, wait!" Arabella begged. "Aritzia has to come with me."

Pride swelled in Aritzia's chest. Arabella had always been resourceful and persuasive. Whatever she was thinking would definitely work.

It had to.

"Why?" Lukas seethed.

"She's my guard, I need her with me at all times," Arabella's sterling gray eyes pleaded to reassure Aritzia.

"a... and Cole!" Arabella added, making Cole shift slightly. He had mentioned he was having memory gaps, but he had to be compassionate towards Arabella's situation, even enough to not want to let her be dragged away.

"No." Lukas responded after looking them over briefly.

"Then I'm not going," Arabella demanded.

"I missed the part where you thought you had a choice." Lukas gritted his teeth and pulled her scrapping heels across the black sand. "I'll get you a new guard. Call it a wedding present."

"No, she's loyal, and you of all people should know that loyalty is important. She's coming with us." Arabella seethed.

Lukas hesitated, looking between the three of them, his scowl unmoving, "fine."

His lackey's released their grip on the two of them. Removing her swords from their hands, forcing her and Cole to walk behind Lukas, who now firmly held Arabella in a choke hold.

"Wait!" Cole demanded, before running back to his brother's lifeless body. Choked sobs echoed from where Lukas held Arabella. She was fighting against him again as Cole hoisted Stanis body over his shoulder and carried him to the river's edge.

Silence swept across the cavern as a small light emerged from Stanis's chest. Cole moved to place his body into the river, the orbs bobbling through the subtle waves, with anticipation.

With a snap of Lukas fingers, Stanis body was lit ablaze. Orange and blue embers engulfed him like an incendiary grenade. Cole stumbled back, barely escaping the flames. Aritzia's horror matched the screams coming from Arabella. The light formed from Stanis's soul flew through the air, impending into Arabella's chest with a glorious flash.

Cole held his shoulders firm as he walked back to where they all waited, cast in a blazing aura. He made sure to stick close to Aritzia as they marched back towards the tunnels. Moisture kissed his cheeks, but his scowl was so firm she was sure it would break stone.

"Where are you taking us?" Arabella demanded through sobs.

"Don't you want to see your blonde friend again?" Lukas retorted, and Aritzia stiffened at his words. She doubted he knew how to get to her, Aritzia knew more than most, but she couldn't see the future without Arabella's help, and she couldn't create a direct path to their solution now that they were prisoners.

Yet.

When no one responded, Lukas laughed his devious snarl that reverberated around the cavern one last time. "She's headed for Idyll, and I know just how to get us there."

The man on her right waved his hand in the air, and a glowing passage appeared in their trail. Her astonishment was short lived as Lukas dragged Arabella through the portal, forcing them to follow her into the unknown.

Epilogue

Humans are sensitive creatures.

Even the darkness of Abyss and the burning celestials of Idyll can't dampen their souls. They are fighting back against the fates, taking claim over their own souls, claiming their departed lovers and depraved souls.

The evidence of their rapture was clear, but decades of naiveties hindered their escape from distortion. Some have seen the truth, some have survived to be enlightened, and some souls have been burned down near the River Styx.

Death welcomes all of them, but he appreciates to feed on complete begging. Alas, this mess that my beloved Dolofonia, has created will be affecting even the gods. The gods who sit up above Idyll know the side effects, as the god dwelling under ground is flooding the gates with soullessness.

Lack of population growth may be better than an unsustainable over growth, but when no one can find love in an admirable existence, does one truly gain any power. Who will mend this breaking world, rekindle its flame and wash away its suffering?

It may seem the Gods are playing with puppet strings, but are the puppets really playing us? Will they fight against the odds to defeat the wills of the over rulers, the defenders of disparity.

The fates have divided our heroes, their power should be enough to overcome their tortures, but existences now separating them from one another.

Or have the Fates pushed them closer together?

Acknowledgements

Thank you to my dearest friend and fellow author Jordan, for sifting through the darkness of self publishing with me over many bottles of wine. Soul mates aren't always lovers, and you have shown me that even two unstable women can find stability in one another. You are the bewitching standard that I measure up to, thank you for giving me solid truths and bitch slapping advice. I know you think no characters resemble you, but there is a little bit of your wisdom in each sentence of this work.

I also have great thanks for all my beta readers for finding the tiny plot holes for me and diving into the dark minds that trek through Lafornas's underbelly.

To my dear husband, Aaron, I appreciate you supporting my passions, always. For being the podium to which I measure all my greatest achievements against. But most of all for being the light outside my tunnel, the wind beneath my wings, and my chest to cry into when the loss becomes to big sometimes. Thank you for supporting my wild relationships with fictional characters, so that they can all be adored as deeply as you love me. You are the other half of my soul and I'm so glad I didn't have to wait years to find you. Here's to us handsome, and all the adventures to come.

About the Author

Audrianna married her high school sweet heart right after they graduated from college. They spent their early 20's travelling across Europe. Then, in the early months of 2023 they welcomed their beautiful baby girl. Granting them a tiny travel companion, who has already been to Iceland at the age of 9 months old. Through the years, Audrianna has dabbled in many creative worlds, from culinary arts, to marketing, all the way to writing Adult Fantasy. Her trio of friends is never far. Having grown up with her two best friends, and maintaining those relationships through adult hood, has helped her through all of the times when she's felt a little lost.

Upcoming Books

All updates about upcoming books within the Lost Isles Collection will be first announced on the Author's Substack.